the dark part o

Belinda Burns was born in Brisbane in 1974. She studied English Literature at the University of Queensland and a Masters in Creative Writing at Bath Spa University College. She lives in Australia after seven years in London.

the
dark
part
of me

belinda burns

Atlantic Books
London

For my mother

First published in Great Britain in trade paperback in 2006 by Atlantic Books, an imprint of Grove Atlantic Ltd.

This paperback edition published by Atlantic Books in 2007.

9 8 7 6 5 4 3

A CIP catalogue record for this book is available from the British Library.

978 1 84354 501 9

Design by Helen Ewing
Printed in Great Britain by Clays Ltd, St Ives plc

Atlantic Books
An imprint of Grove Atlantic Ltd
Ormond House
26–27 Boswell Street
London WC1N 3JZ

'A man beholds the beauty of the world, is reminded of truth and beauty, and his wings begin to grow.'

Plato, *Phaedrus* 249e

Too bloody hot for cappuccinos. Thirteen days till Christmas and still no sign of rain. A state of disaster outback and it was pretty dry in BrisVegas, too. Grass crunchy brown underfoot. Bushfire warnings on the news. No sprinklers allowed. The river was low and swampy, dead cat-fish bobbing on the surface. Cicadas droning on and on. Blowflies buzzing in my ears. Everything was withering away.

Too bloody hot for cappuccinos. That's what the real-estate men from across the road said when they came in to the café to watch the Test in the air-con. Bearded men sucking on iced-chocolates, strawberry milkshakes, eyes slapped on the box. Extra ice-cream, would ya, girly? A wink, a wet lip lick. Later, after knocking off, it was beers they always wanted. Extra cold, would ya, girly? Wink. Lick.

Trish was in the basement carpark, smoking a joint. I was at the counter, peeling paper doilies and zoning out on the cricket. There was something about the soothing 'chock' of the bat hitting the ball, the soft clapping and the lullaby voice of Richie Benaud that sent me off into a doily trance. *Pick and peel. Pick and peel. My nails are painted blue today. Pick and peel.* Old Richie took me back to those hot Sunday afternoons when I was just a kid and Dad sat on the back patio drinking beer and listening to the match...

Mum was in her bedroom, napping in flesh-coloured bra and knickers. I was made to nap too, although not once did I close my eyes. It was boring lying next to Mum in my undies, my chest bare and sticky, staring up at the ceiling fan, which spun so fast I couldn't see the blades. From outside, I could hear the chink of stubbie against stubbie, the rise and fall of excited voices on Dad's pocket radio. He would've watched it on the telly except Mum wouldn't let him smoke his rollies in the house.

I wriggled off the bed.

'Don't disturb your father,' Mum murmured, rolling over, her stretchy boobs mashed between her arms. 'Not when he's listening to the cricket.' From the side of the bed, I watched Mum fall asleep, breathing through her mouth, lips slightly parted, before I turned and padded out of the room.

Dad was pitched forwards alert as a fox on his yellow folding chair, staring across the swimming pool, waiting for the willow crack. His elbows rested on his knees, a squat, brown stubbie bottle clenched in his hands. I reached for the catch on the sliding door but even on tippy-toes I wasn't tall enough. Squashing my nose up to the glass to make a pig's snout, I pummelled my fists against the pane to get his attention. He swivelled in his chair and stared at me blankly as if he had never seen me before in his life.

'Let me out!' I yelled, my hot breath misting up the glass,

grinning, thinking this was some new kind of game. But he took another swig of beer and turned away.

I sat cross-legged at the door and waited. It seemed like ages I was there. When my bottom got sore I lay down on my stomach, my chest pressed against the cool, white tiles. I folded my arms and rested my head on them like a pillow. Staring sideways out of the glass, I watched the backs of Dad's Volleys as his feet swung back and forth, back and forth. When he struggled to his feet I shot up, thinking he'd decided to let me out, but he just wandered over to the fence for a wee, then headed back across the lawn. He took another stubbie out of the esky and plonked down in his chair. Later, Mum came out from her nap, pillow creases on her face.

'C'mon, Rosemary,' she said. 'He's not interested.'

I was wondering what'd made Dad such a bastard, when a cheer went up from the beardies. Ponting had hit a six.

Trish ran in from the back with a joint between her lips. 'Earth to Rosebud. Come in, Rosebud.' I hadn't heard the phone ringing. 'Don't worry,' she said, grabbing the receiver. 'It'll be the Coke man.' I looked out at the tables still littered with dirty lunch plates and thought about going to clear them, but a second later, she waved me over. I asked her who it was but she just winked and handed me the phone. From the grin on her face I had an inkling.

'Rosie?' It was him alright, but with a slight accent.

Blood throbbed in my ears. My armpits sweated. Trish pinched my butt. She knew the score. She'd had my romantic history in truckloads.

'Yeah. Who's this?' I said, pretending I didn't have a clue while inside I was rioting.

He laughed down the line, confident, cocky. 'You remember.' Like fuck, no. Like fuck I'd wiped him clean out of my head. 'Thought you'd have quit that shithole by now,' he was saying. 'Aren't you nearly finished uni?' He didn't know about me dropping out. I hadn't told him about dropping out.

'Where are you?' My voice came out gruff and low, like a man's.

'Back home. Mum and Dad's.'

'Since when?'

''Bout a fortnight.' He paused. 'I'm having a welcome home barbie tonight at the oldies'. Thought you might like to come.'

Cold spiders skittered up my spine. He'd been back two weeks and he was only calling me now? Trish was poking me in the ribs.

'Say something, Rosebud,' she whispered, but I couldn't.

'You around?' he prompted.

'Yeah. Maybe. It's hard to say.'

'Cool, babe. See you around eight.' He'd assumed, arrogantly but rightly, that wild fucking goannas couldn't have stopped me.

'Hang on—'

But he was already gone and that was it – the precise moment I'd been waiting almost two years for, since I was seventeen. I slumped into one of the booths, a quivering lump of jangles. *He'd called me babe. I was still his babe.*

'That was Scott,' I said, my hand trembling.

'No kidding.' Trish lit a fag and inhaled hard. She was five years older than me and already had little crow's-feet around her eyes. With her short, spiky hair and the silver bar through her eyebrow she looked like a dyke, but guys still went for her. Trish thought I was insane to wait all that time for Scott. She said I'd regret it when I was old and wrinkly. But then Trish had one-night stands and snorted coke and thought true love was bullshit.

'When'd he get back?' Trish ashed into an empty latte glass.

'Yesterday,' I lied.

'How long's it been?'

I shrugged. He'd been gone nearly two years and it was a year since he dumped me over the phone. At the time, I'd kind of lost the plot. Mum called it my 'breakdown' but it wasn't like that. I was just a bit hacked off with life. Trish helped me through the bad times, though, kind of like a bigger, tougher sister. She got me into new shit like chatting up dense rugby-fuckers for kicks and dancing to trance and drinking sneaky scotch and smoking pot in our breaks at work. She took me to get a butt-tattoo in Elizabeth Arcade and told me about all the different kinds of sex she'd had, like anal and asphyxiation and dressing up, how she loved being spanked on the arse and pashing girls when she was on E.

Apart from hanging out with Trish, I hated working at Temptations. But I'd stuck it out, ferreting away every last bean, thinking I'd surprise Scott by showing up in London. I'd already saved ten grand, helped along by Trish's nifty knack for till-skimming. She was biding her time, too, planning her escape. It wouldn't be long now, we both kept saying, before we bailed, except now Scott was back I didn't need to go to London after all.

I looked Trish in the eye. 'What the fuck are we doing in this shithole, hey?'

'Not for much longer, babe.'

We went out the back and sat on the steps by the industrial bins. Trish rolled while I stared across the Woolies carpark, water mirages shimmering above the rows of cars, metallic bodies roasting in the midday sun-blast. Beyond, the city floated, murky and hazy. It was a poor excuse for a skyline, just a few scrapers stuck in the middle of a petering ramble of mid-size office buildings, smudging into vast purplish plains of burbia. It depressed me; the heat, the weed, my place in it all. There was no room to be different, no room for any freaks of any kind. It was all about conforming and having a flash car and a big, brick house and kids and pets and a massive widescreen.

'So, what'd he want?' Trish passed the joint.

I took a deep drag. 'He's invited me to some crap party.'

Trish scowled and took back the smoke. 'Reckon he's keen for a root. Calls up his old girlfriend who's still mental as shit for him.' She assumed that all Aussie blokes were the same, rooting around, drinking beer, watching porno. 'So you gunna do him?' she asked.

'Might.'

'If I know you, Rosebud, I'd put good money on you banging him tonight.'

I grinned because of course I wanted to bang Scott asap. I imagined the look on his face when he opened the door and saw me standing there. For a few seconds, he doesn't recognize me because I look different to when he last saw me. Instead of tiny tees and denim minis, I wear long flowy skirts and muslin tops, a serpent armband and beaten silver rings from the Valley market, purple glitter on my eyelids and a butterfly sticker on my left cheekbone. I've grown my hair long and wear it braided in Heidi plaits with a fresh pink hibiscus from the backyard stuck in each end. I've had my belly-button pierced with a ruby stud and I am skinnier, too, much skinnier than before. But then, he twigs and wraps his arms around me, pashing me wild with tongue. We go inside to his bedroom, where he undresses me and pushes me down on the bed. He tears off his shirt and his body is pale from the lack of sun in London and a little thinner without his mum's fry-ups. We root for ages.

Trish would have died if she knew I'd only ever fucked Scott. She thought I was like her, rooting for kicks whenever I got the urge. When Scott and I broke up, it was Trish who tried to convince me that the only way to get over him was to screw heaps of other guys. Like the time I went home with this arty-looking guy called Jed I met at Ric's Bar in the Valley. All night I'd been checking him out, real sly-like. He was bean-thin with longish black hair and smudgy eyes. I liked his bright yellow bowling shoes, and the way he leant against the bar, drinking red wine, blowing smoke rings, taking in the scene. He looked the complete opposite of Scott. When I pointed him out to Trish she cock-sucked her finger and dared me to pash him. So, I did. I sidled over and grabbed him round the chops. His breath was foul, like he'd never owned a toothbrush, but when he said, 'Let's go screw,' I went with him, winking Trish goodbye, telling myself, *this is good, this is good for me*.

We walked fast along Brunswick, past Super Deluxe and the Press Club, not holding hands. A bit further on and we turned down Harcourt, past the hookers strutting back and forth outside the 24-hour Laundromat – some trannies, some straight, all in heels, sickly-skinned under the fluoro. Jed's bedsit was a few doors down, along an alley on the ground floor. We went in and he switched on the light. A naked bulb illuminated: one brown-vinyl armchair, a banged-up telly, various half-eaten containers of take-away food (blowflies hovering above) and, underneath the window, a single blue-striped mattress. What the fuck was I thinking?

'You at uni?' I asked.

'No,' he said, snapping off the light, 'I'm a poet.'

He took me by the hand and led me towards the bare mattress.

'Let's fuck,' he said, a poet of few words, and started tugging off my clothes. He fumbled with the hooks on my bra but I flinched at the touch of his fingers.

'What's the problem?' he said.

'Don't.' The problem was he wasn't Scott.

'But you smell so good.' He kept on like a rodent, snorting and sniffing around me, his arms pale, weedy sticks. 'You said you wanted to screw.' Next thing, he was naked, skinny as a monkey, clambering all over me, sucking hard on my neck. It was dark but I could see his penis as he squirmed back and forth across a thin blade of streetlight. It was small and mottled, crinkly-crumply uncircumcised, like an old man's, not like Scott's thick, rounded tip, buffed and shiny-smooth.

'Stop! Just stop! Get off me!'

I ran away. I couldn't do it. Scott was in my blood and I couldn't get him out. I wasn't like Trish. I lacked the 'casual rooting' gene.

A bellow came from inside the shop. 'Trisha!'

'Fuck. Slob's here,' Trish said.

'Shit.' I jumped up, stubbing out the joint and lobbing the scotch glass into the skip.

Slob (real name Bob) was Trish's uncle. Hairy, foul-mouthed and always reeking of Kouros, he'd made a packet out of his poxy coffee shop franchises which'd sprouted like killer weeds all over the western suburbs. 'We Greeks,' he'd say, puffing on a fat cigar, 'are as good at making money as we are at making sex.'

'Trisha!' Slob roared, again. 'Get your arse out here!'

'Just stick your tits out,' said Trish. 'He loves your tits.'

We sauntered inside; Trish in front, me behind.

Red-faced and cursing, Slob was blustering around making milkshakes for a fresh pack of beardies queued at the counter. He went berko at Trish but except for a pervo squiz at my boobs, said nothing to me.

2

Mum blamed Scott for me dropping out of uni. She reckoned that if I hadn't met him, I'd still be studying law, not wasting my life at Temptations. He was a man, she used to say, and deep down all men were rotten. I'd argue that they weren't all drunk losers like Dad but she wouldn't have it. When Scott went overseas, she said he'd pulled a fast one. When he broke up with me over the phone, she said I told you so. She was right, but at the time I swore she was just bitter.

The night I first met Scott, I was sixteen. Mum had shouted me to Valentine's all-you-can-eat food buffet for finishing my final school exams. We hardly ever went out for dinner – Chinese take-away was our usual Friday night treat – but Mum had a two-for-one voucher which she wanted to use. We'd driven past Valentine's a million times on the expressway (there was this huge, pink, inflatable heart strung up outside to attract passing traffic) but never been in. It was hardly my idea of a fun night out but Mum thought she was onto a winner. We went early to avoid the crowds but the joint was still packed. Compared with the rest of them in Bonds singlets and stubbie shorts, we were totally overdressed, especially Mum, who was decked out in one of her eighties pastel suits plus heels. I hated the place and the way everyone gawped at us as we walked to our table. Worse though, as soon as we sat down with our first round from the buffet, Mum went off on one of her rants.

'You can be anything you want,' she said, working a Wet-One into a lather, 'so long as you don't stuff it up.' She waved the packet at me. 'Go on. Give your hands a little wipe.'

'No.' I was fed up with her treating me like a five-year-old.

'Please. Do it for me.' She shook a Wet-One in my face. 'You'll be using your fingers.' She nodded at my plate of calamari rings.

It was so humiliating the way she brought out her hand-wipes supply in public but I'd learnt, over the years, that it was a hell of a lot easier to go along with it than resist. I snatched one off her, gave my mitts a half-hearted pat. Mum kept yabbering, as a fat teenage boy walked past with a wobbling tower of soft-serve, showered in hundreds and thousands and drenched in strawberry syrup.

'Rosemary, are you listening to me?'

'What?'

I willed fat-boy to stack it, for the tower of soft-serve to go all down the front of his big fat-boy belly, but he plonked the dessert down safe on the table.

'There's only one thing that will stand in your way.' Mum was fishing around for an anchovy on her plate. 'Do you know what that is, Rosemary?'

'Mum, not now, OK? I've heard this all before.'

'No, you listen to me. I know what I'm talking about.' She

pointed her fork at me, the hairy slug quivering on the end. 'Men, Rosemary, once you get to university they'll be everywhere. Hanging around you like a bad smell. Wanting to... ' She bent over our plates and whispered, 'get in your undies', her frosted apricot lips spitting out the words.

'Mum!'

The fat-boy and his no-neck family turned their heads our way. Mum smiled and waved back at them. The no-neck mother paused mid-crumbed-prawn and leant over.

'I just *love* your suit. Where'd you get it?'

'DJ's half-yearly clearance.' Mum preened in her pistachio candy-stripe. 'Half-price.'

'No, really?' the no-neck gushed. 'Well, the colour really suits you.'

I stared out the window at the traffic bumping along Moggill Road, wishing that I was far, far away, in some more exotic part of the world.

'What a lovely lady.' Mum popped the anchovy into her mouth and chewed. 'Now, where was I? Oh, that's right. Men. You've got to be careful. They'll get you pregnant or worse, infect you for life with some dreadful... '

Mum was always going on about germs and diseases and other nasties, those microby blighters you can only see under a supersonic microscope, that breed on toilet seats and door handles and dirty money. But the germs she hated most were the ones that feasted on dead bodies. Every day she used to study the funeral notices in the paper so she could work out what time a hearse would be on the road and make sure we avoided it. Once, when I was about seven or eight, we were driving back from Shoppingtown, the boot packed with the week's groceries, when a huge, black hearse slid past in the other direction. I could see the coffin inside, shiny walnut covered in white lilies. It gave me a chill just thinking about the cold dead body, laid out stiff as a pencil in its Sunday best. Mum went all silent and when we got home she chucked all the groceries straight into the wheelie bin. She dragged me down the side of the house to the backyard and ordered me to strip off my favourite frilly dress.

'But it's not dirty, Mummy,' I said, hands on hips, stamping my foot.

'It's contaminated.' Mum stepped towards me, arms outstretched. I backed up towards the fence.

'What's contaminated?'

'It's got germs.'

'Where?' I lifted up my skirt and inspected the soft, pink fabric at close range.

'You can't see them but they're there.'

'Did the germs come from the dead person?'

'I'm losing my patience with you, Rosemary.'

'Are dead person germs worse than normal dirt germs?'

'Don't upset me like this.' She rubbed at her face. 'It's all your father's fault.' She lunged at me and yanked the dress off over my head. I screamed but she told me to be quiet in case the neighbours came snooping over the fence. She took off my undies and even my sparkly, red Dorothy shoes. She stripped off her clothes, too, and tossed them on top of mine so there was a little pile on the grass near the shallow end of the pool. Mum ran towards the house and I ran after her, giggling at the sight of her naked in the yard. Inside, she dragged me to the bathroom and ran a boiling shower.

'But it's too hot,' I complained.

'Stand still while I scrub you.'

'You're hurting me,' I sobbed, more for the thought of my favourite dress lying on the lawn.

'It's the only way to get rid of them.'

After the shower, Mum dressed me in around-the-house clothes and sat me down in front of my *Jetsons* video while she went back outside in an old terry-towelling dressing gown and a pair of yellow rubber gloves. Curious, I wandered over to the sliding glass doors and looked out. Mum was circling the pile, splashing the contaminated clothes with methylated spirits from an old tin of Dad's. Next, she pulled something from the pocket of her dressing gown and fumbled with it, head bowed, shoulders hunched. The clothes burst with a whomp into multi-coloured flames. Crying for my frilly dress, I tried to get out to rescue it, but Mum'd locked the door from the outside. As she stood staring into the pink and blue and orange tongues of fire eating away the clothes, I thought at least she'd forgotten about my Dorothy shoes and thanked Our Father Who Art in Heaven, but then, as if reading my mind, she swooped down and picked them up. I hammered at the glass but she'd already tossed them on the pyre, the red sparkles spangling bright as jewels for a split-second before melting into goo. I never hated Mum more than at that moment. And then, as if I'd summoned the fire to punish her, the hem of her dressing gown caught a light. She sprang back, screaming. From inside, I watched, bug-eyed, mesmerized by the spectacle. Hopping mad as a rabbit on the scorched grass, she flapped at the flames licking up the side of her gown. With a shriek, she leapt into the pool, surfacing a few seconds later, hair plastered all over her face. She dog-paddled to the edge and climbed out, sodden, shreds of charred terry-towelling hanging off her. There's still a brown patch where the grass doesn't grow and we joke about it now – the day Mum set herself on fire – even though, for a long time, it and other germ-related incidents were strictly taboo.

But that late October evening at Valentine's, Mum was focused on a whole new family of germs. Not dead ones, sex ones. 'STDs. Herpes. Gonorrhoea. Chlamydia. Or those warts, big as grapes, that you have to get burnt off with a laser beam.'

'Shut up, Mum. People are listening.' She was so embarrassing to be with in public.

'I don't care,' she said, sliding a smooth lozenge of ice-cream back onto her spoon.

'I hate the way you do that,' I said. 'It's so disgusting.'

'What?'

'Regurgitating your ice-cream like that.'

She closed her eyes and sucked the ice-cream back through her lips.

'You know, I'm really sick of your germ thing,' I shot.

Her eyes flashed open. 'This isn't about germs, Rosemary, this is about your future.'

'Yeah, right.'

'I'm serious.' She reached across the table but I slipped my hands onto my lap.

'You still treat me like a child. I'm nearly seventeen, Mum. Besides, you're hardly an expert on sex.'

'And you are?' She smirked because she knew I was still a virgin. I'd never even had a boyfriend.

I lie in bed, Valentine's spaghetti and wedges and soft-serve jumbling around in my belly like clothes in a washing machine. My door is open wide for signs that Mum has gone to bed. I catch the flush of the toilet, the snap of the light switch, the same heavy sigh she makes each night when her head, full of germy worries, hits the pillow. Tonight, I'm going to go clubbing like the cool girls at school. That'll teach her. That'll show her. I think about ringing Hollie, my best friend, and getting her to come with me. But just once, I want to do something on my own. Something bad. Something Mum wouldn't like me doing.

For a few seconds, I let the darkness swim around me, filling out the corners of my room, settling in the tiny crevices along my body. Geckoes squeak and chirp from the bricks. Holding my breath, I flick on the bedside lamp, slip out of bed and dart across the room. Softly, I shut the door.

I watch my giant shadow self undressing against the wall; the arch of my back, the point of my left nipple like a huge cherry on a fantasy cupcake, my hair cascading down my back. I brush my fingers lightly across the stomach of the giant shadow me, then touch the real me. Ring-a-ring-a-rosie round and round my belly-button until I feel nice.

It's ten-thirty on the digital. Fifteen minutes till the bus comes. From my top drawer, I pluck a clean pair of Bonds undies, pull them on with a snap. Drown myself in Safari. Wiggle into my new denim mini. On top I wear a low-cut black sparkly with lacy choker. In the mirror, I smear foundation, thick on my freckles and the scar above my right eyebrow. Then, for my eyes, smudgy kohl with Japanese tails out the sides, waterproof Maybelline on my lashes, top and bottom, no gluggies. Eight flaps over on the digital. Seven minutes till the bus. One last squiz in the cheval. I look good. Tarty-sexy with my legs all fake-tanned and skinny. On with the lippy getting the bow just right, bleed them together, tissue in between, mwah, mwah. I wink at me in the mirror and the big shadowy me on the wall. A green flash of bad-girl eye.

Up on the bed, I'm prising out the fly screens, ditching them on the carpet. I chuck my platform strappies out the window. They land, clunking in the pebbles so the mongrel next door starts up yapping.

Shut up. Shut up.

I crouch down in the shadows, listening hard for stirrings from Mum's room, vibing her to stay asleep. The bus is rumbling in the distance, monstering along the wide, flat street. I'm sliding back the window as far as it will go and straddling, one leg over, tippy-toes touching the gravel. My second leg flies up like a ballet dancer's and I crash down on the pebbles.

Hobble. Hobble.

Into my shoes.

Strap. Strap.

Stand up. Brush off the knees. Leap across the fish pond.

Mongrel growling, low growls set to explode.

Nice doggy. Nice doggy.

I hear the bus slowing down, wheezy squeezing on the brakes, nearing the stop. Night sounds crowd in, bug noises buzzing round my ears. I slap at a mosquito, blood on my arm. Possum hissing, eyes gleaming off the roof. Mongrel barking at bug racket and the crunch of my strappies down the gravelly path. I look back at the house all dark and humpy like a termites' nest. The smell of rotting mango makes me want to spew. A rustle in the bushes.

Snake. Snake.

I run along the path, mongrel barking non-stop now.

Fe. Fi. Fo. Fum.

Out the gate. Click. Clack.

On the driveway, smooth as sand, drenched in moony light, sunny bright.

Pelting for the bus.

Wait. Bloody well wait.

Lickety-split. My tiny cross-the-body bag winding round and round my neck.

Hurry. Hurry.

Engine up a pitch.

Ready steady.

Round the corner. Skirt riding up and up. Tug it down, down.

On the bus.

I flash my student pass at the driver.

'Big night on the town?' He winks at my cleavage and sucks on the gingery tip of his beard. His beer gut is rammed hard against the steering wheel.

'Yeah,' I say, glancing back to see who else is on board. There's a pack of skegs and their skateboards littering the back seat, and a pair of poxy bevans pashing with salivary tongues. The bevan girl is dressed in tight white lycra with six gold hoops in each earlobe. The bevan boy is skinny and zit-infested with mullet hair.

'Where you off to?' the driver says.

'Just out.'

'Clubbing?'

'Yeah.' Like I do it all the time. I sit halfway down the bus, wedged in against the side. Out the window there's nothing but blackness, huddled houses and a face which, for a split-second, I don't recognize. The eyes are too big, the lips too red and pouty. A sexy, grown-up me. A thrill of badness shoots through my groin and I smile. We pull away from the kerb and gather speed. The bus hurtles through Merri-Merri estate, lurching around corners, flying along the straights. There's no need to stop. Even though it's Friday night, it's sleepy in burban heartland. I get out my red nail polish and paint my toes, two times over, to make the time go quicker. At last, we hit Moggill Road and there's something to see outside my window apart from my face floating in the darkness.

Up a gear and we're rumbling along past the car

dealerships bathed in fluoro light and past my old primary school, the buildings dull and tired and flaking paint. The Flying Fish flies by and the air-con shop, which tells me it's a hottish kind of night at twenty-one degrees. Down the overpass to our first stop: Shoppingtown. We pull in up the top, near Macca's and the BCC Multiplex. The pashing bevans disengage and get out. A stinking drunk gets on and sits in the seat behind me and I have to peg my nose against the putrid stench. He starts singing that 'Henry the Eighth' song which Dad used to sing when he was drunk. The dero taps me on my shoulder and mumbles something in my ear, but I ignore him as we circle the huge, brick monolith of Shoppingtown and head towards the city.

Next stop: the R.E. It's packed with university students spewing out from the beer garden and onto the footpath. The drunk gets off and staggers into the public bar and I think how Dad is probably in there, drowning his sorrows, shoulders slumped, gazing into his beer glass. Some uni guys get on. They're wearing checked shirts and plaited belts. They order the skegs off the back seat and, as they barge up the aisle, I recognize one of them from the BP servo – a gangly guy with sideburns and a weak chin. He points at me like a cowboy firing two pistols. I visualize the name badge he wears when pumping petrol into Mum's Holden: Gavin.

'Nice tits,' Gavin says.

'Piss off, Gavin,' I say, just above a whisper.

But he's heard me and he stops, resting one knee on the seat beside me. 'Do I know you?'

I shake my head. His mates are hooting and jeering from the back. Gavin wedges in next to me. He slides his arm across the top of my seat. His breath is hot and stale against my neck. I turn my back on him and stare out the window.

Gavin taps me on the shoulder. 'What's yer name?'

I swivel around, my legs sticking to the vinyl seat. 'Gertrude.'

'Hey, Gavin and Gertrude. How 'bout that?'

'Hilarious,' I say, withering him. 'Do you mind racking off? I'm meeting my boyfriend in town.'

'Now, don't get all nasty on me, Gertie. We were getting on real good.' He squeezes my knee with bony fingers. 'You're just my type, you know. Knockers with attitude.'

I give him the silent treatment as the bus rockets along Milton Road past the Night Owl and the dilapidated tennis courts and the Fourex beer factory, choking yeasty fumes out into the night.

Gavin smiles. 'You don't really have a boyfriend, do you, Gertie?' His hand climbs warm and clammy up my thigh. I knock it away but he puts it right back where it was.

His mates shout, 'Go on, Garvo. Stick it to her, mate.'

'How 'bout it, babe?' He grins. His front tooth is chipped.

I glance at his crotch and wiggle my pinky at him like I'd seen the cool girls do to ugly guys who try to hit on them at the bus-stop. And, just like that I say, super-smooth and arsy, 'Sorry, but I like my wieners a bit bigger, thanks.' Crash and burn sound-effects come from the back.

Gavin stands, sneering down at me. 'Slut,' he spits,

before swaying back up the aisle to his mates who are doubled over, cacking themselves.

Next stop, everyone else gets off. We're in Paddington. To my right, there's the Suncorp Stadium lit up like a giant jewellery box. The skegs cruise down the hill to the skate-ramp. The uni wankers unload. Gavin comes around the side of the bus and gives me the finger through the window, before they head into the Paddo Tavern. It's twenty past eleven and I sit on the bus, peering out. The pizza place is closing up, a girl stacking chairs on top of tables. A street lamp flickers on the blink, illuminating a halo of bugs in strobes. Out the other side of the bus, a guy urinates against a Besser-brick wall. His piss trickles, filling out cracks in the pavement, amber then cochineal-pink in flashes from the Café Neon sign strung overhead.

'Last stop, girly,' the driver sings out to me. 'Unless you want to go back home.'

'No,' I say to myself as much to him. 'No way.' I rocket off the seat and run down the aisle.

'You meeting friends?' he says to me but I'm already out the door, the soft, warm air wrapping around me, the pink light licking at my toes, as I dash across the pavement, jumping over the piss-stream. Hectic red arrows pulsing like arteries lead me up a dark set of carpeted stairs into Café Neon and a square-headed bouncer whose collar is too tight. With no fake ID my chances are slim. But I bluff it with my walk, shoulders back, hips swinging. Square-head lets me in. No questions asked. No cover before midnight.

Inside, it's not what I expected. A dingy L-shaped room

with a low ceiling and shabby carpet. The walls are painted matt-black. There's a bar but I can't see a dancefloor. There's no music. I scan the joint in case there's someone I know. The odds are remote. The cool girls go raving in the Valley. Café Neon doesn't look like their scene. A few guys in their late twenties are smoking and drinking bottled beer in battered couches along the back wall but apart from that it's pretty dead for a Friday night. At the bar, three shiny-faced men in suits are drinking pots and eyeing off the bar-girl. She is standing on a stool, reaching for a whisky bottle from the top shelf. Her denim mini grazes the bottom of her butt-cheeks. Her legs are short but slim and deeply tanned. She's not quite got the neck of the bottle. Her fingers flutter in the air, grasping for it. One of the suits shouts out, 'Nearly there!' They all want to see her knickers. She's straining on her tiptoes. A flash of vermilion crotch sends them off in fits of back-slapping titters. She's got the Johnnie Walker Blue, firm around the neck, and clambers off the stool.

I buy a drink, kahlua and milk, and sit by the windows looking down at the yobs staggering up and down Given Terrace. I picture Hollie, tucked up in her white cotton night-dress, dreaming her fantasy dreams in her canopied bed. She would die if she knew I was here. I make my mind up not to tell her, for this to be my secret, when static buzzes over the speakers. A mechanical squawk, then Deee-Lite's 'Groove Is in the Heart' kicks in. I get the urge to dance. Around the corner, past the bar and up a few steps, there is a dancefloor, small and forlorn and kind of out of the way, coloured squares flashing orange and pink and green across the vacant faces of the suits. I head towards it. The suits follow me with their beady eyes, checking me out, but I pretend not to notice as I strut out into the middle, swinging my hips, shaking out my hair, tracking the bass beat low in my stomach.

I close my eyes and I'm a little girl dancing with Dad to Blondie the nights Mum used to work. We'd stay up late, Dad sucking longnecks from the bottle, music squawking from his old tapedeck. He'd grab me under the arms and spin me round and round until I crashed out dizzy. Once, he spun me too hard and I slammed into the wall, my bum making a hole the size of a soccer ball in the fibro. I'd been about to cry but then Dad burst out laughing, a great roaring laughter that had us both in stitches. We pushed the bookcase across the hole to cover it up. It was our little secret until the next day Mum asked me why the bookcase had been shifted. She thought he'd punched a hole in the wall like he did sometimes when he came home maggot. She wouldn't listen when I said it was my fault for dancing.

I go hard for more than an hour, queen of the dancefloor. The club fills up a bit, but no one else is dancing yet. My favourite tracks keep coming. 'Cream' by Prince. 'Tainted Love' by Soft Cell. 'Devil Inside' by INXS. I spread my feet wide and shimmy low to the floor. When the chorus kicks in, I spring back up, whipping my hair around in circles, snapping my hips left and right, step-ball-changing and stretching my arms high above my head. I become aware of people around me, moving onto the dancefloor, but I ignore them and, as the beat quickens, I close my eyes. It's like I'm swimming between the notes, diving down deep for the base, breaking the surface like a mermaid. I wish Hollie could see me now.

'Hey, what d'ya know, it's Gertie.'

I recognize the voice immediately and, when I open my eyes, there is Gavin leering at me with his pack of loser mates behind him.

'Piss off,' I say, turning away from him and dancing off towards the front edge of the floor. I scan the club, spread out below, and there's something odd about it. Then it hits me that there's no women – except the barmaids and me – just a sea of grey-haired suits and younger guys in polo shirts.

'Love Shack' starts up and I can't resist doing my sixties moves, hopping from foot to foot, doing the swim, holding my nose like I'm going down underwater. I keep thinking I should go and get the last bus home but the music is addictive and my legs won't stop. Someone touches me, hot fingers across my stomach. Gavin. I try to ignore him and just keep dancing, head flung back. The smell of cheap aftershave and stale beer fills the air. A hand clutches at my butt, holds it, squeezes hard. Fear snags in me. I stop dead. My arms drop to my sides. They're all around me, winking and nodding, drunk from the Paddo. Dark jeans and checked shirts. Boots and plaited belts.

Gavin grins, fang-toothed.

'Just fuck off, OK?' I shout at him above the music, trying to act tough.

They laugh, mouths red and wide, but no sound comes out as they move in closer. I back away, off the dancefloor, into an alcove, but they follow me. I smack against a table. They crowd in, the press of hard legs against my body. A rasp of stubble burns my cheek. Gavin forces me down, back flat on the table. They're laughing and chanting, over and over, 'Show us yer tits, Gertie. Show us yer tits.' I want to kick and bite and spit but I've clammed up. Gavin climbs up on the table. He straddles me, his thighs clenched either side of my waist. 'Love Cats' by The Cure is playing and it's just about my favourite. I scream, this time for real, flailing my arms and kicking out with my legs. Gavin's hand crawls up my skirt. I look over my shoulder, towards the dancefloor, but no one's looking my way. In my head, I'm screaming. *What happens now? This can't be happening.*

The music lurches to a halt and the house lights come up. Someone is shouting. Gavin steps back. The others look up. I twist my head to see what's happening. The bar-girl with the vermilion undies is running across the dancefloor, the square-headed bouncer close behind.

'Get the fuck off her,' the bar-girl yells. The bouncer lurches in like an action hero, picking Gavin up and throwing him halfway across the floor. The others slink away gutless, as I peel myself off the table and bolt to the loos.

I'm standing, shaking against the wall. I catch my reflection blurred and tiny in a graffitied mirror opposite. I step up to it and I look just fine but not much like me either. Like they didn't rape you or anything, I tell myself. The toilets are feral. I turn a tap on with my fingertips, splash water on my face. What a mess. I want to be home, tucked up in bed in my PJs. I re-apply my lippy and try to adjust my top to hide my cleavage. The foundation has melted off my face, exposing my freckles and the jagged white scar which sits above my right eyebrow. It's past midnight and the last bus has gone and I don't have enough money for a cab. I could call Mum to come and get me but it's not worth the grief. A toilet flushes and I jump. From the cubicle, one long, blue Converse appears. I scan the room and catch the urinals in a bank along the wall. I've never seen a urinal before. Ha! I'm in the men's. I head for the door.

'You 'right?'

I wave a hand over my shoulder. 'I'm fine.'

There's a squeak of sandshoes across the floor.

'You just prefer the men's?'

I turn around. He's tall and broad-shouldered. A shock of sun-bleached hair. He's wearing faded Levi's and a plain, red T-shirt. His arms are tanned, hairless and sinewy. He runs his hands under the water. Somehow, he looks familiar.

I smile back, just a little, and make my assessment of the men's loos. 'We've got better lighting and bigger mirrors, and it doesn't smell so... '

'Rank?'

'So bad of piss.'

He shakes his hands dry and wipes them on the front of his jeans. He looks up and flashes me a broad grin. His eyes aren't blue but violet, the colour of squid ink or orchids, black grapes in sunlight. More shocking than beautiful. Something twists in me. I'm sure I know him from somewhere but the line is too cheesy to say. I step closer, drawn by his eyes, as if I might pluck one out to examine it.

'They real?'

'What do you think?'

'Weird.'

He stares back at me. 'You here with mates?'

'No.'

'Who then?'

'I'm by myself.'

'What? To pull?'

'No. To dance.'

'Nice seedy establishment you've chosen.'

'If it's so seedy what are you doing here?'

'Buck's night for some guy from uni. I'm supposed to meet them here.' He checks his watch. 'The strippers'll be on soon.' He winks and heads towards the door. 'You coming, dancing girl?'

We stand at the back of the club. The dancefloor has been transformed into a stage. A girl about my age stands legs apart, completely naked save for a sparkly gold g-string and a long string of oversized pearls around her neck. Her body is child-thin, her skin milky white. Her breasts are small but pert. Something silver glints from the dark aureole of her right nipple and again from her belly-button. Madonna's 'Like a Virgin' starts up as the girl bangs her hips from side to side, blue-ish bone rippling under translucent skin. I lean back against the wall. I can't help staring. As the lyrics kick in, she takes the pearls from her neck and swings them around and around like a lasso. She doesn't smile, not once, just pouts and slides her small pink tongue over her front teeth. Men slouch back at tables and chairs around the stage, drinking beer, swapping sly glances with their mates. I spot the uni wankers crammed along the stage front, leaning forward like teenage groupies at a rock concert.

Gavin waves in our direction and Purple-eyes gives him the thumbs up.

'Is he your mate?'

'What, Garvo? Nah, not really. Mate of a mate. He got some chick preggers and he's been conned into marriage by her oldies. Poor bastard. Nineteen and getting hitched. It's his last night of freedom so we're all out on the slash.' He pauses, looks at me. 'What, d'you know him?'

'No.'

We stand in silence as I'm drawn back to the girl. She is rubbing the pearls, held taut with both hands, back and forth against her golden crotch.

'What do you reckon?' Purple-eyes nods towards the stage.

'What?'

'Does it turn you on?'

I shrug, non-committal, but the truth is, she does make me feel a bit sexy.

'Tell you what, watch the rest with me then I'll drive you home.'

For all I know he could be a complete psycho-murderer but then he seems harmless enough, like someone's big brother, and I need a lift home and I'm still sure I know him from somewhere. Besides, he's real hot.

'What about your buck's night?'

'Got a big match tomorrow so I'm off the turps. Garvo's so maggot he won't notice.'

A slow clap starts up, wolf-whistles in-between. I look back to the stage. The girl has ditched her g-string, showing off a hairless pussy. The pearls are gone, too. Sitar music is playing as she swivels her skinny hips like a belly dancer. She runs her hands over her breasts, then down her body, and sticks her fingers up inside. I wonder how many men, at that precise moment, have erections. The music stops and a hush falls over the room. A drum roll. The girl pushes her fingers further inside, her eyes closed, her mouth hanging open. Purple-eyes gulps. The drum roll finishes and the girl takes one large step forwards to the edge of the stage. She's pulling something out of herself, something small, round and shiny which glistens under the spotlight. Then another shiny thing and another. I squint up at the stage. A roar goes up from the crowd. Loud, eager clapping and then I twig. The string of pearls. Each one coming out quicker now as the crowd goes wild and one man, rushing forwards, snatches the pearls and stuffs them in his mouth.

'That'll be Garvo,' says Purple-eyes.

'That's disgusting!'

'It's not meant for chicks. Unless, of course, you're a dyke. C'mon, want a lift or not?'

I hesitate. 'But I don't know your name.'

'Scott.'

'Rosie.'

He grabs my hand and kisses it like in the movies.

That night, Scott didn't stop talking the whole way home, rattling off a compendium of 'getting to know you' facts about himself while I conscientiously took it all in like I was going to be tested. He told me he was nineteen, three years older than me. He'd just finished second year Human Movement Studies at Queensland Uni. He said his best mates were Bomber and Muzza and that he'd known them since kindergarten; he had an older brother called Nick who played in a band; his favourite colour was Kermit-the-frog green; and his favourite number was seven. He told me he was mad about sport, especially basketball, water polo and cricket; and his Mum's beef lasagne was his favourite food, followed closely by Big Rooster's chicken fillet fingers. By then, we were turning into my street.

'Here's fine.' I pointed at the kerb, feeling like a little girl being driven home from school.

'That your house?' He pulled over, switching off the ignition.

'Yep.' I prayed Mum wouldn't come storming out in her chenille.

'Still scabbing off the oldies?'

'Yeah,' I admitted, trying to sound tough.

'Me, too,' he said. 'Mum and Dad mind their own business, though. My bedroom's downstairs so I pretty much do what I like.' I pictured my tiny, pink room, smackers in the middle of the house, and my single bed.

We sat in the dark interior of his 1979 Gemini, listening to the engine contract, the cool night air slipping in around our bodies. I pressed my palms against the bare tops of my inner thighs. A new sensation burned in my gut. Sick excitement. I felt his eyes on my neck, my shoulders, my legs.

'Lucky you don't live far,' I blurted out.

Scott grinned. 'Lucky for what?'

'Nothing,' I said, burning up. 'I'd better go. Thanks for the lift.' I fumbled with the door handle.

'Door's fucked from the inside. I'm afraid you're stuck in here, babe. Unless of course you want to climb over me.' His tone was light and playful but when I tried the door again it wouldn't budge.

'No kidding. This car's a piece of shit.' I thought about winding down the window and opening the door from the outside but instead I undid my seat-belt and, flipping onto my knees, crawled over the hand-brake. I wrapped my arms around his neck for leverage and hoisted myself on to his lap. The steering wheel dug into my back and my head butted against the ceiling. My chest was level with his nose.

I turned to the door but it was locked, the button wedged beneath his elbow.

'Move your elbow, please,' I said. But his hand was behind my head, pulling me towards him. Our lips met and I was amazed at the softness of his mouth. He held the kiss then pushed his tongue inside, sliding it over my teeth and my gums. His mouth tasted sweet, of red cordial mingled with something even sweeter, like caramel. His tongue was smooth and slippery, gentle yet insistent. I pulled back.

'What's up?'

'Nothing.'

What's up was that I hadn't kissed anyone since I was nine. It was Friday morning cookery class when Frank Castelli, a chubby Italian boy, held the blunt side of a carving knife to my neck and poked his tongue in my gob while Mrs Hodge had her back turned rolling out pastry for our strawberry tarts.

'I know this sounds silly but you look familiar,' I said.

'Really?' he said.

'Yeah.' We stared at each other, a beam of streetlight slicing between us.

'Maybe out. Brisbane's not that big, hey.'

'No, that's not it.' I drummed my fingers against my temple. 'Wait. It'll come to me.' A memory hook snagged in my brain. 'I know! You were mates with Danny Bailey, weren't you? You went to Grammar.'

'Yeah. Nah.' He tilted his head back, out of the light, and I couldn't see his eyes. 'Only for a bit.' His voice had gone quieter, low and kind of distant.

'I'm best friends with Hollie, his sister. God, I remember now. You used to come round to the house. That's right. How funny.' I thought back to the time, as a kid, I'd spied on them: Danny and his school mates, watching porno vids and drinking Mr Bailey's vintage piss out of the cellar. But right then, I was too shy to mention it so I just smiled and blinked and tossed my hair back over my shoulder.

'He's still inside, isn't he?' Scott ran his fingers through his hair a few times. I still couldn't see his eyes.

'Yeah,' I said. 'Were you there when it happened?' Hollie had never told me who was there that night in the changing rooms after footy practice. The school and the parents had made sure that the boys' names, except, of course, Matty Taylor's, were kept well out of the papers.

'Yeah, nah, but I wasn't in on it.' Scott cleared his throat and stretched out his legs. His face was back in the streetlight. He stared at me, tracing a finger down the side of my body, brushing against the edge of my breast, giving me awesome tingles. I could feel his erection against my thigh so I flashed him some bad-girl eye, but he'd spotted my scar. I turned away, patting my fringe down over it, but he pulled my hand off and ran a finger along the ridgy bit.

'Don't!' I batted his hand away.

'Whoa, sorry. What's the big deal?'

'I just don't like it, alright? It's ugly.'

'Nah, scars are cool. It makes you look dangerous. Like you've been in a fight or something. How'd you get it?'

'I fell off a bike when I was seven,' I lied. 'Nine stitches.'

'Impressive.'

We pashed again. Our tongues synchronized better this time. He wrote my phone number in pen on the inside of his arm and I got out. He rolled the car backwards down the street without the engine on. I crept around the side of the house and climbed back through my bedroom window.

I stand in front of the cheval with my legs wide apart. There's music in my head, a throbbing beat which starts slow but gets faster. I swing my hips from side to side, watching the bones ripple beneath my skin. My naked body excites and disgusts me. Last night, I met a boy with purple eyes.

Mum's pearls are much smaller than the stripper's; elegant, rosy buds which shimmer when I hold them up to the sunlight. She says she won't ever wear them ever again because they were a present from Dad, but a few times I've caught her standing in the mirror with them on.

It's easier than I thought getting them up inside me. I'd been worried it might hurt but it doesn't. They sit up there nice and snug as I dance around my bedroom, flicking my hair and kicking out in my strappies. When I've had enough of that, I squat down on the floor, just like the stripper, and fish around for one end. As I pull them out, I pout and wink at the mirror and lick my lips. I imagine Scott watching me and I feel real bad, real sexy. I wonder what Hollie will say when I tell her I've pashed a real guy.

3

Even though I knew it was the last thing she'd want to hear, I couldn't resist going round to tell Hollie that Scott was back. Since he'd been away, we'd slipped back into our old, childish habits of dressing up and doing Shakespeare and pashing in the cave. But with Scott back, all that would have to change. I thought it best to break it to her gently, or else she'd go all dark and gloomy.

I pulled up outside Hollie's place, the last on the cul-de-sac which backed onto Mount Coot-tha national park. It sat, all dark brick and wrought-iron fancywork, like a fortress at the top of the hill. It couldn't have been easy for her then, all alone in that big, draughty house with Danny locked up and Mr Bailey on business in the States half the time. As I got out of the car and walked up the steep drive, the bush was raucous with crickets getting loud and arsy as the sun went down. The gum trees quivered in the itchy heat as a crow, big as an eagle, broke through the scrub, swooping low and glinty-eyed to settle on top of the fence. My heart was tight and bursting with the thought of Scott, but I was sure Hollie wouldn't be so ecstatic.

Before I met Scott, Hollie and I were inseparable. We did everything together. At All Hallows, the other girls thought we were weird. They used to call us names like 'The Loony Lesbos' and 'The Dyke Duo' but we didn't care. We thought they were all dumb sluts anyway, destined to marry half-witted men and spawn quarter-witted babies. Whereas Hollie and I, we'd set our sights loftily high. Hollie wanted a kind, gentle-natured fellow with soft, blond curls and deep-blue eyes who would read her Milton at bedtime and brush her hair. I fancied a darker, broodier Heathcliff type, who would die for me. Up in the cave, we'd close our eyes and practise pashing for hours, imagining each other as a fantasy lover. We thought love was like in the movies; all thumping hearts and sonnets and red roses. But that was all before I met Scott. Before I got thinking I wanted a taste of the real thing. From day one, Hollie never liked him. He didn't fit our fantasy mould. Once I started going out with him, Hollie refused to see me. It wasn't until Scott went overseas that we started hanging out again.

I jabbed the doorbell a few times but there was no answer. Hollie slept at odd times of the day so I went around the side, which was always unlocked. I went in through the parlour, filled with tall palms, gold-framed mirrors and white wicker furniture, and headed up the marble stairs to Hollie's bedroom on the top floor. Her door was closed. I knocked softly, and when there was no reply, pushed inside. The room was dim with the crimson-brocade curtains drawn against the western sun. On the dressing table, a single candle flickered, dappling the fairies, goblins and fire-breathing dragons which stared out from the forest wallpaper, unchanged since she was a little girl. I padded across the rug to her canopied bed but it was empty, the cream-lace spread smooth without a wrinkle. I blew out the candle and threw open the curtains. The view through the window was too perfect; the top half of a giant orange sun caught between the crimson folds of the Great Dividing Range. I left Hollie's bedroom, heading further down the muffled hall. At each door, I stopped and listened, my ear pressed against the heavy oak. All sounds were deadened, sucked up by the thick carpets, the velvety wallpaper, the mustiness.

At the furthest end of the hall was Mrs Bailey's bedroom. The closer I got to it, the faster my heart pumped. It was the last place I wanted to go but I had a feeling Hollie was in there. I stopped at the door first and took a few deep breaths to calm my nerves. I closed my eyes and strained for the tiniest noise. The tick of a clock. The shouts of kids playing in the street. Nothing. It was enough to send you crazy, the quiet.

My memory of Mrs Bailey is pretty sketchy, but I remember the way she used to stand, tall and willowy on the deck, gazing up at the bush, smoking with her long black cigarette-holder, her dark hair flying in the warm wind. She seemed to float through the house in her pale, chiffon dresses. Wherever she went she left the same faint smell of cinnamon. She was nothing like your typical burban mum. She never did tuckshop or reading group and I never once saw her in the kitchen. Apart from her parties, she never had any female company around. She must've been lonely with Mr Bailey often away, or depressed, or maybe, like me, she wished she were someplace more exciting. Perhaps she was just plain old nuts. Whatever, Hollie and I were only six years old the day we found her.

Danny is waiting for us by the tennis courts. 'You're late,' he grumbles, holding his watch up to Hollie's face. 'You're always late.' But we run fast and make it to the bus, just in time. Hollie and I are puffing. Danny dumps us at the front and heads down the back to his grade-four mates. Tomorrow it's Ekka Holiday and it's noisy like a Friday. The bus swings out onto Moggill Road. Hollie leans into me, squashing me against the glass.

'My mummy's a famous actress,' she whispers in my ear. 'She's being Titania, Queen of the Fairies.'

'No, she's not,' I say, because my mum doesn't do anything special like acting in plays or dressing up or throwing fancy parties. My mum just works in an office and cooks dinner and yells at Dad and worries about me having clean hands.

'Is too,' says Hollie.

'Is not,' I say.

We keep this up until the bus drops us at the bottom of the hill. Hollie strides ahead in a huff because I don't believe her mummy's as famous as Judy Garland or Audrey Heartburn. Danny talks to me, though. As we trudge up the steep hill, he tells me how his mum is taking him to the Ekka and he's going on all the scary rides in Sideshow Alley and he's going to get the Transformers bag and the Violet

Crumble bag and stuff himself on hot dogs and fairy floss and strawberry-farm ice-cream. And I'm getting really jealous because Mum won't take me because she says I'll get sick from all the germs even though I've begged her a squillion times to take me just once to see what it's like.

'Mummy's home!' Hollie yells back at us.

Mrs Bailey's big, white car is parked on the drive with its windows so black you can't see inside. Danny uses his special key to unlock the front door and we all clatter inside and up the marble stairs.

'Mummy!' Hollie sings out.

'Mum!' says Danny.

There's a whiff of homemade biscuits in the air but the house is silent. Hollie and I go into the kitchen where there's a huge plate of chocolate-chip cookies on the counter top.

'There're still warm,' says Hollie, gobbling one down.

'But your mummy never cooks biscuits,' I say.

'She must've gone for a walk,' says Danny, flicking on the telly. *Monkey Magic* is just starting. I sit down beside him, my mouth full of biscuit, waiting for the bit when the giant egg cracks and out pops Monkey.

'I'll check upstairs,' says Hollie. 'She might be having a nap.' She trips up the staircase, singing the school anthem we'd learnt in music class that day. *'Daily we go to our school on the hill. Ready to try hard and work with a will.'* Overhead, her footsteps pad, dull and muffled along the hall. The monkey intro finishes and the princess on her donkey and the pig-snout man are wandering through the wilderness. Danny turns to me, his finger pushing up the tip of his nose, and snorts. I laugh, and reach for another cookie.

Hollie screams. She is screaming. One big, long scream that doesn't stop. Danny tears off the couch and I follow, flying up the stairs. Hollie's scream is coming from Mrs Bailey's bedroom at the end of the hall. The door is open. Everything slows right down. The cookies gurgle and melt inside me. My legs are heavy, my fingers thick and fat, as I bound down the hall. And still Hollie is screaming, but Danny doesn't scream. He doesn't do anything, but stands frozen in the doorway as I hang back in the hall, not wanting to see what they are seeing. But something pulls me inside and I'm staring at Mrs Bailey's waterbed and the blood and the gun and Mrs Bailey's head all blown up into little red bits on the white, satiny pillows and on the lovely, purple walls.

Hollie blamed it all on her father. Over the years, she'd convinced herself that he'd been having an affair even though there was no hint of it in the suicide note. When Mr Bailey was at home, Hollie rarely spoke to him and if she did it was only to call him a liar or a traitor or a spineless, philandering cheat. It was no wonder he kept such a low profile around the place. He spent most of his spare time locked away in his home cinema watching Westerns or in the cellar tending to his prized collection of Bordeaux.

Sometimes, I wondered what Hollie and Danny would be like if it hadn't happened, whether they'd be a bit more normal. Every year, just before Christmas, Hollie hosted a kind of do in memory of her mother, who used to love throwing fancy-dress parties. She wanted to be just like her mum. Often, I'd find her in Mrs Bailey's boudoir, flopped on the bed reading poetry or dressed up in her dead mum's outfits. The room was spacious and high-ceilinged, done out in sumptuous Hollywood glam circa 1986: the carpet white shag-pile; the curtains plush, gold velvet. One side of the room was fitted with floor-to-ceiling mirrored doors behind which Mrs Bailey's designer outfits and theatre costumes were stored. Centre-stage was the giant circular waterbed, piled with fluffy, pink cushions and covered in a glitzy white s atin bedspread (the blood dry-cleaned out). On either side of the bed were two black lacquer bedside tables, which gleamed from Hollie polishing them every morning. On one table there was a steel-stemmed lamp. The other was scattered with Mrs Bailey's things as she'd left them: a slim volume of Elizabeth Barrett Browning's poems; a red silk scarf; a scotch glass with a few sips still left in it; a solid gold zippo; a framed black and white photo of Mr and Mrs Bailey on their wedding day. The way Hollie used to keep it like a shrine gave me the heebie-jeebies.

I turned the cut-crystal doorknob and pushed inside. The air-con hummed full-blast and it was cold, icy. The curtains were drawn back, but the room was cast in deep shadow.

Rubbing warmth into my arms, I stood, blinking. I looked over at the waterbed. Hollie was sleeping on her side, facing away from me. The tiniest breath quivered up and down her slip of a body. Her boy-hips barely dented the chintz. She was wearing one of her costumes: a long white muslin dress with a high collar and a row of pearl buttons up the back. Her dainty feet, small as a child's, poked out from the hem of her skirt and her thick, black hair cascaded down the side of the bed.

I tiptoed towards her, then stopped. There was someone with her. A man. Hollie had a man in bed with her. She was pressed up against him, one arm flung about his middle. Sweat broke out from each root of my hair, instantly cooled by the air-con draught. I darted to the end of the bed to take a closer look. The man slept, lying flat on his back with his arms pinned to his sides.

Danny.

Danny. Fuck. It was eight years since I'd seen him.

With all the buzz of Scott phoning, I'd clean forgotten he was getting out. Not that Hollie hadn't told me a million times. She'd spent the past month getting ready for his homecoming; spring-cleaning the house, buying him designer clothes to wear, planning an elaborate dinner party for his first night home. She'd even bought him the latest PlayStation as a welcome home present, charging it to the family Amex which Mr Bailey paid off each month, no questions asked.

I snuck round to his side of the waterbed and knelt down to look at him. From a scrawny teenager, he'd become a fully-grown man, although still gaunt and skinny. He'd be twenty-two, the same age as Scott. His face was pale and angular, framed by a shock of matted hair so black it was almost blue. There was something girlish about his long, thick eyelashes and his lips, which were too red for a man. He was like Hollie with short hair. But he was not so much feminine as androgynous, sexless. He had on a crisp white shirt, open at the neck, and black tailored trousers. His feet were bare and bony, his toenails painted with emerald-green varnish. Although he was fast asleep, his hands, large white hands, fluttered by his sides as if he was having a bad dream. Fuck, those hands. I got a bit freaked thinking about what they'd done.

Outside, it was getting darker. The sky was turning a deep, backlit indigo that made me uneasy. Dusk was seeping into the room and the air felt suddenly old and stale like the inside of a church. I looked back at Hollie and Danny sleeping in each other's arms, like Romeo and Juliet. Like twins. They both looked so peaceful. They had a certain aura of innocence, the faintest white glow about their skin.

'Oh, Danny. Danny.'

I started but it was just Hollie sleep-talking. Her eyes were closed. Danny didn't stir. If it had just been Hollie there, I would've woken her, but I didn't want to disturb Danny. He gave me the creeps. Instead, I sat down at the mahogany desk under the window and wrote Hollie a note with her tortoise-shell fountain pen:

Hey Hols,

Didn't want to wake you. You must be so happy Danny's home. He looks just the same but a bit more manly, don't you think? Guess what? Scott's back, too! He called me at work and invited me to a party so I won't be able to come to your dinner tonight. Sorry. Promise I'll make it up to you with some Shakespeare on the weekend.

Love lots

Rx

I folded the note in half and laid it next to Hollie's head. Pillow marks creased her cheek and I was struck by how little she had changed since I'd first known her. Not thinking, I leant over and kissed her softly on the lips. She opened her eyes.

'Rosie,' she murmured sleepily, looking up at me with clear blue eyes.

'Go back to sleep,' I whispered, creeping backwards towards the door. 'I left you a note.' I knew she'd be upset about me not coming to dinner and I didn't want to get into an argument with her. She pushed herself upright and I thought how beautiful she was with her angel face so pale she couldn't sit in the sun, and her lips like the pink inside of seashells.

'Look.' She beamed across at Danny, who was still fast asleep, tranquil as a carved knight atop a sarcophagus.

'Don't wake him,' I said.

Absently, Hollie picked up my note from her pillow. I paused, my hand resting on the doorknob, waiting for the inevitable storm. She read it quickly, her smile fading to a look of hurt and confusion and then anger. Crumpling the note in her hands, she crossed the carpet and pushed me outside into the hall, closing the door gently behind us.

'Hollie, please, try to understand,' I entreated, but she pulled me down the stairs into the parlour where we stood face to face, about a metre apart.

'I can't believe it. After the way he's treated you. You're going to go crawling back to him just like that. I won't let you do it. I won't let you make such a fool of yourself.'

'But he rang me,' I protested, lamely.

Hollie scoffed, theatrically. She looked just like her mother. 'He never loved you, Rosie. He just used you for sex.'

'Like I didn't want him too! For fuck's sake, Hollie, I've been celibate for two whole years.' I sighed, realizing it was a pointless argument. 'Not that you'd have any idea what I'm talking about. You haven't even pashed a guy, let alone rooted one.' It was a low blow, one which I immediately regretted.

Hollie turned on her heel and was flying, two steps at a time, up the marble staircase. I called out to her, pleading with her to forgive me, but all I heard was the door to Mrs Bailey's bedroom slamming behind her.

4

When I got home, Mum was on her knees rolling out the plastic runners across the lounge room carpet. It was a ritual which went back a long way in our household, as long as I can remember, and meant only one thing – that someone was coming over, a rare occurrence which caused Mum great anxiety and an entire day of preparation.

Mum has a 'decontamination procedure' of military precision: clear plastic covers with elasticated edging for the couches; disposable plastic tablecloths; a hand-made sign positioned in the entry at direct eye-level – 'Welcome to our humble home. Please remove your shoes before entering' – then an arrow pointing down to a pair of 'jiffy' slippers vacuum-sealed in a plastic bag. In the bathroom, she disguises industrial-strength anti-bacterial liquid in a Palmolive 'Gentle On Your Hands' pump container, places a scrubbing brush next to another sign which reads, 'Please Use Vigorously', and hangs disposable hand-towels.

'Expecting visitors?' I asked.

She spun around. From under her bathrobe, I caught a glimpse of black lace.

'Oh, no one in particular,' she said, smoothing out the runner with her hands.

'C'mon, Mum. You haven't let anyone in the house since the plumbing broke last year.'

Mum got to her feet. With android meticulousness, she scanned the room for any remaining tasks. Satisfied, she turned back to me. 'I've got a date.'

'Who? How?' Mum hadn't dated since the sixties.

'Sit down and I'll tell you.' She dragged me onto the plastic-covered couch. 'I'm really excited.'

'I don't have much time.' I glanced at my watch.

'Sit down.' She patted the seat beside her.

I sat, my thighs squeaking hot and sticky against the plastic.

'I went to see Clive this week.'

'I thought you were done with him.'

'No. He's got this new therapy he thinks could really help.' Her cheeks were flushed. Her eyes glittered. 'It worked on one of his other patients, a woman who couldn't stop pulling out her hair. She was a lost cause, but then Clive recommended she join a dating agency.'

'Come off the grass.'

Mum wasn't listening. 'Clive calls it his love therapy technique. Learning to love again. You know I never loved your father. But now Clive says it's time I went out and found myself a nice man, before it's too late.'

'That's great, Mum.' I stood up but she yanked me back down.

'So, this morning, I went to a dating agency in Spring Hill. A lovely woman called Jeanie asked me all these questions like, "What's your favourite movie?", "Are you an early morning person?" and "Do you like spicy food?", and inputted my answers into a special computer which came out with my "compatibility partners". It was all very hi-tech.'

'I'm sure.'

'Then I watched the videos and picked out my favourite one.'

'Did he say how big his—'

'His name's Andy Bronson and he's a widower with no kids. His first wife died of cancer, very sad, but now, three years later, he's ready to move on. He's into ballroom dancing and fine dining. He's after a sensitive, caring woman who's not too tall.'

'What? Is he a dwarf?'

'Don't be smart. He's picking me up for dinner at eight so I need you to help me decide what to wear.'

She pulled me into her bedroom. Arms crossed, she stood in front of the built-in wardrobe, her pastel suits hanging like corpses in see-through plastic body-bags.

'I'm going for classy and sophisticated.'

'Mum, can't you do this yourself?' It was already six-thirty. 'I've got to get ready, too.'

She turned around sharply. 'Why? Where are you going?' Like I didn't have a life.

'Just out. With friends.'

'What friends?'

I stared back at her, defiant. 'You don't know them.'

'Don't lie to me, Rosemary. I know you're going over to Scott's. He rang here this afternoon looking for you.' My heart sang with those three little words – *'looking for you'*. She turned back to the wardrobe and started throwing suit after suit down on the bed. 'I hope you're not going to jump straight back into bed with him. I hate to think where he's been putting his thingo. Bet he's picked up all sorts of venereal diseases overseas. I read in the paper that syphilis is making a comeback.'

I squeezed my fists into tight balls and tried hard not to lose it. How dare she talk about Scott like that. I hated her with a passion. I hated the revolting apricot damask suit with gold buttons and grid-iron shoulder pads she was holding against her small rounded frame. I willed Andy Bronson to be a small-dicked loser with a lisp, hairy earlobes and bad personal hygiene.

'What do you think?' She pivoted back and forth between the mirror and me.

'Whatever. I don't really care.'

Her face collapsed like a crushed petal. She looked at me, her doe-eyes baleful with hurt like she was going to cry. 'I thought you'd be happy for me. It's not easy, you know. After all this time.' She put the apricot damask back in the wardrobe and picked up another one, sky-blue chiffon.

My rage sludged into guilt. 'I'm sorry, Mum, but you said yourself you've never been in love so how would you know anything about Scott and me?'

She addressed her reflection in the mirror. 'Face it, Rosemary, he treated you like dirt. You must have rocks in your head.'

'You've got no idea.'

'After all we've been through... '

I let her ramble on about all the stupid, psycho things I did when Scott broke up with me. Like the nights I slept in her bed because I couldn't bear to sleep alone and the time I went walking the streets in my PJs. I can't believe now how mental I went. For months it went on. Thanks to Trish, I got better in the end. She toughened me up, got me into new things like tatts and pot and not taking life too serious. But I never stopped thinking about Scott. I knew he'd be coming back, sooner or later.

Mum put the sky-blue chiffon back in the wardrobe and held a purple paisley number with pearl buttons up against her.

'How about this?' she said.

'It's hideous,' I said, and strode out of the room to take a shower.

I washed my hair, shaved my bikini line in to a thin porno-strip (how Scott liked) and plucked the spider hairs from around my nipples. Later on, after everyone had left the party and his parents had gone to bed, Scott would lead me into his bedroom, push me down on the bed and, not saying a word, undress me in the dark. He'd lick my breasts and tug at my nipples and bite my neck, whispering how much he'd missed me, how much he still loved me. I positioned the stream of hard hot water up into me and waited for the shock, the little weakening in my knees, then did it again. I turned off the taps. Fuck. No towel. I stuck my head out the door.

'Mum! Can you bring me a towel?'

Her heels clacked across the tiles. The linen cupboard squeaked open and closed. I stuck my arm out into the hallway, my body shielded behind the door. Mum didn't understand that once you got to a certain age it was no longer OK to see each other in the nude. A soft, lavender-fresh towel landed in my hand but then Mum was inside, decked out a pink gingham ensemble.

'How about this?' She twirled in the steam.

I shook out the towel and wrapped it around me. Too late, she'd seen two things she wasn't meant to see:

My butterfly butt-tatt.

My porno-strip bikini.

For a moment I thought she would pull the towel off me for a closer look. I waited for the inevitable onslaught – the risks of catching AIDS from the tattooist's needle, the slutty hairlessness of my pussy. She switched her gaze to the mirror, wiping a circle for her face in the mist. As she checked her frosted lips, her head shook like she was fighting some inner demon. For a few seconds it looked as though she was going to speak but she just gave a little restrained sigh and exited the bathroom.

Naked, I surveyed the pile of clothes on my bed. Should I wear what I used to wear? Denim minis and tiny tees. Or my latest look? Long hippy skirts and muslin tops. Underwear was easy – the black g-string he'd sent me from Harrods and a push-up, Grand Canyon setting. My body buzzed as if I'd been mildly electrocuted. Of course he still loved me. He'd called me babe, and why else would he invite me to his party? And what about the postcards he'd kept sending, even after we'd officially split up. Brief and chatty but always signed 'love Scott', with three kisses and three 'R's for roots. That was his little sign to me – *wait for me, babe, I'm coming home for you.* On the walls around my bed, I'd Blu-tacked each one of his postcards (seven in total) with the writing facing out. Over the past two years, his handwriting had changed a lot, from neat upright letters, to a broader freer hand. I lay down on the bed, my head on the pillow, and re-read for the zillionth time the last postcard he'd sent me. It was from Paris, dated July that year:

Yo babe!

Bonjour from Paris! Today we went up the Eiffel Tower and visited Notre Dame. Yesterday was Bastille Day and we stayed up till late partying and letting off hand-grenade firecrackers with these black dudes in the street outside our hotel. Like everyone says, the Frenchies are rude wankers but I still reckon you'd love it here, especially shopping on the Chumps-Elysées.

Love Scott xxxRRR

P.S. Hope uni is OK and you're keeping out of trouble.

I'd become expert at decoding Scott's hidden meanings, buried deep within his deceptively shallow prose. 'Keeping out of trouble' was his way of saying, 'I hope you're not with anyone else', and 'you'd love it here' meant 'in the future, we can go back here together'. He didn't know about me dropping out of uni to save money to go and see him, but with him back I figured none of that mattered. The only thing I worried about was that little 'we'. I hated that 'we'. Why couldn't he just say 'I'? 'We' made me edgy, that and the fact that he was in Paris, my number one overseas destination. I was pissed he'd gone without me. I mean, what a waste going to the most romantic city in the world with his mates.

I opted for the sexy look: a black, pleated mini with a gold sparkly halter-neck, which showed off my summer shoulders, and my new black strappies with wedge heels. Mum was in the shower when I left so I wrote her a quick post-it and stuck it to the fridge:

Mum,
Good luck on your date with Randy Andy. Hope you find true love. Don't do anything I wouldn't do!
Love R xxxooo
P.S. Sorry about before.

Outside the shadows were creeping in. There was not the tiniest breeze, the heat clinging to every inch of my skin. Across the street, I could see Mrs Leyland from number ten, silhouetted in the bright fluoro of the kitchen, her head bent over the sink. I took off my shoes and tossed them onto the passenger seat. The driveway was warm beneath my feet.

So, this was it. After all the waiting.

I got in my car and reversed out. A quick glance back at the house and there was Mum standing in the illuminated doorway dressed in a canary-yellow suit with square, black buttons. She looked like the Queen but she didn't wave so I honked the horn and she gave me a little smile. I felt sad for her, all lonely and timid in the doorway. She'd had a rough time of it with Dad. As soon as he started hitting her she should have left. She said she'd stayed because she got pregnant with me and I hated her saying that. As she turned back into the dark interior of the house, her shoulders stooped. I pumped the accelerator and sped away towards Scott, my head crammed with sex thoughts about the first time we rooted.

I'm sitting next to him at the kitchen table. Sweat runs down the back of my thighs, collecting in little pools behind my knees. Outside, the air shimmers in a heat mirage. Scott wrestles with the edges of the sports pages, which flutter in the currents from the ceiling fan. I place two empty tea mugs at the top corners of the paper. He nods and reads on, his full lips pursed in concentration.

'Mum'll be gone by now,' I whisper so that Mrs Greenwood, whisking eggs in the kitchen, doesn't hear.

Today we're doing it for the first time. At my house while Mum's at work. I think about doing it on her bed because her room's got air-con, but she'd find out somehow. She'd sniff out the sex germs. I wonder if I'll look different after we've done it. More like a woman. Less like seventeen. I wonder if my breasts will get bigger and if Mum will be able to tell I'm not a virgin any more. But I'm ready. We've been going out for almost three months and I've got my driver's licence now.

'C'mon.' I try to sound calm but my words are light and breathless.

'OK. Let's go.' Scott takes the tea mugs to the sink and kisses his mum on the cheek.

'Where are you two love-birds off to?' she asks.

'Rosie's place for a swim,' says Scott.

I stare at the table, studying the spiral grains in the wood. In my stomach, my nerves jitter like bugs around a fluoro.

'If I didn't have to make these bloody sponges for the Women's Auxiliary, I'd join you. It's like a sauna in here.'

Scott urges me down the stairs, through the rumpus room and outside into the blinding midday light. We stand bare-footed on the grass: me with my freckly arms folded across my bikini top; Scott bare-chested in tartan boxers. I stare up into his purple eyes, smudgy in the heat-haze, and I think about all the hours we've spent pashing until my jaw ached and ulcers burned in my mouth. I think about him pushing his fingers up inside me.

'Whose car?' he says.

Scott's rusty Gemini sits in the garage. Behind it, the brand-new Laser which I'd bought with Grandma's will money, its shiny, red body roasting in the sun.

'I'll drive,' I say.

'No. I want to.' Scott swipes for my keys.

'My car's in front.'

'Yeah, I'll drive yours.'

'No way. It's new.'

'But you just got your licence.'

'So?'

'I'm a better driver.'

'Crap. You drive too fast.'

'Slow drivers cause as many accidents as fast drivers.'

'I don't believe you.'

'Babe, just give me the keys. Stop being a silly little girl.'

'Stop being a silly little boy or I won't keep my promise.'

'You want it, too.'

I grin because I do but don't give in. 'C'mon, Mr Stubborn, get your scrawny butt in the passenger seat.'

'I'll race you instead.'

'But your car's a shitbox.'

'You'll be crying.' He dashes into the garage.

I climb into my car, fasten the seat-belt and reverse out on to Jacaranda Avenue. Scott pulls out alongside me. He leans across and shouts through the window.

'I'll give you a handicap, OK? Because you're just a chick.'

'No way. I don't need one.'

'You'll be sorry.'

He spends a long time lining his front wheels up with

mine so there can be no unfair advantage on either side. When satisfied, he says, 'On the count of three. I'll hold my hand up like this to signal go.'

I nod and picture the new sexy lingerie – black lace bra and matching g-strings hidden in the bottom of my jumper drawer – and, as Scott revs the accelerator on his 1979 bomb-mobile, a thrill rips through my body. His hand goes down and he shoots off towards the traffic lights, his head bent low to the steering wheel, smoke billowing out of the corroded exhaust. He beats the lights on amber but I miss them. As he streaks ahead, gathering speed along the straight parallel with the train tracks, he shakes his fist out the window, whooping like a maniac.

Crossing Indooroopilly Bridge, he's nowhere in sight, so I accelerate, flooring the pedal with my bare foot. The road is quiet as is usual for a hot weekend when BrisVegans flee to the coast or hang out in the backyard pools. Puddles of imaginary water vibrate on the tarmac as I turn left at Big Rooster – *who wants hot chicken now?* – and race up the hill towards the black, steaming bricks of the Uniting Church. On the crest I catch a familiar flash of silver, its tail end resisting then twanging round the bend as if made of chewing gum. But the traffic lights stop him and I pull up alongside in the other lane. Scott turns and winks, running his fingers through his hair like the Fonz. I lick my lips and pout. He looks ahead, pretending to ignore me, so I lean out the window and flash my right tit at him. He sees it and drops his gob. The lights change and I speed off, leaving him for dead. Ha!

Down the rollercoaster hill and up again. A slow choking mini approaches but I nip through. Adrenaline courses in my veins. My hair, loosened from its ponytail, flies around my head, trailing out the window, sticking to my lips, whipping my bare shoulders. I shout into the breeze and check my face in the rear-vision mirror, grimacing at the dark freckles, the pale refusal of my skin to go brown, and the scar which cuts in a diagonal gash above my right eyebrow. I hope there'll be time to re-apply Max Factor before we get down to it.

Around past the Toyota dealership, car bodies glint like jewels and I slip dreamily down into Russell Terrace. On the right, my old primary school is empty, under the sun the squat fibro classrooms bake like square sponge cakes. How fast I've grown up, I think, pressing my foot hard on the accelerator, speeding away.

At the bottom of the hill, I check the rear-vision. Scott's right on my tail. He honks and waves out the window, weaving about behind me, laughing and trying to overtake. We're passing under the freeway when he darts out like a fish, shooting over the double line onto the wrong side of the road. A blue car's coming the other way. It swerves, horn blasting, but Scott's already gone, tearing out of sight. I strain to see his car but the sun smashes and explodes on the burning crest of Green Hill. Faster! Faster! I cry, riding the car seat like a saddle. The sun-glare knocks out everything but I go harder, galloping into the white. I can't wait to get home, to show off my new underwear, to slam him down on the bed. He's going to love it, I just know. He's so going to love it. The engine wheezes as I change gear with a jaunty thrust and pull of the stick, and then I'm charging up the hill. My stomach floats, bumping soft against my heart. It all feels so good, so right. Scott loves me. *Why me with my ginger hair and freckles, my too-big feet and skinny legs, my scar?* I ask the shadowy grove of trees whose leaves turn wide and waxy to hear my question. They rustle back an answer but I'm already gone, dashing nifty into the bend. Curving into the apex, the wheel at its limit, there comes a spark of fear, a little quaking in my belly, a subtle shift in the car's bulk and a horrible sliding out of control. The steering wheel whirls through my fingers and I pump the ball of my foot against the brake pedal but it makes no difference. The road buckles and loosens, billowing free from the earth like a streamer. I'm flying out across western burbia, soaring up and up through the tree-tops, and it's all so quiet like my ears are jammed with cotton wool. Then it hits me, a gentle spreading, like a revelation or something I knew deep down already.

I'M GOING TO DIE.

The words appear giant, forged in tungsten, hovering silent in the air like a UFO. But I've got a calm, lullaby feeling, like I'm comfy with death. I see a single fluffy cloud, low-slung on the horizon, and a flash of rainbow lorikeet makes me grin. How strange, how beautiful the world is. But then, a pang that I hadn't fucked Scott sooner. The bonnet peaks, sniffing at the heavens. A beat, no more in which I beam some love vibes to Scott and a couple to poor old Mum and Hollie, too. And then I'm hurtling down to earth, the car pitching sideways through the air. I'm screaming, my eyes scrunched tight, my finger bones locked around the steering wheel, queen of my firey space-ship.

The car slams against its side with a heavy boom and crunch of metal. We flip onto the roof and, for a blink, I'm hanging like a bat in a cave, limbs flailing. And then we're spinning over and over, right ways up then upside down again, the seat-belt rasping at my neck, and it's like we're rolling down a mountain and I think it's never going to end.

We stop. We're upside down. Silence, complete as a vacuum. Am I dead? Ha. I could be dead. It strikes me as funny, being dead. Ha, again. I wriggle my toes, my fingers. I open my eyes. Grass is growing from the sky. Sounds come to me. The pretty tinkling of glass. Static on the radio. The hiss of air escaping. A breeze blows through the shattered windscreen, carrying a dank smell of soil, vegetation. Petrol. I get a vision of the car and me inside it, exploding into action movie flames.

Fuck. Get out. Quick. Gotta get out.

I unfasten my seat-belt and my body slumps forward. My legs crumple into my chest and my knees bash against the steering wheel. I twist around to fumble with the lock. My hands are shaking, my fingers slippery with panicky sweat. The door swings open, flattening the knee-high grass.

Curled like a foetus, I tip sideways out of the seat and onto the ground. I flip onto all fours and crawl fast through the spiky weeds. At a safe enough distance, I slump against a gravel incline and gaze over at the car lying, hidden from the road, in the middle of a vacant block. It's on its back like a Christmas beetle, its wheels pawing at the air as if struggling to get upright. Its sides are buckled, the windows shattered, but it hasn't exploded yet. A lone kookaburra peals with laughter and I tilt my head to the sky. Greenish storm clouds have gathered thick above, sun burnishing the edges.

I'M ALIVE.

The hum of freeway traffic. The rev of a lawnmower. Blue-skinned skinks chirping in the grass-roots.

Scott.

I turn and scamper up the bank, slipping and falling against the rocks. A strong gust sweeps across, blotting out the sun. A heavy raindrop splashes on my bare bikini-ed back and all the time I'm thinking, *Scott, Scott*. As I climb out onto the pavement and start walking, the storm hits with tropic force, rain pinging off the tarmac. My skirt sucks around my thighs and my hair hangs in wet clumps over my face. A car approaches, tyres hissing on the wet. Scott's Gemini mounts the footpath, breaking onto a grassy verge. He leaps out and dashes over to me, his eyes wild.

'What happened?' he shouts above the storm. Water droplets stream off my face as I stare at him blankly. He grabs me by the shoulders. 'I've been looking for you everywhere. Where the fuck's your car?' He shakes me and a pain rips up my left arm. I wince and fold it like a broken wing between my breasts.

'Babe.' His voice softens. He strokes my cheek and looks down. 'What's wrong with your arm?'

But my tongue is dry and useless. I nod back down the hill.

'OK,' he says. 'Show me.'

We skid down the bank. The storm shower has ended but the incline is alive with hundreds of little waterfalls, tumbling over the rocks. The sun comes out, warming my shoulders.

'Jesus fucking Christ.' Scott spots the car, lying heavy, sinking into the soil. Its metal underbelly glistens wet from the rain. 'C'mon, stunt-woman.' He's laughing as he sprints over to it. I float behind in a trance, mud squelching between my toes, the long, wet grass licking at my calves. I look up at the sky. The storm clouds scud away, leaving a sky so blue it makes me want to cry.

When I get to the car, Scott is lying inside, his bare legs sticking out of the wreck. I crouch down on the ground and tug at his shorts with my good arm.

'Did you land upside down or did it roll over?' His voice is muffled from inside the cabin.

I pinch the skin on his thigh, aching for him to hold me.

He wriggles out. 'Here. Show us that arm.' He takes my fingers, gently pulling until my arm is fully extended. 'Tell me if it hurts.' He presses the soft pads of his fingers along my arm, bending down as if to listen to the bones, working his way from the wrist up to the elbow joint. Pain shoots through me, up to my neck. He frowns. 'Yep, it's broken alright.' He stands and pulls me gently by the armpits, but I shake my head and lie down on the ground with my bad arm cradled into me. I'm so happy here in the sun, in the sweet-smelling grass.

He crouches over me, brushing my hair out of my eyes. I struggle to sit up. He inches closer, wrapping his arms around me. I press my face to his bare chest, lick his salty skin. I find his mouth, falling on to it open-jawed like I'm biting into a peach. My tongue searches out the walls, the teeth, the gums, his silky palate.

He pulls back. 'C'mon. We better get you to a hospital.'

I look into his eyes and suddenly the world is purple – the grass, the sky, his skin. Such a beautiful colour. With my good arm I push him down into the grass and pull off his boxers and all the time he's staring at me, unblinking.

'Oh, babe,' he murmurs. His purple cock is pointing at the sky.

Holding my arm stiff as an oar behind me, I dip down to lick and kiss the smooth, rounded tip of his penis. He groans, slipping back the triangles of my bikini top and twisting my nipples into buds. I crawl further up his body, straddling his thighs. With one hand, he reaches down, slides the crotch of my bikini bottoms to one side and pushes his fingers up into me. I close my eyes and tip my head back towards the sun, kaleidoscope reds and orange swirling behind my lids. I pull his fingers out of me and rear up, my pussy hovering over his dick, nudging and brushing against it.

'Oh, fuck.' He bolts upright and pashes me. Then he stops, draws back and looks at me. 'What about your arm?'

I push him back down again. His eyes flutter shut. I wait, one, two, three before sliding on to him. At first, it hurts. I bite hard on my bottom lip. But then, I'm spreading, opening, and he's in me and I want to get inside him, too. Right deep inside him. A soft, dark drowning in his blood. I'm having strange thoughts of being consumed, absorbed, devoured by him.

'I love you,' I say.

'I fucking love you, too,' he says.

I kick and shudder. My spine sways and teeters and I collapse on to him, just like I'm dying.

5

It was nearly nine by the time I parked under the leopard tree a few houses up the road from Scott's. From inside the car, I watched a pack of his old uni mates shouldering cartons of VB across the lawn. I patted some extra foundation on my scar, opened the door and stuck my legs out on the road to do up my strappies. I had a wild thought that maybe later, after the party had ended, Scott would take me down to the bottom of the backyard and fuck me under the mango tree where we'd done it heaps of times before. But I told myself to play it cool. Straightening my mini, I sashayed down the footpath and across the lawn. I knocked on the side door which everyone, except Avon ladies and Mormons, used instead of the front.

Mr Greenwood appeared, stubbie in hand. 'Well, hello there, stranger. Long time no see.' He was wearing a 'World's Best Barbie, Mate' apron. Since retiring from the police force, he'd aged a lot. His face was thinner and his hair white all over. He must've been pushing sixty. Slurping on his Fourex, he motioned for me to come inside.

'So, how's life been treating you, Rosie?'

'Not too bad, Mr Greenwood.' I scanned the room for Scott but he wasn't around.

'Call me Bill.'

'OK.' It was weird being back in the house but in two years nothing had changed. Down one end, the mirrored bar with the same old sign, 'No Sheilas or Darkies Allowed,' which Mr Greenwood had found at a garage sale and strung up as his idea of a joke. There was the vintage record player in the corner with stacks of LPs – Buddy Holly, Elvis, Neil Diamond – on either side. In the middle of the room was the pool table, set with Tupperware bowls of coleslaw, potato salad and mixed beans, buttered bread rolls for the snags, and two casks of Fruity Lexia wine.

'Er, what'll you have to drink, Rosie?'

'Wine, thanks... Bill.'

A ripple of male laughter drifted in from the backyard and I pricked up my ears for Scott's voice. As Mr Greenwood squirted some cask wine into a plastic cup, I edged closer to the screen door to see if I could spy him amidst the groups of guys standing in faded jeans and T-shirts on the lawn. I spotted Bomber, and Muzza with him. They were leaning back in their chairs, sucking on stubbies, grinning from ear to ear at some private joke. Bomber looked like he'd been pumping iron – his shoulders were busting out of a retro seventies shirt – and he'd swapped his thick Italian curls for a blade two crew-cut. Muzza was just the same as before, except skinnier. His clothes hung off him as he slouched back in the chair, his John Lennon specs perched on the end of his nose. Scott wasn't with them.

'Here you go, love.' Mr Greenwood shuffled over with my drink.

'Glad Scott's home?' I sculled the ropey stuff.

'Yeah, but after all his gallivanting he better bloody well simmer down and get himself a decent job.'

'They say it takes a while to settle back in,' I rallied, anxious to defend my man.

'Nah, I've got one no-hoper for a son. Don't need another one.' He waved his stubbie in the direction of Nick, Scott's older brother, who was setting up on the lawn with his band. 'Sure, he's not brain surgeon material but I always thought Scott'd make something of himself.' He drained his beer and sighed heavily. 'Isn't that what he went to uni for?'

I turned back to the pool table and re-filled my cup.

'Here, chuck us another stubbie, would you, love? I'd better go fire up the barbie since no other bugger's gonna do it.'

I handed him his beer out of the esky. He cracked the top off against a corner brick, took a long pull and exhaled, his red cheeks deflating like a balloon. 'Why don't you pop upstairs and see Shirl? She'll be tickled pink to see you.' He prodded me in the small of my back. 'Go on.'

But I didn't want to go upstairs. I wanted to find Scott.

I knocked back the rest of the wine, which was starting to taste not too bad, and, once Mr Greenwood had gone, headed around past the mirrored bar towards Scott's bedroom. I had a vibe he was in there.

How could I forget the skull and cross-bones sticker, with the words, 'SCOTT'S BEDROOM: ENTER AT YOUR OWN PERIL' scrawled in black texta. Its childishness made me smile and a warm glow spread from my guts down to my toes.

Pressing my ear against the door, I could hear music. I opened the door and went in. The room was dark save for a pulsing green coming from the controls on the CD player, which was pumping out low-volume techno. This was different. Scott'd always hated hardcore, refusing to go to clubs in the Valley because all they played was 'that stupid ravey shit for poofs and speed-freaks'. London must have changed his music taste.

I stood still, my ears straining to the possibility that he might be in the room. As my eyes adjusted, familiar objects took shape – his student desk under the window, the double bed shoved up against the wall, his bookcase, which displayed sports trophies on the top shelves, and a battered collection of textbooks and muscle mags on the lower shelves. I flicked on the desk lamp and, turning back around, stubbed my toe on the sharp corner of an open suitcase. I crouched down to check out the contents: a pair of new Nikes, a sleeping bag, a duty-free bottle of scotch and a couple of French porno mags. His clothes were all new – an assortment of designer T-shirts and silky shirts, tartan trousers and a pair of y-front undies – even though he always wore boxers. I plucked an orange hooded jumper from the pile, held an armpit to my face and inhaled deeply for his smell – that salty, scalpy smell that never ponged, just grew more intense the less he washed. I pulled the orange jumper over my head with the hood up, feeling safe and alive in his dirty clothes. It was a stinking hot night, even hotter in the room, but I couldn't help myself. I turned back to his suitcase, in case there was anything else I'd missed. In the side pocket was a packet of photos.

A thrill of the forbidden ripped through me as I pulled off the rubber band and settled back with the snaps in my lap. Most of them had been taken when Scott first got to London. Fucking Bomber was there, hanging off him in every photo, at every landmark – Buckingham Palace, Big Ben, the Tower of London – wearing his devil grin, posing rapper-style with his fingers splayed like a tosser. You could have picked them a mile off; two Aussie backpackers fresh off the plane. After six months, Bomber had come home, but Scott had stayed on.

Seeing those early photos slated me big-time. It should have been me, not Bomber, sightseeing around London, Paris, Berlin, Amsterdam with him. But then, I already had a plan. With my ten thousand smackeroonies, I'd convinced myself we could do it all over again but better, with style. Staying in nice hotels with king-sized beds and crispy sheets and chocolates on the pillows. I kept flicking through – Bomber and the Eiffel Tower, Scott and Stonehenge – and that's when I saw her. My heart dropped to the pit of my ribcage like a dead bird falling from the sky.

She looked half-Japanese. Late twenties. Her face a perfect oval framed by a sleek black bob and a short fringe. She was wearing a pair of white lace knickers and nothing else. Her breasts were small and white with pale nipples. Her limbs were long and gangly, her legs draped over the arms of a wing-backed chair. In the background was a tall bay window with a view of the countryside; a low slate sky threatening rain. Her skin glowed gossamer in the strange, northern light. She had a confidence, an ease, the way she lounged in that armchair. She was smiling, a knowing sparkle of superiority in her black, almond-shaped eyes, no more than a teasing curl on her lips. *Yes, look at me. Aren't I beautiful? Aren't I sophisticated? I'm older, smarter, better in bed. I know things. What do you know about the world, Rosie?*

Nothing but BrisVegas.

I grabbed Scott's duty-free scotch, broke the seal and took a big, burny slug. I stared at her satiny cheek, her glossy hair, her dainty crotch. Next thing, I was tearing the photo in half, then quarters, like my hands had taken over. They kept going until there was nothing left of her, just shredded bits of leg and eye and nipple scattered on the carpet. *Don't laugh at me, you bitch.* I couldn't just leave her there so I picked up all the pieces and shoved them down the crack between the bed and the wall, hoping Scott would never find them. Then, I went back out, half-cut and hunting for my man, wearing his orange jumper.

Out on the lawn, The Grubs were playing Beatles covers. Scott's brother, Nick, was singing, his dreads flying about like snakes. Mr Greenwood was on the barbie, tossing steakettes on the grill, his sweat dripping onto the meat. The men stood drinking and eating snags stuffed into long bread rolls, washed down with warmish beer. The women sat on plastic chairs, arranged in a semi-circle facing the band, paper plates piled with salads, balanced on shiny knees. It was hot and itchy in the jumper and I felt light-headed, a bit tipsy. The band sounded warped and distorted as if they were playing underwater. I trailed the border between light and dark, where the arc of floodlight ended and the green grass turned black. It wasn't long before I spotted him. He was standing near the fence, chatting to Bomber and Muzza. He had his back to me but I knew it was him. He was wearing a green T-shirt and a pair of baggy shorts. His hair was long, tied back with an elastic band. My armpits prickled with instant sweat. The lawn seemed to tilt forwards, tipping me towards him. I was close enough to reach out and touch him. My hand floated towards his right shoulder. It landed but didn't register. I squeezed the bone and he spun around, blinded by the glare of the floodlight. I drank him in. Stubble on a sharpened jaw. His chest meatier, harder. He blocked the light with his arm, squinting at me.

'Oh. Hi, babe. You made it.'

Babe. He called me babe.

Leaning forwards, he pecked me, once, on the cheek. His growth grazed my face. The smell of him filled me with want.

Say something. But my tongue sat fat as a lizard in my gob. *Fuck, I wanted him.* He was checking me out, I could tell.

'Looking good,' he said, giving me the once-over. 'You've lost weight.'

'I joined the gym.' Scott used to say he liked my curves, but from the way he was eyeing me off it was obvious he appreciated my newer, sleeker figure. My hard work had paid off. 'You've put on a bit,' I said, jabbing him in the belly, giving him grief to disguise my rapture.

'Yeah, I know. That'll be the beer.'

Before I could stop it, my hand shot out and stroked his sandpaper jaw.

'Like it?' His voice light and cheery. 'I'm growing a beard.' He fondled his chin.

'It's alright,' I said, mesmerized by his lips. 'You look like a fisherman.'

'Most chicks complain about the prickles.'

'I could handle your prickles.'

He laughed and his eyes sparkled. I couldn't stop smiling. Behind him, Bomber and Muzza were smirking, but I ignored them.

'Hey, Woody, she's wearing your jumper!' Bomber gawped like a drongo.

I looked down at the jumper like I didn't know what he was talking about.

Scott turned to me. 'Where'd you get that?'

'She just wants to be close to you, man. Isn't that sweet?' Bomber puckered his rubbery lips and made a sucking noise. I could've kicked his nuts to a pulp.

Muzza chipped in. 'I've read somewhere about this weird mental condition where people confuse hot and cold temperatures. They think it's cold in summer and hot in winter. Maybe you've got that, Rosie.'

'Yeah, right, thanks for that, Muzz, but I'm not mental,' I said, even though I knew I was acting pretty weird.

Scott said, 'When we were in India, we saw a yogi walking over burning coals. They imagine the coals are chunks of ice and that's how they do it. We made one guy show us the soles of his feet. Not one scar. It was incredible.'

The dirty little 'we' was there again, crapping on everything, but I pushed it out.

Scott turned around to face the band and I stepped up beside him, acting like I was really into the music, too. He was just about to say something to me when Mrs Greenwood screeched over the mike, 'Come on everyone. Gather around. Time to cut the cake.'

'Better do what the old lady says. Catch you later.' Scott nodded and sloped off. Bomber and Muzza followed him.

I stood rooted to the spot grinning like a loon, the world spinning around me; a blur of green lawn and shiny, sweaty faces huddled around the cake table. It was so hot in the jumper that I could feel foundation running off my face, my fringe pasted in clumps on my forehead. I pictured my freckled scar-face next to the Asian chick's cool oval of perfection.

'Rosie, do you want some cake?' Mrs Greenwood sang out to me and everyone turned to stare at the red-faced girl in an orange jumper, stuck in the middle of the lawn.

'Nah, I'm OK,' I squeaked, willing my legs to function; a jerky walk, a skip, then a run across the lawn and into the house. Back in Scott's bedroom, I ditched the jumper and re-did my makeup, wondering how long I'd have to wait till Scott and I were alone.

I spent the next few hours downstairs, sitting in a corner of the rumpus room, drinking Fruity Lexia and watching old codgers play shit pool, waiting for the party to end. Scott didn't come near me but I figured he was flat strap catching up with his friends – there would be heaps of time for us later. Around midnight, the old codgers went home. Mrs Greenwood marched upstairs to wash up and Mr Greenwood went to bed maggot. I headed out the back, fairly wasted by then.

A slight breeze rustled through the tree-tops but the night was dense and muggy. It was hard to breathe. Scott was standing around with his mates, polishing off the last of the beers with Nick and the rest of The Grubs. I lingered by the doorway, waiting for him to see me and come over, but despite some intense vibing, he didn't. The coloured lightbulbs throbbed like crazy fruit growing off the fence. I sauntered over to check them out. The red ones looked good. Plump and ripe and bursting as rampant tomatoes. But when I reached out they were so fucking hot I burnt my fingers. I ran inside and iced the poor suckers in the esky. Feeling stupid and a fair bit agitated, I carted the empty salad bowls upstairs.

Mrs Greenwood was bustling around, wrapping the leftover bread rolls in Gladwrap, transferring the cold snags and burnt steakettes onto smaller plates for the fridge. Kirstie, Bomber's on-off squeeze, was at the sink washing up. She was gossiping in a whiney voice to Mrs Greenwood but stopped midstream when I appeared at the top of the stairs.

'Rosie! Thanks for bringing those up,' said Mrs Greenwood.

'No worries,' I said, dumping the salad bowls on the bench.

'Hi.' Kirstie waved one blue rubber glove in my direction and smiled sickly sweet. We'd been in first-year law together until I dropped out. I shot her a fake smile, then turned back to Mrs Greenwood, who looked more youthful than when I'd seen her last. Her hair was streaked with gold highlights and she was wearing a daring shade of hot pink on her lips which matched the giant hibiscuses on her dress. She was way more glamorous than Mum.

'Kirstie and I were just talking about you,' she said.

'Really? That's nice.' It pissed me off no end to see them so chummy. I plonked myself down on a stool. 'Good to have Scott back?'

'Oh, yes,' said Mrs Greenwood, untying her apron. 'I've missed washing his dirty footy socks, making his cooked breakfasts.'

'I heard he had a girlfriend over there,' said Kirstie. 'Some Asian chick.'

A spurt of vomit came in my mouth but I swallowed it down, gripping the bench. Kirstie's beady eyes vultured for a reaction but Mrs Greenwood, never wanting to cause a scene, came to the rescue.

'He hasn't mentioned anyone to me.' Her voice dropped to a whisper. 'Besides, I can't imagine Scott with an Asian, can you, Rosie?'

I shook my head and breathed. *Good on ya, Mrs Greenwood. Nah, I can't imagine Scott banging an Asian. No way. No fucking way.* And even though I'd seen the photo, I believed her 'cause she was Mrs Greenwood and she was like my second mum.

Kirstie sniffed and turned back to the washing-up. 'Well, that's just what I heard.' I scowled at the back of her small, peroxided head.

'Anyone for bourbon?' Mrs Greenwood pulled a tray of ice-cubes from the deep-freeze.

'Better not,' said Kirstie. 'I've got to study this weekend.'

'Rosie?' Mrs Greenwood cracked the ice-tray against her thigh and bashed the cubes out onto the bench.

'Sure.' I jumped up off the stool, eager to talk more about Scott.

Armed with a bottle of Jim Beam, a litre of Coke and two glasses with ice, we went out to the front veranda. Mrs Greenwood lit a citronella candle for the mossies as I kicked back in a low-slung deck chair, my feet up on the railing. The night hummed around us. A streetlight flickered out front. The last train to Ipswich rattled in the distance. Mrs Greenwood mixed our drinks. I was wrecked before we even started. We chatted for a good hour or so about all kinds of rubbish. Like the new dress she was making to wear on Christmas Day, the best way to make pavlova, and her menopause. She told me all about the hot and cold flushes, the nausea and the periods of forgetfulness and neurotic behaviour. She said you could feel your eggs drying up inside you. It was strange how Mum never talked to me about these kinds of things. She was only a few years younger than Mrs Greenwood so she was probably due her menopause quite soon.

'But listen to me droning on,' Mrs Greenwood said, mixing herself another bourbon. 'I'm starved for female conversation.'

'We used to chat all the time.'

'That's right. Scott used to complain that I hogged you.'

'So, d'ya reckon he's changed much since he's been overseas?' I wheedled.

'He's got that dreadful beard.'

'I don't mind it.'

'It's terrible.'

'What about what Kirstie said?'

'Don't worry, love,' she said, patting my lap. 'He'd have told me if there was anyone serious.'

'But do you think...' I wanted more, some extra reassurance but I held back. 'Do you think he'll stay here for a while?'

'If he so much as mentions going anywhere we'll chain him to the bed!'

We laughed and, after finishing our second bourbon each, Mrs Greenwood yawned.

'Nearly two!' she said. 'I'll turn into a pumpkin. Do you want me to call you a cab?'

'No... I'll be alright.' Why couldn't I just stay over like all the other times when I slept in the spare room, sneaking downstairs to Scott's bedroom once she'd hit the sack? What was different now? I felt cheated, like she'd been leading me on.

'But how will you get home?' She stood up. 'You'll be over the limit.'

A knot of steel twisted in my chest as it dawned on me that things were different between us. 'Mum said she'd pick me up,' I lied.

'At this hour?'

'Yeah, she doesn't mind.'

'Well, say hi to her for me.'

'Yeah, OK.'

She said goodnight, bending over and kissing me on the cheek. Her lips were sticky with booze.

After she'd gone inside, I emptied the rest of the bourbon into the half-empty Coke bottle and went down the front steps, around through the side door and across the rumpus to Scott's bedroom. I'd had a fair bit to drink but I felt alright considering. There were low voices and music coming from inside but the door was locked. In the past, Scott'd only locked the door when we were having sex, in case Mr Greenwood, mistaking grunts and groans for burglars, came downstairs swinging his riot baton. I rapped lightly. The music went dead, followed by hushed whispering and muffled footsteps across the carpet.

'Who is it?' An edgy whisper. His.

'Rosie.'

A pause, then the door opened. Scott's face appeared in the crack.

'I thought you were Dad.' His eyes were bloodshot and he was grinning.

'Aren't you going to let me in?'

'But we're—'

I barged past him into the room. The curtains were

pulled tight, held together by a clothes peg. The air was thick and hazy with smoke, the smell of pot overpowering. Bomber and Muzza sat cross-legged on the bed: Bomber puffing on the biggest joint I'd ever seen, Muzza smiling with his eyes closed, his head tipped back against the wall. Kirstie had gone home.

Scott locked the door again, pressed play on the stereo with his big toe and sat down on a broken swivel chair, feet up on the desk. The suitcase had been shoved half under the bed. I thought about the photo, ripped to shreds down the side of the wall. There was nowhere to sit so I undid my strappies and sat on the floor with my legs stretched out, toes pointing in Scott's direction, not daring to look at him. I stared at a square centimetre patch of murky-green carpet. Awkward silence filled the room. I took a slug on my Coke-bourbon combo.

'So, you back for good?' I said, shooting him a sneaky glance.

He shrugged, tipping back in his chair. 'Hope not.'

'You gonna get a job like your old man wants?' Bomber sucked greedily on the joint, holding it in then opening his mouth wide as a goldfish, blowing smoke rings. His face swam in and out of focus.

Scott reached for the joint and Bomber passed it over. 'I've got some debts to pay off. But I'm not staying in this shithole for long.' He took a drag. 'Tell me what there is to do here except go on slurpee runs to the seven-eleven.'

'Man, it's not that bad,' said Muzza. 'You should check out the Valley.'

'Yeah, Woody,' Bomber added, 'there's a big rave next Saturday at Arena. Oblivion or some shit like that. They're headlining some decent DJs from Europe. I can hook us up with some A-class.' Bomber thought he was the fucking business but he was just desperate to appear cool in front of Scott. But then, we were all a bit in awe of him just because he'd been living in London for two years.

'Yeah, maybe.' Scott re-lit, toking hard to get it going. Before, he'd always been against drugs, even pot. I watched him inhale. No coughing or spluttering. Perhaps the Asian chick had got him into it. I pictured him fucking her stoned, rolling around in some king-sized hotel bed, and it made the bourbon bubble inside me.

'Give us a go,' I demanded, trying to focus on a stubbly patch of his jaw.

Looking straight at me, he took another puff, pinching the remaining stub between his thumb and middle finger. 'Since when do you spliff?' he said, exhaling smoothly.

'Fair while. At work, mostly,' I said, enjoying his attention.

'The coffee shop?'

'Yeah. Trish and me. When we're bored or fucked off.' It sounded like bullshit but it was the truth. 'What about you? You never used to.'

'Things change.'

'We were wasted all the time over there,' said Bomber, talking through the smoke. 'Weren't we, Woody? And not just weed. Every weekend, off our tits raving. It was mental. And the chicks... '

I looked over at Scott but he was studying the carpet, picking fluff out of it with forced intent. I wanted to get up and shake him, until the truth about the Asian chick came tumbling out, but I sat there, my eyes boring into the top of his sandy head.

'Yeah, man. We had ourselves some prime pommie pussy.' Bomber jabbed at the air with his rapper fist. 'Muzz, you sure missed out, man.'

'Yeah, thanks for reminding me,' said Muzza.

'If it was so good, why didn't you stay, then, Bomber?' I flared, knocking back some more bourbon.

'Too cold for him,' said Scott, looking up at last. 'He might look like a hard man but he couldn't hack the winter, could ya, mate?'

'That's crap. I was skint.'

'Yeah, that's your story and you stick to it,' Scott grinned.

'Fuck yers all,' said Bomber. 'Just remember who gets your gear, hey?'

'It doesn't matter. I've got myself a new supplier.' Scott kicked me gently. 'Hey, babe?'

'Who?' said Muzz, confused.

Scott passed me his dying joint. 'So, how good's your shit?'

I sucked hard on the soggy end but it was dead. 'What? Yeah. Not bad. Pretty good.'

'Great, 'cause your shit's shit, Bomber,' said Scott. 'All leaf. You should have tried the gear I was getting before I left. From this Paki guy who grew it in his basement. Fuck, I miss London.' Scott turned to me. 'So, can you get us some off this Trish girl?'

'Sure,' I said. 'No problem.' I didn't know what Trish could get but in the next breath, I'd promised him ten ecstasy pills and a fifty bag of speed. Right then, I would've promised the heavens and oceans and all the fucking universes in between.

'Fab.' He bent down and kissed me on the cheek. His face was close enough for me to pash him. His mouth hovered on the edge of my vision like a gorgeous bird, his lips all glossy. I imagined reaching out, touching them, my finger tracing the top, then the bottom lip, slipping inside, his tongue soft and wet, warm and pink and lovely. In and out. Round and round. Scott was back in his chair, acres away from me.

I knocked back some more bourbon and wondered how long it'd be before Bomber and Muzza racked off.

'Hey, Woody,' Bomber said. 'What happened to that Asian bitch you were doing?'

I swivelled my back to him, not wanting to hear it, but the bastard couldn't help but revel.

'Fuck off, Bomber,' Scott said.

'You should have seen her, Muzz, she was so fuck-ing nas-ty.'

'Yeah?' said Muzz, egging him on. 'I heard some stories about her, alright.'

'Shut the fuck up,' said Scott, dead serious.

'Yeah, man. Bad like you wouldn't believe. Great arse. Pins up to her cunt. You know it.' Bomber jumped up on the bed and started air-fucking. 'I could hear Woody banging her through the walls. She'd scream and carry on and shit like a filthy fucking chinky-whore.'

I looked over at Scott, wanting him to save me, to say it was all bullshit, but he was staring daggers at Bomber. 'Fucking shut it or you'll be sorry,' was all he said.

'Nah, Woody. Admit it. You were one lucky prick getting your cock into that every night. Oh, man, she had the tightest fucking arse I'd ever seen.'

Scott flashed past me, wrestling Bomber onto the bed, and pummelling him in the stomach. Muzza piled on top. They were all laughing, tangled on the bed like some fucking orgy to which I wasn't invited. The room smudged and blurred a myriad dirty colours. A flaming comet of booze rocketed from my gut, burning up my oesophagus. I peeled myself off the floor and raced, arms streaming, feet thundering, out through the rumpus and the side door to the front lawn where I spewed all over Mrs Greenwood's prize marigolds.

I lay down in the middle of the road, pretending to be dead. Even at that time of night the tarmac was warm as the beach. I pressed my ear to the ground and could hear tiny, groaning noises as the bitumen sighed off its heat. When Scott came out, he would see me lying like I was dead on the road, my legs crooked as if they'd been smashed and broken. Then he'd remember how he loved me, just like before. Just like after the car crash when we fucked in the wet grass and I came so hard I thought I was dying.

I could hear a car coming up the road. It approached slowly, its tyres crunching on the loose gravel. I lay still, holding my breath, pinned like a butterfly to the road, waiting for Scott to come flying off the lawn and whisk me up in his arms. The car rolled closer towards me, engine smooth and purring. I melted into the ground. The tar-baby screamed, *'Get up! Get up!'* into my ear, but I closed my eyes and thought about dying, wondering how it would be. The crunch of my bones. The squelch of my skin popping under hot rubber. I smiled and sank further into the tarmac, just then quite happy to die. But the car braked sharply, gravel spraying over me. My body bathed in white headlight. The sulphur pong of unleaded petrol and the clean tang of new chrome filled my nostrils. I lay motionless, listening to my heartbeat, waiting for Scott to save me. Classical music was coming from somewhere, and I could feel heat from the radiator. He bent over me, scooping me off the tarmac. I was all floppy-flimsy as he carried me across the road in his strong arms and set me down on the lawn. The grass was cool and springy beneath my feet.

'What the hell were you doing?'

The voice was familiar but it wasn't Scott's. I opened my eyes. A man, tall and dark, loomed over me. He was wearing a long, grey trench with silver buttons. His hands fluttered like white birds out from the cuffs of his coat. I peered into his face, but it was hidden behind a black curtain of tangled hair.

'Danny?'

I turned at the crunch of footsteps on the drive. Scott was striding towards us. I wondered if he'd recognize Danny from school days.

'Hey, Danny, how's it going?' Scott sounded casual, like he was talking to a mate.

Danny tucked his hair behind his ears. He stared at Scott, his black eyes huge and dilated despite the brilliant light. 'I just got out,' he said.

Scott was nodding. 'Great.' And then, as if searching for something else to say, 'I've just got back from London.'

'I just got out,' Danny repeated as he stepped forwards and patted Scott on the shoulder.

'Yeah?' Scott glanced at Danny's hand on his shoulder. 'You just said that, mate.'

There was a mega-weird vibe in the air.

Danny withdrew his hand from Scott's shoulder. 'London, hey.' His expression was blank. Suddenly, he burst into a kind of jig on the spot. 'They're changing the guards at Buckingham Palace. Christopher Robin went down on Alice.' His voice was low and whimsical, spoken in fits and starts. 'Did you visit Queenie?'

Scott cleared his throat as I grabbed his hand. 'Nah.' He gave a short laugh. 'But it was pretty wild.'

'Wild.' Danny repeated, deadpan. 'Lots of girls?'

'Yeah. Nah.' Scott glanced at me. 'I mean, we, me and Bomber, we had some crazy times. That's all.'

'And how is the old Bomber these days?' Danny asked.

'Not bad.' Scott turned to me, lowering his voice. 'Babe, you'd better go home now.'

But I didn't want to go home. I clenched his hand tighter.

Scott nodded at Danny. 'Mind giving her a lift?'

'Sure.' Danny turned and headed back to the car.

'He's a psycho,' I whispered to Scott. 'What's he doing here anyway?'

'Fuck knows.' Scott shrugged. 'Go on. I'll call you tomorrow.'

'You coming, Rosie?' Danny stood waiting, his arms draped over the open car door.

Scott shoved me forwards.

'But what about...'

'The fellas are staying over,' Scott said. 'I'll call you tomorrow.'

I leaned over to kiss him but he turned his head and my lips caught on his stubbled cheek.

'Prickles,' I said.

'I warned you.' Scott backed away, giving Danny a wave. 'See ya, mate.'

Danny nodded and ducked inside the car.

I stood in the middle of the road, watching Scott cross the lawn and disappear inside the house. Shielding my eyes from the headlights, I looked over at the car. Danny was sitting behind the steering wheel of Mr Bailey's gun-metal Lexus. I wasn't too keen about getting in the car with him. After all those years he was like a stranger to me.

When I'd last known him, he was a pretty normal fourteen-year-old, despite what he'd been through with his mum. When he first started high school, he used to have mates over all the time. Hollie and I would hear them downstairs, in the billiards room, getting drunk on his dad's vintage. One time, when Hollie was having a bath, I crept downstairs with a kitchen stool and spied on them, through the glass panel above the door. At the time, I didn't know their names. They were just Danny's mates. The skinny one with glasses (Muzza) and the beefy one with dark, curly hair (Bomber). The freckly ginger one (Matty Taylor) and the tall, good-looking one with sandy hair (Scott). They sat cross-legged or stretched out on the carpet, drinking burgundy from the bottle, rap music playing low. Muzza puffed on a cigarette, before passing it over to Bomber. Danny sat to the side, his back against the wall, his knees bent up to his chest, watching his mates laugh at something on the telly. I focused on the screen but couldn't make a picture from the pink fuzziness. The sound made no sense either, a series of grunts and groans but no words. I couldn't work it out. The picture froze. Scott got up and went over to the telly, pointing with his finger at something in the middle. The others were all curled up in balls and rolling around, clutching their stomachs. Bomber knelt down and licked the screen with his tongue. That got them laughing even harder. I was desperate to know what was so funny, but Hollie was calling me so I leapt down off the stool and ran back upstairs.

The car horn made me jump. Danny stuck his head out of the window. 'Are you coming or not?'

I staggered over to the Lexus and got inside. The door swung shut with an expensive thud. The taste of vomit sat bitter in my mouth, as I slouched down in the slippery, leather seat and said, slurring my words, 'Drive slow, alright?'

Without a glance in my direction, Danny u-turned and sped off, his knuckles viced around the steering wheel. Opera blared from the speakers and when I asked him what it was he said it was the most beautiful piece of music he'd ever heard.

'The final scene from *Tristan and Isolde*,' he said. But it filled me with wretched want, so I made him turn it off. I must've fallen asleep because next thing we were pulling up outside my house and Danny was shaking me awake with his cold, cold hands.

Exactly five years since the day Mrs Bailey shot herself, Hollie and I are home alone, eating pizza for dinner and watching *Wuthering Heights* on video for the zillionth time. Mr Bailey is stuck at the office. Danny isn't home from footy training yet.

Hollie takes a half-hearted bite of pizza. 'It's past nine. Danny should've been home an hour ago.' She jumps up and paces back and forth in front of the telly in one of her mum's satin evening gowns and high heels.

'Hollie! Get out of the way. This is my favourite part.' It is the bit when Cathy dies in Heathcliff's arms.

Hollie waves at the screen. 'Why couldn't he just be nice?'

'But he's mysterious,' I say. 'Women love that.'

'He's too moody.'

'You're so boring, Hollie.'

'No, I'm not.'

The doorbell rings. 'There, I bet that's him,' I say.

'He's got a key,' says Hollie, scampering down the stairs.

I press pause on the remote and follow.

There are two cops in uniform at the door. They are serious with grey faces.

'Can we speak to your father?' the taller, meaner-looking one says. His eyes dart from Hollie to me like he's trying to work out if we're sisters.

'Dad's not home,' says Hollie, arms folded.

'Your mother, then?' says the shorter cop, shifting from one leg to the other as if he needs to do a wee.

'Mum's dead,' says Hollie, matter-of-factly.

The cops exchange a look.

'Mr Bailey will be home later,' I say.

'How old are you girls?' the meaner cop asks.

'Eleven,' I say.

'You shouldn't be here on your own,' says the shorter cop.

'We'll wait for your dad,' says the mean cop.

'What's wrong?' I ask, a chill spreading through me.

'Where's Danny?' Hollie shouts. 'What's happened to Danny?'

'Calm down,' says the short cop.

I wonder if I should invite them in but they push inside anyway. Hollie runs upstairs to her bedroom, slamming the door. The cops wait in the parlour, sitting upright on the yellow chaise longue, drinking cups of tea and eating fruitcake which I bring them. When Mr Bailey arrives back and sees them, he rings Mum to come and pick me up. It's not until the next day that I find out Danny has killed his schoolmate, Matty Taylor.

6

'Go away.'

'But it's past noon. You can't lie in bed all day.'

'Mum, just leave me alone.'

'Hollie's been on the blower wondering where you are.' Mum was drawing up the venetians. The midday sun streamed in, fierce and burning.

'Don't do that! I'm really tired, OK? Just get out.' I shoved my head under the pillow and waited for Mum to scat. My chest ached under a heavy weight, as if a huge black crow was sitting on my ribcage. Blurred visions from the night before crammed my brain:

The Asian chick.

The orange jumper.

Bourbon. Pot.

Vomming in the marigolds.

Lying down dead on the road.

And then Danny, turning up out of nowhere like he was Scott's long-lost mate. Did that really happen? But thinking just made my hangover worse.

'Are you upset about something? What happened with Scott?' Mum plonked down on the edge of the bed, her soft hip squashing up against my backside. 'As long as you didn't sleep with him, that's the main thing.'

Inside my head I chanted, *fuck off fuck off fuck off* over and over, my molars grinding against each other, my eyes screwed tight as bolts. I dug my nails harder into my thighs.

'Well, don't just lie there. Tell me what happened. Has he got another girlfriend, is that it?' From under the pillow, I could hear the muffled sound of next door's kids shrieking and thrashing around in their pool. Mum was prodding me in the back, but I wasn't going to let her win. 'Well, if you're not going to talk to me you can at least get out of bed and call Hollie back.'

I knew why Hollie was calling. It was Saturday and I'd promised her a session of Shakespeare in the cave. Any other day but not today, not after I'd fucked it all up.

Mum wrenched back the top sheet. I hadn't bothered to change out of last night's clothes.

'You didn't even take your shoes off!' she squealed. 'I'll have to disinfect the sheets. Just how much did you drink last night? Your car's not in the garage.' She ripped the pillow off my head. I could just imagine what my face looked like; racoon-circles under bloodshot eyes, smudged lipstick, my fringe sticking up all over the place. I stared at her, wild-eyed, feverish, wanting her to be disgusted.

'You'll end up like your father if you don't watch it,' she said quietly, as if she barely dared.

My hand shot out and slapped her across the face. 'What did you say that for?' Mum jerked back in alarm, a prick of fear in her eyes. Her shoulders hunched. My fingers were stencilled bright red on her cheek, like an aboriginal hand-painting. She pressed her hand to her face as she got up from the bed and walked stiffly towards the door. My palm stung from the smack. I couldn't believe I'd hit her.

'Mum. I didn't mean it.' She turned around and stared at me, her lips tight. I drew my knees up against my chest, bowed my head, letting out a sob of remorse.

'Don't cry.' Mum came and sat down on the edge of the bed. She touched my arm.

I looked up. 'I'm so sorry.'

'You're nothing like him.' Mum hugged me, her forehead touching mine. 'I'll go and make you a cup of tea and some toast.'

When she returned, I asked her about her hot date with Randy. A broad smile spread across her lips.

'You mean Andy.'

'Yeah. Randy Andy. Was he randy?'

'It wasn't like that at all. No. He was a perfect gentleman. He took me to this really swanky restaurant overlooking the river and then we went ballroom dancing.'

'Yeah. And then after the dancing?'

'He drove me home.'

'Did he kiss you?'

'He kissed me goodnight.'

'On the lips?'

'On the cheek.'

'Good girl, Mum. Don't do anything rash now.'

'Don't be smart.'

'Did he come into the house? Did he see the plastic everywhere?'

'He didn't come inside.'

'Didn't he want to?'

'Stop it, Rosie. He's a perfectly lovely man. He's picking

me up tonight at six-thirty to go and see *Phantom*, so you can meet him if you like.'

'I'm working.' It was my plan to avoid meeting Randy Andy for as long as I possible.

'Oh, that's a shame.' She sounded disappointed. 'I've told him all about you.'

'What does he do?'

'He's some kind of a scientist out at the university. But he didn't really go into it.'

That was right. While I was killing the Asian Bitch and vomiting my guts out, Mum had been tangoing with some nerdburger who hadn't the balls to give her some decent tongue.

I am six years old, lying in bed listening to Mum and Dad fight. Tomorrow is Easter so I'm trying hard to get to sleep, worried that the Easter Bunny won't come if I'm awake. I stick my fingers in my ears and cover my head with a pillow but I can still hear them shouting. *Shut up. Just shut up.* I say it over and over, my fists tight as rocks against the mattress.

Their voices are muffled but I can tell them apart: Dad's booming thunder; Mum's timid squeak. It's like Dad has grown into a giant and Mum has shrunk to the size of a mouse. I can hear Dad kicking the lounge chairs around and punching the walls, the fibro crumpling like paper. Each time he makes a hole, Mum goes to Shoppingtown and buys a new laminated poster so that there are posters all over the walls, Blu-tacked at odd heights: a clown with diamonds for tears; a ballerina with pink legwarmers; a 'Life Be In It' one with Norm the fat guy; the Daintree rainforest with the slogan 'Queensland – Beautiful One Day, Perfect the Next'. But my favourite is the talking vegetables with smiling faces and shiny button-eyes. It's in the hallway, hiding one of Dad's kicking holes. In my imagination, the carrot says, 'I'll make you see in the dark', the fat potato with specs says, 'I like sitting on the couch', and the family of peas say, all in happy unison, 'We love it in our cosy pod.' Sometimes I sit down cross-legged to chat with the friendly veggies. That night I am scared and want to talk to them, but they are fast asleep, being good for the Easter Bunny, too.

Dad tears through the house like Cyclone Tracey. Mum begs him to stop. Then, I hear a big smashing sound. I scamper out of bed, down the dark hallway, past the sleeping vegetables, towards the living room. I hang back in the shadows, wondering where Dad is, afraid. Mum is slumped in the corner near the sliding door which is shattered, shards of glass hanging like icicles from the frame. Her head is bowed to her chest, and her feet, twisted at a strange angle, are cut and bloody. I want to run to her but Dad is kneeling beside her, speaking in a low voice. His back is to me so I can't see what he is doing. I creep out into the light, softly, softly, so he can't hear me.

I can see better now. Mum is breathing, her breasts straining in and out against her flowery, cotton shirt. She stares at Dad, her eyes blank and stony. A streak of blood, red as paint, runs down her left cheek. I crawl in closer, crouching down in the shadows under the kitchen table, scrunched in a ball, watching.

What have you done to my mum?

But Dad's words are gentle. His fingers are tender as he picks splinters of glass from her legs and her feet. 'Janice, I'm so sorry. I didn't mean to hurt you. I never meant to hurt you. Janice, I love you.' He kisses her forehead but she winces and pulls away. He is crying. I haven't seen Dad cry before and it makes me feel so sad.

From the floor, he takes the neck of a broken beer bottle and twists the jagged edge into the white inner side of his forearm until blood spurts out of his skin. Without thinking, I dash out from under the table yelling, 'Stop, Dad! Stop!'

He looks up, unseeing, as if he doesn't know who I am.

'Rosemary! Go back to bed, pet. Go back to bed!' Mum says, struggling to get up.

Dad turns and runs out of the house, blood dripping from his arm onto the carpet.

In the morning, I wake up early. At the foot of my bed, in a basket lined with yellow tissue paper, are six Easter eggs wrapped in brightly coloured foil. I run with the basket of eggs into Mum and Dad's bedroom, but Dad isn't there and Mum is fast asleep. For a long time I watch her sleeping, her face peaceful but covered in cuts and bruises. Any other day, I would wake her up by jumping on the bed or tickling her feet. But that morning I just watch her sleeping. I pick out the prettiest Easter egg, wrapped in nice pink foil, and snuggle it in the crook of her folded arm.

7

After a cool-off dip in the pool, I chucked on cut-offs and a boob-tube and headed around to Hollie's. It was no more than a ten-minute stroll, but the heat made me cranky and, by the time I got there, I was in no mood for Shakespeare.

Hollie was sitting cross-legged on a shady patch of the driveway, the *Complete Works* open in her lap, a wicker basket at her side. A wide straw hat eclipsed most of her face save her lips which were busy mouthing lines from *Midsummer*. After the way she'd carried on the day before, I decided not to mention Scott unless she brought him up. I strode up the drive and stood, casting a giant shadow over her.

'My Fairy Queen.' I bowed.

Hollie was so engrossed that I startled her. She leapt up. 'Darling, I've been waiting ages for you.' She was wearing a long, white dress and lace-up boots. 'But, no matter, you are here at last.' She sometimes had a peculiar, old-fashioned, pommie way of speaking, like she'd been taking her English Lit lectures too seriously. Offering me her hand, she said, 'Shall we henceforth attend our forest chamber, my noble Oberon?'

'Listen, Hols,' I said. 'How 'bout we go and get a chocollo at Shoppingtown?'

Chocollo was Hollie's favourite low-fat chocolate ice-cream. But she wouldn't have a bar of it.

'As Titania, Queen of the Fairies, I order thee, my noble Oberon, to uphold thy sacred vow to lie with me in our leafy chamber. I even made us a special picnic and everything.' She lifted a gingham cloth off the top of the wicker basket. 'See?' There was a bottle of pink champagne, two crystal flutes, a baguette and a pot of the vile fish-spawn Hollie adored.

'Oh, alright,' I sighed. 'But only for an hour or so.'

Hollie picked up the wicker basket and tucked the *Complete Works* under her arm. She slipped her hand in mine and, like two English ladies taking a turn in the garden, we set off up the bush track into the national park, a scrubby tract of bushland which stretched from Chapel Hill north towards The Gap and west towards Enoggera State Forest. From the end of Hollie's cul-de-sac, the guttered dirt track rose steeply up the hill to a flat clearing at the top. Turn right and you ended up on a road which led to a tourist look-out point where Scott and I used to go to pash and eat ice-cream. Further up the road were the television stations, all four of them, their steel satellite towers blinking snazzy red lights across the prehistoric terrain. But Hollie and I would always turn left at the clearing and crash headlong into the bush, zig-zagging between the stringy barks, rocky outcrops and dried-out gullies, following our secret way to the cave.

'Darling!' Hollie was calling back to me. As usual, she was ahead, slipping like a ghost between the silver gums. 'After the picnic we'll do Act Two, OK? Me as Titania, you Oberon.'

'Fine.' I was always the man but I didn't care. Fighting waves of hangover nausea, I kept plodding up the track. I wanted to ask Hollie about Danny being outside Scott's last night but I needed to wait for the right moment.

The further we climbed, the louder the cicadas and the fiercer the sun. The scrawny eucalyptus offered little shade and I could feel the top of my scalp burning. In the cooler months, the track was a busy thoroughfare for bushwalkers but in the height of summer it was deserted. Every so often, there were bush fire warning signs, nailed into tree trunks. The week before there'd been some emergency services guy on the news predicting bad fires by New Year if the drought persisted. The track was reaching its steepest bit and I kept skidding backwards on the loose gravel. I leant against a paperbark for a quick breather and looked out.

The dusty soup-bowl of BrisVegas lay beneath me: a far-away sprinkle of skyscrapers encircled by endless suburban plains; the river basking dull and brown like a giant snake in the sun. On all sides the mountains, once green, were hazy purple and parched. I closed my eyes and could hear the hum of traffic on the Western freeway and a distant chainsaw, but around me it was quiet and still. Up in the bush, far above the ant-like scurry of burban lives lived in brick boxes, cars, gyms, shopping centres and multiplexes, I could imagine I was different, set apart, a cut above the rest. I turned and kept going, pushing off my knees for extra momentum, until I reached the clearing. My heart was racing like crazy, my face itchy with sweat, but my hangover wasn't as bad. I sat down on a burnt-out stump. Despite the heat and the bugs and the effort of climbing, I always felt better up there; freer, lighter, more alive.

'Is something the matter?' Hollie knelt beside me and stroked my brow. Her fingers were powdery-soft and cool. She was wearing a new perfume which was too musky, too grown-up for her, and it made me feel sick. Her eyes flitted over my face as if trying to read something in me. I could tell she wanted to ask me about Scott, to hear that things had gone badly at the party; for some tale of betrayal or bitter disappointment that would prove she'd been right about him all along. She'd been joyous when he dumped me. That first night, after the phone call, I'd climbed out my window and ran barefoot in my pyjamas to her house. I threw stones at her window and she came outside in her long cotton nightie and hugged me and told me that everything would be alright because we had each other. She said she loved me and we pashed like pretend lovers and she made me swear on Lady Shalott's watery grave never to speak of Scott again.

'Did you have a late night?' It was her coy way of asking if I'd slept with him.

'Yeah, kind of,' I said.

Hollie got up and wandered off but not before I caught a frown of annoyance cross her brow. 'Did you sleep with him?' she shot, petulantly, from across the clearing.

I turned to face her and lied, 'Yes.'

'How could you?' Her pretty mouth twisted in disgust.

Indignation burned in my chest. 'Just because *you* don't have anyone!'

She stared at me, eyes blazing. Her lips twitched as if she was about to say something but instead she snatched up the basket and tore off through the bush until I caught up with her. I grabbed her by the back of her skirt and spun her around. She looked at me coldly, but I slipped my hand around her waist and waltzed her about in a circle. Her body was stiff, unyielding in my arms, but as we danced, lacing between the trees, kicking up clouds of dust with our feet, her face softened into a smile. I set her down on the ground like a doll.

'Do it again,' she panted. I picked her up and twirled her around, and she threw her head back and laughed like a little girl, her eyes shining out from beneath the wide brim of her hat, her cherry lip-gloss sparkling in the sun. She took me by the hand and led me towards the cave, the scorched leaves crunching beneath our feet. Our footsteps fell into sync; her kid-leather boots; my stinky sneakers, sweaty-slimy between the toes. There was a rustle of a goanna or a snake in the lantana which grew in tangled clumps along the way. Hollie let go of my hand and charged ahead, all forgiven, as I followed behind her to the cave.

Danny, Hollie and I discovered the cave by accident one September holidays not long after Mrs Bailey died. We were up in the bush, playing explorers, pretending to be lost and slowly dying of starvation. We had stopped to rest in a small clearing, which was partly shaded by a granite outcrop. The base of the rock face was overhung by ferns growing out of the cracks, and carpeted in soft moss. Exhausted, we leaned back in the dappled light against the cool green fronds, only to fall backwards, all three of us, into the cave. You'd never have known it was there. We scampered inside where we found yellow, orange and white hands stencilled into the rock and, on our third or fourth trip, a babysized human skull. Imagine our delight! This was all we needed to believe that real aborigines had once lived there. We placed the skull on top of an egg-shaped rock, which rose up from the centre of the cave, and there it stayed for years, our sacred talisman. We swore on Mrs Bailey's grave never to tell anyone else about the cave and it became our secret place.

Hollie was waiting for me at the entrance, the lace border of her skirt covered in orange dust, her straw hat drooping like a giant sunflower. Over the years, we'd knocked away the hole so that, as we got older, it was always big enough to squeeze through. We crawled in, one after the other. Inside, it was cool, shaded from the sun by the overhanging vines, and still just high enough to stand up in. We'd decorated the interior with satin cushions along the walls and a red velvet curtain which hung from a steel rod wedged between the rocks. In the afternoon, only a small amount of light penetrated the cave, giving the impression of night when outside the day blazed with heat.

Hollie raced around, lighting the ring of candles. 'I can't wait for you to see Danny,' she said, excitedly.

I grabbed the pink champagne out of the basket, popped the cork and took a slug.

'No, wait.' Hollie dashed over to the basket for the flutes. I filled them up, but too quickly, so that the bubbles ran over her wrists. She laughed as I licked the champagne off her skin. Hollie spread a gingham rug over the dirt floor and unpacked the gourmet delights, while I leaned back with a cushion against the egg-shaped rock in the middle of the cave, sculling and watching her dainty movements.

'Actually, I saw Danny last night outside Scott's,' I said casually, pouring myself another glass of champagne – it seemed to cure my hangover.

'Don't be ridiculous,' Hollie scoffed. 'He was with me all night.'

'No, it was him. Scott and him spoke. There was this weird vibe between them. It was like Danny was dropping by to let him know he was out.'

'You must have been drunk, imagining things.'

'Look, Hollie, I'm telling you it was Danny,' I said, exasperated. 'Ask him yourself.'

'Impossible. Danny and Scott stopped being friends a long time ago. It's a mystery to me why you keep throwing yourself at him. He's hardly what we dreamed of for each other.' She was so bloody irritating. The number of times I'd tried to make her understand that real life wasn't all pink champagne and floppy-haired gentlemen.

'You just don't get it, do you?' I said. 'Aren't you curious?'

'About what?' Hollie looked up, flushed.

'You know, about guys and sex and stuff.'

Hollie glanced at me, a swift, icy flash. She lowered the silver spoon from her mouth and leant across the rug for her Complete Works. She opened it at a book-marked page and started reading.

'Don't you want to know what it's like?' I persisted. 'You know, all that romantic stuff's just bullshit. Waiting around forever until your tits get saggy and your teeth fall out. Who's going to want to do you then, hey?' My voice echoed around the cave, our shadows shuddering in the candlelight as if under my command. Perhaps I was harsh but sooner or later she had to quit living in her fantasy world. I goaded her with a line from *Midsummer*: '*To live a barren sister all your life, / Chanting faint hymns to the cold fruitless Moon.*'

But Hollie ignored me and continued reading. It was infuriating. I leapt up, snatched the *Works* off her and flung it away. The book sailed across the cave and slammed with a thud against the back wall, dislodging a miniature avalanche of dust and rock and landing in a puddle of muddy water. Hollie sat mute, her face draining whiter and whiter. She bowed her head and smoothed her skirts over her lap.

'Be gone. Thy heart is tarnished, black as stone, ill-deserved of thy Queen's purity.' She sniffed and turned her back on me, fishing her Shakespeare out of the puddle. I watched as she wiped the spine off on her dress, leaving muddy streaks down the front of her white skirt. I felt my heart opening up, flip, flap, with feelings of love, and I wanted to bundle her up and keep her safe and tell her I was sorry for being such a bitch.

'Come here,' I said, gently. 'Please.'

Setting her Shakespeare down on the rug, she came over and laid her head on my lap. I ran nice spider fingers down the inside of her arm.

'Kiss me, Oberon,' she murmured. 'Kiss me like we're lovers.'

It was our cue. Hollie sat up and I clasped her face between my hands. I leant in, my breasts pressed against the stiff bodice of her dress. I felt her heart beating fast as a newborn kitten's as we pashed, open-mouthed like lovers, like we'd done a thousand times before, except this time Hollie was more impassioned, more urgent, and when I pulled back, she whispered, 'I'm not as innocent as you think.'

Leaning in, she kissed me again.

'Jeez, what a sight for a bloke just released from captivity.' A dark figure was silhouetted against the bright entrance to the cave.

'Danny!' Hollie sprang back from me, wiping at her lips, and rushed to embrace him. 'Where've you been?'

'Hunting,' he said, straight-faced.

Hollie and I laughed as he entered the ring of candlelight. His face was sickly pale with big, black circles under his eyes like he hadn't slept in days, and he was wearing his thick army trench even though it was nearly forty degrees outside. When he turned around, I caught a glimpse of his body, naked underneath. Hollie saw it, too.

'Where are your clothes?' she demanded.

'Huh?' Danny acted dumb.

'The new clothes I bought you.'

He opened his coat and looked down. I took a quick peek, comparing his to Scott's, which, as I remembered it, was a fair bit bigger.

'Oops,' he said. 'Must've forgot to put them on.' He laughed, whipping off his coat and raising his long, gangly arms up to the ceiling. Naked, he capered about, shrieking and scratching at his armpits like a monkey. He'd always been a bit zany but he'd never acted as weird as this before.

'Danny, please,' said Hollie, grabbing hold of his arms and pulling him down next to her. 'Rosie doesn't want to see your parts.' She threw his coat over him, but he tossed it off again.

'It's better naked,' he said, grinning. 'Clothes block the flow.'

'The flow of what?' I asked, genuinely curious. He looked at me for the first time and I wondered if he even remembered picking me up off the road the night before.

'I've been communing with the spirits.' He nodded, emphatically.

'Stop it, Danny,' Hollie chided. 'You're talking nonsense.'

I turned to Danny. 'What spirits?'

He grabbed my fingers and squeezed them so tight I thought he'd crush my bones. 'The spirits of the cave.' He glanced at Hollie and lowered his voice to a whisper, drawing me into his confidence. 'You see, inside, there was this aboriginal guy called Micky. We were in the same cell and late at night, when we couldn't sleep, he'd tell me about his people and how they used to live, here, on Mount

Coot-tha before they all got killed off. Some died of smallpox and other "white-fella" diseases, but the rest got murdered by white farmers who left out gifts of poisoned sheep and flour laced with strychnine, or by the Native Mounted Police who were given open slather to shoot any aborigine they fancied. He told me how his people had lived on this mountain and how their spirits still lived here. So, I told him about the cave. He wanted to know where it was and how we had found it and if anyone else knew about it.'

Hollie jumped up. 'But we swore on Mother's grave!'

'I told him it was a secret and he promised not to tell.' Danny lay down, his head on one of the cushions. He looked exhausted.

'Have you taken your pills?' asked Hollie, her voice gentler than before. I wondered what he was taking drugs for.

'Yes,' Danny murmured. 'I'm a good boy, aren't I, Hollie?'

'Yes,' Hollie soothed. 'You're a very good boy.'

I nudged his leg with my foot. 'What about these spirits, hey, Danny,' I said. 'Can you see them?'

He rolled onto his side, fixing me with his black liquid eyes. 'No, but I can hear them.' He cupped one hand against his ear. 'Listen.'

I did the same but all I could hear was water plinking at the back of the cave. His eyes were wide and bright, his body rigid.

'They're coming out of the rocks,' he whispered. 'Up through the earth. The young spirits are quick. But the older, wiser ones, they take longer. They have a long way to come.' Still naked, he lay down flat on the ground, his eyes closed, his legs and arms splayed like a starfish. He was all skin and jutting bones. His lips started moving rapidly but no sound came out.

Hollie got up and came over. 'Come on, Danny. We're going home.' She stuffed his arms into the coat-sleeves and did up the buttons. Together, we coaxed Danny to his feet. His body was floppy. Despite his skinniness, he leaned heavily on our shoulders as we dragged him down the hill, the red roof of Hollie's house glinting in the distance below.

Back in the parlour, we lay Danny on the yellow chaise longue. The room quivered with rainbow prisms of light from the crystals hanging at the top of the window as Hollie stroked Danny's brow and sang him a lullaby. Before long he was asleep. Somewhere deep inside the house, a clock chimed five times.

'I have to go to work,' I said.

Hollie looked at me, eyes bright. 'Please stay with me a bit longer.'

I felt bad leaving her with Danny like he was but I was eager to get away.

'I can't,' I said, pulling back from her. The afternoon in the cave had left me uneasy. When we'd pashed in the cave it'd felt different, like it wasn't a game any more. All I wanted was for us to be normal and talk about guys and sex and clothes and music.

'Kiss me,' Hollie murmured, coming up from behind.

I turned and kissed her quickly on the lips, then headed

out the side door and down the spiral staircase to the garden where I broke into a sprint, my tits bouncing everywhere in my boob-tube.

8

It was almost a whole day since Scott's party and he hadn't called. I was busting to ask Trish about how I was going to get back with him, but work that night was mental-busy. The pavement tables at Temptations were teeming with stuck-up bitches wearing chunky silver fob-chains and Ray-Bans on their heads. They laughed way too loudly, sucking Corona through lime wedges and smoking 0.1mg Dunhills. Most of them were from law school. Kirstie waved at me from the sea of blonde bobs and orangey fake-tan faces but I snubbed her. She thought she was so cool in her hipster jeans and pink Lacoste with the collar turned up, but everyone knew Bomber screwed around behind her back.

It was past eleven before the madness died down. Trish called me over for a break. We sat outside, at the other end of the footpath from Kirstie and the law bitches.

Trish lit a fag. 'So. Scott. Spill. Did you root?'

'Ummm, sort of.'

Why not tell her the truth? You chundered then lay down in the middle of the road, pretending to be dead.

'You *sort of* rooted?' She exhaled into the mugginess. 'What kind of root is that?'

'You know, we had to be quick.'

She flicked ash on the pavement and grinned at me. 'Was it ultra dirty?'

'Yeah, well, we—'

'Hey, Rosie.' Kirstie'd come over. 'You alright, sweetie?' She touched my arm, acting all chummy like she wanted something.

'Why wouldn't I be?'

'Last night, at the party, you seemed pretty upset.' Kirstie stood, hands on skinny hips.

'I was fine.' I knocked back the rest of my drink.

'Well, if you're sure you're OK, can we get another round?' She did a cutesy circle hand gesture to show off her French-manicured nails.

'Counter service only,' I said. 'Read the sign.'

'But there's no one at the counter.' Kirstie smiled down at me and, lowering her voice, said, 'I would have warned you but I thought you knew.' Mock-concern creased her perfect brow. 'He should have told you.'

'Told me what?'

Trish interrupted. 'We're closing soon.'

'What about our drinks?'

'I'll be over in a sec,' I snapped.

'Thanks, gorgeous. Same again. Don't forget the lime.' Kirstie clicked off in kitten heels.

'How'd you know *her*?' Trish scowled.

'Bomber's squeeze. We did first year together.'

'I'll sort her out.' Trish stood up. 'What does this Bomber guy look like?'

I filled her in and she went inside to get their beers.

Back at the table, Kirstie was whispering to the others. I watched them, my skin prickling with intense paranoia. She was slagging me off, telling them all how pathetic I'd been to wait for Scott when he'd been banging some other chick the whole time. Trish came back out with the Coronas on a tray. I followed her over.

'On the pull tonight, girls?' Trish set the tray down.

'We've all got boyfriends,' said Kirstie, real smug.

'Where're they now?' Trish asked.

'Boys' night out,' said Kirstie.

'And you think, if some real bad pussy comes up and ask them for a root, they're gonna say no?' Trish winked at me. I was catching her drift. 'Just the other week, I was out in the Valley and there was this guy. Fuck, what was his name? Dark hair. Big pecs. Cheeky grin. You know the type. So, I asked this guy, Bomber, that's what he called himself, back to my joint.' Trish paused for maximum effect. I looked across at Kirstie. Her face paled under the fake-tan. The others were glancing at her, sipping on their drinks, acting like they didn't know Bomber fucked around on her. 'Anyway,' Trish continued, 'we rooted like fucking psychos. He sucked me out like a fucking hoover. It was insane, you know, but then, in the morning, he tells me he's got a girlfriend. Some blonde bimbo studying law... hey, you girls might know her.'

Kirstie jumped up and slapped me hard across the face. 'You pathetic slut.' She grabbed my arms and dug her acrylics into the skin. Trish pulled her off me, pinning her against the bricks. Kirstie thrashed and screamed and Trish kicked her in the shins. The bimbos looked on horrified. I stood back, wondering whether or not to get the dish-pig out to break it up. Part of me was pumped like I wanted Trish to cream her but I felt bad, too. A pack of long-haired bevans in a yellow Escort, Iron Maiden blaring out of the back-seat speakers, pulled up along the kerb and cheered. Trish let go of Kirstie's wrist to give them the finger and in that second Kirstie bent down, grabbed an empty Corona bottle and hurled it at Trish. She ducked as the bottle flew through the air, smashing into the café wall. Shards of glass ricocheted across the pavement. The bevans went berko, mooning out the window. The bitches swooped on Kirstie, hugging her as they left the café. The Escort burned off from the lights, horn honking.

'Fucking slags,' Trish cursed.

'They didn't pay either,' I said.

We sat down at an outside table and were silent for a while. I felt dazed and jittery.

Trish lit a fag. 'Don't you fucking hate working Saturday nights?'

'Yeah, it's shit.'

'One of these days, when I've finishing ripping off the Slob, I'm gunna tell the bastard to shove this job up his slimy arse and I'm gunna piss off to southern India where they have those awesome outdoor raves and I'm gunna to rave my tits off and root heaps of sexy boys.'

'Yeah, cool,' I said, although fucking scrawny rave-heads wasn't exactly my idea of heaven. 'I meant to ask you.' I leant forward. 'Scott wants some drugs.'

'Oh, yeah?' She grinned. 'What's he want?'

I told her.

'I'll need the moula up front.'

'How much?'

'Five hundred.'

'No problems.' I dashed across the road to the ATM.

'Nice,' she said, counting out the cash. 'Hey, that reminds me, there's this rave on in the Valley next Saturday night called Oblivion. It's at The Arena. We can both swap for day shifts. How 'bout it? I'll hook us up with some green elephants. Bit smacky but gets you rank as shit.' Trish had asked me a million times before to go raving but I'd never been that keen. But if Scott was going to the same rave, no way was I missing out.

'Yeah, alright then.' It was the same night as Hollie's memorial party for her mum, but I reckoned I could go for a bit then sneak off to the rave.

Trish picked a speck of tobacco off her pierced tongue. 'So, what's Scott like to root? He must be some kind of fuck-machine for you to wait all this time.'

'Ask the Asian Bitch,' I said, not meaning it to pop out like that.

'What?'

'Nothing.' I gulped down my scotch. 'There's someone at the counter.'

'Fat Helen can deal with it.' Trish pointed her fag at me. 'I'll get us another round and then you're telling me everything.'

So I told her everything, except the bit about pretending to be dead. I got in a real state, mascara everywhere, my nose all runny. Trish had to calm me down with two more scotches and a couple of drags on her cig. By then, it was nearly one and all of the customers had gone.

I turned to Trish. 'So, how can I get him back?'

'Too easy,' she said. 'With cocks it's just too fucking easy.'

9

Trish dropped me off at my car, which was still parked under the leopard tree outside Scott's house. After five or six scotches, we were both pretty maggot but Trish was heading down the coast to catch the last set at some illegal rave. Her dealer was going to be there so she was confident of getting the drugs for Scott. As I watched her hoon away, techno beats rattling the rust-eaten exhaust of her Suzuki, I thought about her advice. It seemed fair enough, coming from someone who'd had heaps of blokes. I got in my car, switched the cabin light on, and read over the shopping list she'd given me:

1. One pair of crotchless knickers (red lace preferable)
2. One sufficiently large (but not larger than his) glow-in-the dark dildo
3. One pair of 'police' (not those cheap fluffy ones) handcuffs
4. One blindfold (black PVC)
5. One leather whip or, if not available, teacher's cane
6. Several candles (for dripping hot wax on his nipples)
7. Johnson's baby oil
8. One over-ripe banana (use your imagination!)
9. One pair of black strappies (stilettos preferable)
10. One pair of fishnet stay-ups (red or black)

No wonder Trish had guys after her left, right and centre. BrisVegas wasn't that big a place and word, no doubt, had got around. Scott and I'd never had kinky sex. We tried anal once but it hurt too much so we stopped. We liked experimenting, though, with different positions – doggy and standing up and the one where I faced the other way on top. That suited us fine, we didn't need any weirdo shit. Sex toys were for married couples who'd lost the magic or old men who couldn't get it up. I mean, what the fuck was I meant to do with an over-ripe banana? I hated bananas and so did Scott.

I tossed Trish's list on the floor and looked across at the house. The bricks seemed to expand and contract as if they were breathing. He was in there, I could smell him, splayed starfish on top of the sheets. I should have driven straight home but I couldn't resist the thought of slipping into bed naked with him, his hands all over me in the dark, our legs entangled. I took off my sandals and got out of the car. The air outside was as warm as sea water, and it felt like I was swimming through it. Avoiding the sensor light, I trailed the edge of the front lawn until I hit the pebbled driveway which led to the side door. The pot plant was still there, dead now. Tipping it to one side, I hunted around for the spare key, trying not to think about redbacks. There it was, on the same rusty old keyring. I crept inside the rumpus, closing the door gently behind me. For a few moments I stood still, waiting for my eyes to adjust to the dark, listening for any sounds from upstairs. The old Kelvinator chugged in the corner like a big white bear. The pool table took shape, then the built-in bar, from behind which I half-expected Mr Greenwood to come popping up like a jack-in-the-box. My feet slapped against the cool tiles as I headed towards Scott's bedroom. It was just like old times when I'd surprise him, driving over in the middle of the night to root and sleep spooned until sunrise.

His door was shut, which was strange on a night so hot and muggy. What if *she* was in there? I imagined her thin, blue-ish legs entwined in his, her black hair strewn like seaweed across the pillows, her buff-coloured nipples small and erect as cherry seeds. I turned the doorknob but it wasn't locked. Inside, it was stuffy, the air heavy with the smell of stale pot and unwashed clothes. I shut the door and tiptoed towards the bed, taking off my top and slipping out of my skirt. I ditched my bra and undies until I was cool and naked, skinny-dipping under the sheet. A lovely floaty feeling swept over me as the pores of my skin opened up. I crawled top and bottom, searching for him under the pillows and at the end of the bed where I found an odd footy sock and curled-up porn mag. Where could he be? The red digits on his alarm clock flashed 2.25. He was probably out raving in the Valley. He'd come home eventually, after the clubs shut at five, and I'd be waiting, strung out naked on his bed, the sparkle of my ruby belly-button leading him to his prize. I lay on my back, my ears pricked for the crunch of his footsteps up the drive. My brain charged with visions of us having wild and dirty sex. I watched the minutes flipping, then the hours. At 4.02, I remembered the spare key and dashed outside to replace it in case Scott needed it to get in. By 5.16 it was getting light and I hadn't got a wink. Around the room, shapes were emerging, outlined by the first seeping of sun through the curtains. I had a sick, prickly feeling like a cactus was lodged in my stomach. But then, it wouldn't be long before he walked through the door. I closed my eyes and waited.

The air-con's on the blink. The men have sweat patches down the spine of their shirts. The women fan themselves with programmes folded into concertinas. March can be the hottest month sometimes. I sit between Mr and Mrs Greenwood in the university concert hall, wearing a new white linen trouser suit which I reckon makes me look twenty-five instead of seventeen. It's three months since the car crash and it hurts to sit for too long because the pain in my neck comes back. But I grin and bear it, clapping polite as an opera-goer as the chancellor walks across the stage, because it's Scott's big night and I'm so proud of him.

I uncross my legs, thinking about varicose veins, but then re-cross them, thinking surely it's more important to look sophisticated. Mrs Greenwood has her legs crossed and, despite the heat, she's wearing flesh-coloured pantyhose. From where I'm sitting, most women, even the grannies, are bare-legged, swollen feet jammed into sandals or court shoes. Mr Greenwood's in his one and only suit, a shiny seventies number with wide lapels and flared trousers. As he leans across me to whisper something to

Mrs Greenwood, I catch a flash of his hairy tummy, spilling through a gap in his shirt.

'This speech's been going for bloody half an hour. I came to see the boy, not this idiot drone on about bloody funding. If anyone needs funding it's me after paying for him to come here.'

'Sssshhhh. Don't be so rude, Bill,' chides Mrs G. 'He's the head chief of the university and a damn sight smarter than you.' She arranges her face in a perfect show of concentration and turns back to the stage. I do likewise but Mr Greenwood's got ants in his pants. He jabs me in the ribs, narrowly missing my left breast.

'So, when are you two love-birds going to tie the knot, hey?' He pats my linened thigh. Mr and Mrs Greenwood were childhood sweethearts, growing up on adjacent farms west of Ipswich. They got married when they were both just sixteen and Mr Greenwood still thought it was the norm. 'Christ, when I was the boy's age—'

'Sssshhhh.' Mrs Greenwood shoots him a death stare as the chancellor finishes his speech with an apology for the broken air-con.

Mr Greenwood nudges me in the side and whispers, 'He's got some silly idea about going travelling with that no-hoper mate of his, Bomber, but I'll set him straight. He'd be a complete dimwit to leave a pretty girly like you behind. Don't you worry, love, I'll have a word with him.' *Scott is going overseas with Bomber.* He winks at me and I force a saccharine smile while Mrs Greenwood's special lasagne does backflips in my stomach. Excusing myself, I squeeze out through the tightly packed aisles and dash outside, as up on stage they start calling out the graduates' names in alphabetical order.

I miss Scott getting his degree. For the rest of the ceremony, I sit on the lawn, not caring about the grass stains on my white linen bum. You see, it was me and Scott who were meant to go overseas. We had a pact. We'd made a plan. I wrote everything down in a special notebook – Scott's number one destination was Amsterdam, mine Paris – and we had a date of departure, in four years' time, after I'd finished my degree. That night, after talking it all through, we were so excited that we made love for hours in the dark. We did it slow and gentle because my arm was still in plaster. At first light we drove up to Mount Coot-tha to watch the sunrise. We stood looking out over the city, my feet wedged between the railings with Scott behind me, his arms around my shoulders. There was something about the puny skyline, winking lazily in the pink light, which gripped me with an intense longing to escape. I leant my head against Scott's chest and said, 'We're too cool for this place,' but he just laughed and said, 'Take it easy, babe. We've got a few years here, yet.'

They are coming out of the hall, a sound like swarming bees from the quadrangle. Mr and Mrs Greenwood appear, squinting in the sunlight. Scott goes up to them, hugs his mum, slaps his old man on the back. All I want to do is talk to him so I know it's not true. I spot Bomber and Muzza sitting on a bench a little distance from the crowd, watching Scott with his uni mates. Pushing up off the lawn,

I head towards them, but Mrs Greenwood's coming up to me with a frown. She leads me by the crook of my arm a little distance from the main gathering.

'Are you alright? You're white as a sheet.' She presses a palm against my forehead. 'And you've got a bit of a temperature. Were you sick?' She scans the grass for incriminating evidence.

'I'm OK. Really.' I glance across at Bomber and Muzza, busting to go and interrogate them. Mrs Greenwood stands there gripping my arm, searching my eyes. I can see where she's painted her fuchsia lipstick beyond her actual lip-line.

'You're not...'

I look at her blankly.

'You know...' She bends her head closer to me.

With a nervous laugh, I tell her I'm not pregnant. Mrs Greenwood turns to see Scott having his photo taken with his year. She is so chuffed with him getting a degree; the first Greenwood ever to go to university. He's not smart, like me, but still he'd scraped through and there are heaps of jobs for personal trainers. The western suburbs are stuffed with rich, overweight housewives desperate to loose excess flab, or so Scott was always telling me.

'But, they'll all want to fuck you,' I'd say.

'So long as they pay me,' he'd tease.

I'd punch him in the arm. 'That's not allowed. Besides, they'll all be fat and disgusting.'

'Not when I've finished with them. They'll be super-toned and terrific. Then, only then, will I let them sleep with me. I'll be their reward.'

I break off and head towards the guys, my jaw clenched with foreboding.

'Are you going overseas with Scott?' I ask Bomber straight out.

'What's it to you?' Bomber's dark-brown eyes are defiant and his chest is puffed up like a rooster in an oversized Chicago Bulls singlet. Muzza says nothing. I wonder why they are here.

'It means a fucking lot to me.' I glare back at Bomber, hands on hips. 'So tell me or I'll tell Kirstie you've been rooting around.'

'Give a fuck? She's with the programme but it makes no difference,' he says. 'With a cock like mine she ain't going no-where.' He grabs at his crotch and, through the baggy fabric of his shorts, jiggles his balls. 'No other nigger can sa-tis-fy the bitch like me. Nice and hard up the arse. Yeah-yeah, you know it.' He punches the air with a rapper fist.

'Are you going, too?' I ask Muzza, struggling to keep my cool.

'Nah, no moula.'

'That's fucked, Muzz. You think me and Woody do?' says Bomber. 'We're gonna find jobs soon as we get to London. If that fails, Woody reckons we should hook up with some rich pommie bitches we can scum off.' He flashes me a challenge.

'Crap,' I fight back. 'Scott would never say that.'

'You better believe it, baby. Woody's goal is to root a bitch from each different country we visit. He's already taking bets. Isn't he, Muzz?'

Muzza snorts.

'He's calling it Woody's Worldwide Rooting Quest, kind of like a spell-a-thon except it don't matter if the bitches can't spell!' Bomber slaps his thigh. Muzza grins, sheepishly. I tell myself that it's just stupid mates talk which means nothing.

'So, when're you off?' Muzza speaks to Bomber as if I'm invisible.

'Next Saturday,' says Bomber.

'Yeah right,' I scoff, disbelieving. It can't be true. He's lying. But my guts have turned to mush.

'Yeah, we got our tickets last week.' He turns to me. 'Guess now the cat's outta the bag.' He slouches back against the bench, his arms stretched out along the top railing, his legs spread wide. A smile of victory infects his face.

'You're so full of shit, Bomber,' I say.

As I head down the grassy embankment, Bomber's voice carries on the still air. 'What a fucking psycho-bitch! He'd dump her 'cept he says she gives awesome head.'

After the graduation, everyone goes to the R.E. Scott's in the thick of it, sculling beer with his uni mates. Somehow I have to grab him and get him to tell me the truth. It isn't easy. The sporty chicks from his year want a piece of him, too. Tall and tanned, they hang off him like flies. They hate me for nicking the best-looking guy on their course and I hate them for being sluts. Everyone knows that Human Movement chicks are the easiest roots on campus.

'Scott.'

'Hi, babe.' He swaggers over, tipsy but not yet wasted, and kisses me with a hot, beery tongue.

I take a deep breath. 'Are you going overseas without me?'

Scott rubs the back of his neck, looks at his feet. 'Babe, let me explain. It'll only be for a while, a few months or so. Six months max.'

I shove him hard in the chest. He stumbles backwards. His beer sloshes over me as I push past him, tearing through the crowded public bar. He shouts after me but I'm already outside on the pavement. I hail a taxi and get in.

I yawned and opened my eyes to a low, flaky ceiling which was strange and yet familiar. Overhead, someone crossed the floor with quick, efficient steps. A toilet flushed, followed by the groan of rusty pipes. I sat up in bed. Scott's bed. 8.53 on the alarm.

He hadn't come home.

I found my clothes in a tangle on the floor and got dressed, telling myself he'd probably crashed at Bomber's. I made his bed, tucking the sheet in tight and folding down one corner like in a swish hotel. From the pocket of my skirt, I pulled the Baci chocolate 'kiss' I'd stolen from work as a treat for him. I placed it on his pillow, in the dip made by my head during the night. Then I sat down at his desk to write him a note:

To my sexy babe,

I've just spent the night naked in your bed! I thought I'd surprise you but you didn't come home. Where were you? Maybe you crashed at Bomber's place? Hope you had a good night. Did you go raving? Anyway, <u>please</u> call me when you get this note. I'm really sorry about acting psycho Friday night — it must have been the bourbon and pot combo.

Love your (still naked) Rosie xxxRRR

P.S. Trish is getting you the stuff.

I slipped the note under the chocolate and snuck out barefoot through the rumpus room. Mr Greenwood was mowing the back lawn in a pair of paint-splattered stubbies, so I ducked low under the window sill so he didn't see me, and snuck out through the side door. As I walked along the pavement, the boughs of the poinciana trees sagged in the heat. The sun passed through my thin shirt, warming my nipples. There was a Sunday smell in the air. Across the road, the lawn-bowlers were out in force, dressed in whites. Bending and stooping. The lovely 'chock' of balls colliding. Gentle clapping. I scanned up the road for my car. It was still there, under the shade of the leopard tree. Another car was parked a few metres in front. Passing by, I shielded my eyes from the glare and glanced in. There was someone slumped in the driver's seat looking dead, like I always thought people sleeping in cars looked dead. I stopped and peered closer. It was dark inside the cabin, the tinted glass cutting out most of the sun. The window lowered with an automatic hum. A blast of ice-cold air-con hit me. A dark face appeared. I jumped back in shock.

'Danny?' His face was covered all over in brown stuff like boot polish or mud, camouflage-style. 'What the hell have you got on your face? What are you doing here?' I hopped from foot to foot, the bitumen searing my feet. Startled, he rubbed his eyes, brown coming off on his fingers. He stared at himself in the rear-vision as if he had no idea who he was. He turned to me, dazed. His lips were blue. He was wearing the army coat and I wondered if he was naked underneath. He clenched the steering wheel with both hands.

'Where am I?' he said, squinting up at me.

'At Scott's.'

'Oh.' He shook a clump of black hair out of his eyes and looked across at the house.

'Are you stalking him?' I half-laughed. Last night's sneak-in was pretty bunny-boiler, too, but part of me felt uneasy, like there was something major I didn't know about.

'Does he know I'm here?'

'Nah, he's still asleep,' I fibbed, waving towards Scott's bedroom window.

'Good.' He turned the key in the ignition. Opera blared from the multi-track. 'Hey, Rosie.' He beckoned. I bent forward, my arms resting on the sill. 'Don't tell Hols about me being here. She'll freak.'

I nodded.

'Or Scott,' he added.

'OK. Sure.' I reached in and touched his arm. It was cold. 'Are you alright?' He looked so freakish, yet so vunerable with his face all blacked up. It took me back to the times when we were kids playing aborigines in the cave.

'I'll be fine.' He revved the engine into an excited purr. I jumped back and he shot away from the kerb.

It's near the end of the Christmas holidays. We are all in the cave. Hollie, Danny and me. Outside, it's bright, boiling sunshine but inside it's dark. Hollie strikes a match and lights a candle. Our shadows rise giant up the walls, stooping backwards across the low ceiling. An arc of light flickers over the hand paintings, orange and white and yellow aborigine hands. The baby skull sits on top of the egg rock.

Hollie stands naked in the middle, her pale, boy-body caked in dirt. We rub more mud into our faces, up our legs and arms, and apply our markings, taking turns at the orange paste we've made from water and crumbly ochre. Hollie grins. Her hair is knotted and full of dead leaves and twigs. She begins to chant in pretend aborigine. She claps and stamps her feet, filling the cave with dust and strange echoes. I join in, hopping from one foot to the other, singing and waving my arms above my head.

Danny hovers in the dimmest corner, flames reflected tiny in his shiny, black eyes. He takes off his shorts and T-shirt, folds them neatly on the floor. 'I'm keeping my undies on,' he says, but we tell him that he has to take them off because real aborigines didn't have undies. Still he refuses, so we grab him and tug them off. Hollie paints his arms and legs with dots and snakey lines, and I rub dirt into his thick, black hair.

We sit around the candle. Speaking in our tribe's native language, Hollie explains to Danny how the game works. But he can't understand the words so Hollie whispers to him in English while I make music on my imaginary didgeridoo. Hollie says that as chief tribesman of the Mount Coot-tha tribe, Danny-Dilly must go out into the bush and hunt down a big red kangaroo to eat at the corroboree that night. While he is out hunting, Hollie-Wallie and Rosie-Maroo, his two most beautiful aborigine wives, collect witchetty grubs and weave useful baskets out of twigs and long grass.

Danny nods but looks a bit confused.

'And don't forget you're not allowed to speak English,' says Hollie, wagging her finger at him.

'And if any white fellas come then we must hide together at the back of the cave with our spears pointing out in case they are baddies with guns,' I add.

'Let's start,' says Hollie. She pushes Danny-Dilly outside. We kneel in the dirt and dig for yams.

As the sun is sinking, Danny-Dilly comes home with the biggest red kangaroo the tribe has ever seen. The roasted yams are delicious. The men dance and sing songs around the fire and there is lots of gossiping between the women. Everyone agrees that it is the best corroboree ever. When Danny-Dilly is tired, he goes into his humpy with his two most beautiful wives, Hollie-Wallie and Rosie-Maroo. We lie down on either side of him, our arms draped over his middle. We take turns to kiss our brave hunter-husband and tell him, in our made-up aborigine, how much we love him.

10

As soon as I walked in, I could smell smoke coming from the backyard. Dread seized me as I raced through the house and outside. It had been years since Mum'd burnt anything but she was in the middle of the backyard tossing one of her eighties jackets onto a fire. A sleeve of her peppermint pin-stripe protruded like a dead person's arm, its silver cuff-buttons melting in the inferno. I yelled at her from the patio but she was transfixed, her face radiant with the heat of multi-coloured flames. I crossed the lawn and grabbed her by the arm.

'What are you doing?'

'What does it look like?' She spoke like a ventriloquist, her lips pressed into a thin line. The skin around her eyes was puffy like she'd been crying. She didn't even ask me where I'd been all night. 'We were having such a nice time.' Her voice trembled. 'We saw *Phantom* and then we went for a bite to eat at the Lyrebird Restaurant. I asked him all about his first wife, Noreen, who died of breast cancer, and when he'd finished telling me all about that, I asked him about his work.' She picked up the smouldering sleeve and tossed it into the middle of the fire. We watched it writhe and twist, dissolving into nothing. 'There.' She brushed her hands together.

'C'mon,' I said, dragging her inside.

We sat on the couch drinking tea. 'So, what happened?'

She wrung her hands and shook her head. 'He's a germ scientist. What are they called?'

'A microbiologist?'

She nodded. 'He was telling me how he's trying to find a germ that kills cancer. He was holding my hand and I snatched it away. All I could think about was millions of germs crawling all over him. I rushed out of the restaurant. Everyone was staring.'

I could just imagine it; Randy running after Mum across the piazza while she screamed at him to keep his distance.

'Did you tell him?'

'Yes. I told him I had an irrational fear of germs and diseases and that, no matter how much I liked his company, I could never see him again.' She looked at me with big, sad eyes. 'You know, Rosemary, in every other way, he's perfect.' Two dates and Mum was in love. I thought she was pathetic, hooking up with some desperate loser from a dating agency just because her shrink had said so. I looked outside at the fire. Wisps of smoke spiralled in the air. A stray silver button glinted in the midday sun. I turned back to Mum. She had her face buried in her hands, whimpering.

'There'll be others,' I said, wanting to make her feel better. 'Didn't you say the dating agency came up with four compatibility partners?'

'No one as nice as Andy,' she sulked.

'Well... maybe you can work things out somehow.'

'How?' She looked up at me, pleading. 'I can't even bear

to touch him. He grows cancer germs in little dishes.'

'At least he's not an undertaker,' I said, but Mum sat glumly staring into her teacup. The doorbell rang. My legs went numb. Scott'd got my note and come straight over.

'Tell him I've gone shopping,' said Mum, dashing down the hall to her bedroom. Fuck knows why she thinks it's Randy, I thought, as I raced to the front door, delicious waves of expectation surging through me. I wondered where we could go. If Mrs Greenwood had popped out, we could tear back to his bedroom for a quickie. Or we could drive up to Mount Coot-tha and find some secluded grassy patch for an alfresco root. Just thinking about it got me wet.

Through the glass panels either side of the front door, I caught a glimpse of red petals. He'd bought me flowers! I flung open the door. The sun streamed in. A short, balding man with a round, shiny face stood on the doormat. It was Randy Andy for sure. Shielding my eyes from the glare, I gave him the once-over. He was wearing beige knee-length shorts with dazzlingly white knee-high socks and Jesus sandals, just like Mr Magoo. In a pair of hairy hands, he clasped a huge bunch of roses.

'Hello. You must be Rosemary.' He stuck out a gorilla mitt. 'I'm Andy.'

'Yeah, I figured that,' I said, ignoring his hand which hung limply on the end of an apishly muscular arm. By contrast, the rest of his body was incredibly weedy like he only pumped iron on his biceps and triceps. He cleared his throat.

'Janice has told me all about you.'

'She's not here.'

'Oh.' His face fell. 'Do you know when she'll be back?'

'No idea.'

'Do you know where she's gone?'

'Shoppingtown.'

'Oh.' His head dropped to the flowers.

'I'll tell her you came.' I retreated over the threshold.

'Yes. Yes. Please do.' He was rubbing his bald spot in a circular motion, as if stimulating his brain cells. 'And give her these,' he said, thrusting the roses at me. I took them and began to close the door, thinking, *what a total loser!*

'And tell her... tell her... ' Randy stuttered.

'Tell her what?'

He shifted from side to side. 'Tell her that I've scrubbed myself with hospital-strength anti-bacterial liquid, chemical name chlorhexidine gluconate, and sterilized my clothes in boiling water.'

He stepped back and I slammed the door. I turned around and collided with Mum who'd been eavesdropping from the alcove. Her eyes sparkled as she snatched the roses off me, reading aloud from the gift tag: *To my darling Janice, Not all germs are bad. There are good ones, too. Lots of love, Andy x.*

Mum floated into the kitchen, returning with a vase of water which she set down in the middle of the coffee table. She unwrapped and arranged the bouquet, burying her face in the roses and inhaling deeply. A little sigh escaped from her lips. Her face was flushed, as if the colour of the petals

133

had rubbed off on her cheeks, and she looked girlishly pretty.

'Mum?'

She looked up at me blankly then, snapping out of her daze, leapt up, ran to the door, banged it open and bolted outside.

'What are you doing?' I shouted from the doorway as she shot across the lawn, the tails of her dressing gown streaming out behind her. Randy's crappy Beetle was puttering down the road as she raced along the footpath, flapping her arms about to get his attention. A sudden gust of wind whipped off her dressing gown but she didn't seem to care. Poor old Mr Leyland, innocently stepping out for his Sunday paper, got the fright of his life as she thundered past, her loose thighs wobbling in the morning sunshine. But Mum, unsheathed, kept on heedless in her flesh-coloured support bra and tummy-firming undies. As the Beetle swung out of our street, she tore into the middle of the road, jumping and screaming. Randy spotted her in the rear-vision. He braked and tooted the horn. He was half out of the car when Mum pounced on him, ramming him back against the side of the Beetle and pashing him. Randy looked a bit stunned but it didn't take him long to respond with sickening gusto. I turned and slunk back inside the house to call Scott. I'd waited long enough.

On the eighth ring an out-of-breath Mrs Greenwood answered the phone. When I asked for Scott she said that he hadn't come home yet. 'I'll get him to call you when he comes in, OK, love?'

I hung up and slumped back on my bed in a foul mood. It was just past noon. I checked my mobile and there were seven missed calls from Hollie. It was probably something to do with Danny and his odd behaviour but I didn't feel like calling her. Mum and Randy came laughing and giggling into the courtyard, right outside my window. I closed the venetians, but I could still hear every sappo word they said.

'Thank you for scrubbing down,' Mum gushed. 'You smell so lovely and clean.'

'Last night, I couldn't stop thinking about you, Janice. I've been trying to figure out a way to help you get over your... little problem.'

'It's alright,' said Mum. 'You can call it my germ phobia.'

'For hours I lay there, testing different methods and possible solutions.' I imagined Randy rubbing his bald spot and licking his lips. 'And then, about four in the morning, it came to me.' His voice was rich and creamy like in a chocolate ad. 'Knowledge banishes fear.'

'Knowledge?'

'I'm going to teach you all I know about microbiotic life. Then you'll realize that your germ phobia is illogical. It doesn't make scientific sense. It is, as we say in the lab, insupportable. Worse than that, it is superstitious indulgence of the worst kind, a fear of the unenlightened mind.'

'But, Andy, it's not that simple,' Mum sighed, impatience in her voice.

'What do you mean it's not that simple? The best solution is always the simplest,' persisted Randy.

There was a long silence in which I pictured Mum shaking her head and wringing her hands.

'Janice, don't get upset. Everything'll be alright. I'll help you through this.'

'Look, Andy, I appreciate you trying but it's not that easy. You can't just fix me like a broken washing machine. I've been like this for nearly twenty years.' She'd been like this ever since I was born. Randy was kidding himself if he thought he could change her. 'I'm good on my own, you know, and the truth is, Andy,' she lowered her voice as if to tell a secret, 'I've never been very good at relationships. Look, you'd better go. I'm sure the agency will find you a nice normal woman who'll make you very happy.'

A chair scraped back across the pavers. This was Randy's opportunity to walk. Not that I blamed him. Even without her phobia Mum was a handful.

'Put me down! Put me down!' Mum was squealing. I took a quick squiz through the venetians. Randy had scooped her up in his gorilla arms and was carrying her through the sliding doors. She was kicking and screaming but pointing the way to the bedroom. I doubted if she'd ever been ravished (Dad was hardly the ravishing kind) but she seemed to like it alright.

Mum'd told me how she met Dad at Cloudland, a kind of blue-light disco on the top of Bowen Hill. It was the sixties, Brisbane was still pretty tame, and Dad, with his sneaky hip flask of gin and sketchy knowledge of eastern religions, was enough to wow her. After four or five dates and a few furtive pashes at the flicks, Dad proposed. In the wedding photos, Mum was petite and slender with a shy smile. Dad had a blade one crew-cut and a maggot glint in his eye. It wasn't until the honeymoon on Tangalooma Island that Mum realized he had a drink problem. That's when he started hitting her, but she stayed with him, covering her bruises with foundation and saving enough money to leave him. It was only when she got pregnant that she decided to stay. I was born, eight weeks premature, skinny as a rat, too sick to feed. Dad lived at the pub. Mum got post-natal depression. That's when the germs took hold. She was so worried I was going to die that she became obsessed with keeping the blighters away from me.

It was a stinking hot afternoon when they emerged from the bedroom. I was reading in a shady spot under the paw-paw tree at the bottom of the backyard and they didn't see me tucked up in a deck chair amongst the foliage and the shadows. It was obvious they'd been rooting. Mum was all giggly. Randy walked with a post-fuck swagger. I couldn't believe it. After all Mum'd warned me about the evils of men and sexual intercourse, I'd thought it would take her months, if not years, before she'd let anyone stick their thingo in her. What about warts, gonorrhoea and the syphilis comeback? She'd only known him for two days. What a slut! Randy had a fluffy, pink towel tucked around his waist, his narrow chest carpeted in thick, salt and pepper hair. Mum was in an old faded pair of togs with built-in cups. Randy couldn't keep his mitts off her. He kept patting her on the bum. She'd shriek and hop away from him, but then sidle back for more. He tried to pick her up and chuck her in the shallow end but she jumped in instead, squealing as she hit the water. It was years since Mum'd been in the pool although she still insisted on double-dosing the chlorine levels. The water stung like crazy. Five minutes swimming left your eyes sore and bloodshot for the rest of the day.

Mum bobbed around in the shallows, not wanting to get her hair wet. 'Hurry up,' she yelled at Randy. 'It's lovely once you get in.'

Like most men, Randy wasn't content with a measly jump in the shallow end. He wanted to make a big splash. Like driving in the fast lane and assembling Ikea furniture, diving was a test of a bloke's manhood.

'Watch this!' he said, jogging down to the deep end, his muscular arms swinging from his scrawny torso. He stood with his back to the pool, tilting his head from side to side and taking deep breaths like he was going for gold at the Olympics. His jaw was set, his lips pursed in concentration. He inched backwards so that his heels were hanging over the edge. He peered over the back fence to see if any neighbours were about and, with a flick of his wrist, he whipped off the towel.

He was naked.

From her end, Mum gasped. From my end, the sight killed me. His penis was enormous, obscenely large for any man, let alone a man of his restricted height. I was shocked but I couldn't stop staring. Thick and straight as a salami, it hung in all its buffed glory. My mouth went dry. In length and diameter, it was twice the size of Scott's and about four times the size of Jed's, the monkey-boy poet's. It had to be surgically enlarged or some form of abnormality. I forced myself to look away.

Randy yelled to Mum over his shoulder. 'Count me down from ten!'

'OK, but don't hit your head on the bottom,' she warned. 'Ten... nine... eight... '

Randy swung his arms in windmills and jigged up and down on his toes like a pro diver about to reverse triple somersault into a half pike entry.

'Seven... six... five... '

I sneaked another look at his Long John, which was swinging pendulum-style as he bounced up and down, and, at that moment, Randy glanced up and saw me under the paw-paw.

'Golly!' he spluttered, bending over, trying to cover himself. 'Didn't see you there, Rosie.' He lost his balance, hopping from foot to foot, and toppled backwards. Airborne, his giant member protruded from his compact form like a pink tail as he crashed butt-first in an almighty bomb dive. Water gushed over the sides. Mum, who still hadn't spotted me yet, cacked herself, laughing and bouncing about like it was the best entertainment she'd had in ages. I resolved to put Randy's cock firmly out of my mind, and went back to my book.

The rapids subsided to a gentle lapping and the suburbs

went quiet. I glanced back towards the shallows. Mum had stopped splashing about and was anxiously peering towards the deep end. Randy hadn't surfaced. He'd been down there for well over two minutes. From where I was sitting, I could just make out a pink, shifting splodge on the bottom. I had a nasty vision of Randy the quadriplegic, his massive member dangling limp and useless as a dead sausage dog. Although she couldn't swim properly, Mum was paddling into the middle of the pool, choking and spluttering.

'Possum? Are you alright, possum?' She struggled over to the edge and clung on, looking desperately around for someone or something to help. 'Help! Please! Somebody help me!'

It must have been nearly three minutes now. I stepped out from the shade of the paw-paw tree.

Mum shouted, 'Oh, thank goodness, Rosemary. Save him!'

I dived into the deep end. Under the water it was quiet; the lapping flap and suck of the pool filter, the rush of water in my ears, the sunbeams loose and scattered, swaying like reeds. I touched down on the pebbly bottom and looked around. Randy was sitting cross-legged like a monk meditating, a steady stream of bubbles ascending from his nostrils. He smiled and gave me the OK sign. I shot up to the surface where Mum was leaning over the edge.

Assuming the worst, she screamed, 'Oh my god, he's paralysed. Quick, call an ambulance!'

'He's fine,' I said. 'He's just kidding around.'

'He'll have brain damage!'

Randy's bald spot broke the surface.

Mum shouted, 'He's alive!'

He was coughing and gasping for air but grinning like a maniac. Mum leapt in on top of him with a splash. She slapped him on the bicep. 'What a stupid, stupid thing to do.'

'So I had you going, did I?' Randy's eyes were bloodshot from the chlorine.

'You sure did. We thought you were paralysed.' She wrapped her arms about his neck, clinging onto him like a koala.

'No, we didn't,' I said.

'I'm in training for the Queensland over-fifties underwater breath-holding championships in Townsville next month.'

'That's amazing,' Mum raved. 'You were under there for... how long was it, Rosemary?'

I hauled myself out of the pool.

'Four minutes, fifty-two seconds,' Randy said, showing Mum his stop-watch. 'Only two minutes, forty-three off the Andy LeSauce record.'

The weekend was nearly over and Scott still hadn't called. At work that evening, I lied to Trish about my progress, inventing sexual antics deviant enough to satisfy her. It was all bullshit but she believed me and proceeded to describe in graphic detail the sex she'd had the night before with some guy called Zane she'd met at the Norse-Raider rave.

'He went down on me for hours. Kept saying how much he loved eating pussy and he must have because he jerked off while he was licking me out.'

'Was he cute?' I asked.

'Dunno,' she said, 'Everyone looks cute on ecky.'

I wondered if Scott might have been at the same rave. At least he wouldn't have been eating pussy. He always told me how he hated the taste and preferred 'real pump action', but in retrospect he was probably just too bloody lazy to go down there. Not that this ever worried me; I could orgasm every time without fail so long as I was on top with Scott wet-pinching my nipples simultaneously, like the first time we made love after the car crash.

After shutting up shop, Trish got out the stuff for Scott. We stood behind the counter with the lights dimmed low while she unwrapped a square of alfoil. Inside, there were ten white pills, each stamped with an identical green elephant, its trunk trumpeting in the air. Trish flipped them over so all the elephants were on show, lining them up in a grand procession down the bench-top.

'Fucking beautiful, hey,' she said. 'Makes your legs go like honey and your cunt feel all funny.'

I laughed, loving the thrill of being bad. Trish pulled a snap-lock of speed from her bag.

'Want a bit?' She dipped her finger inside.

'Nah, I'm OK.' I was crap enough on pot and booze.

'Relax, babe. It'll just get you a bit buzzy.' She stuck her finger under my top lip and rubbed in a circular motion over my gum. It was a bit like being at the dentist.

'Mind if I go some?' Trish said. She scooped a small amount out of the bag with a latte spoon and pushed and prodded the stuff into a thin line with her credit card. She nicked a fifty from the till and rolled it into a tight cylinder. Then, pressing her finger against her left nostril, leant over the bench-top and snorted. A wide grin spread across her face. She sat up on the bench and lit a fag. I dipped my finger in again. Trish cranked the hardcore. My heart was racing and, although I was buggered from work, my brain was alert and sparky and my body felt hard and springy. I could have gone for a run. The shop took on a new vibe. The counter slick and metal bright. The chairs and tables expectant, like they wanted to dance. I looked up and saw my face, reflected a million times in the parfait glasses which hung upside down from the overhead rack. I got a spurt of childish excitement, like being locked in a toy shop overnight, as if anything was possible.

'Told you it was good shit,' Trish said. 'Hope lover-boy likes it.'

I took some deep breaths and thought about how cool Scott would think I was, getting him A-class so easy. It would be my shout, my welcome home present to him.

Now I had a legitimate, non-desperate reason to call. Still, I decided to wait a few more days to see if he would ring me first.

I got home just after midnight, still buzzy from the speed. Trish had lent me one of her hardcore import CDs and, driving back, I pumped it to the max. The bass thumped low and deep in my stomach as the car shook around me and the steering wheel sent vibrations up my arms. I was feeling mega-supreme-sexy-queen-of-the-road until I pulled into the driveway where, to my ultra annoyance, Randy's Beetle was blocking my side of the garage. I blasted the horn continuous, even though the house was in darkness.

Across the road Mr Leyland stepped out with his pet shih-tzu to suss out the racket. Mum came running out in her chenille, but I kept on with the blasting, which I could barely hear over the hardcore anyway. Mum was yelling and hammering against my window but I wasn't letting up. It was important to make my point. Randy came sauntering out of the house in a pair of leopard-print undies. He said something to Mum and waved across at Mr Leyland. Then, as if he had all the time in the world, he cruised into his Beetle, reversed down the drive and parked on the side of the road. Mum daggered me through the windscreen before following Randy back into the house.

I zapped the roller doors, released the brake-stick and rolled into the garage next to Mum's Holden, the darkness swallowing me up. I pumped the hardcore and butt-danced in my seat for ages, but then the stuff started to wear off and I felt like a bit of a dick so I jabbed it off and sat listening for the tiniest sounds I could hear. The muffled tick of the engine cooling down. The soft crunch of a moth's abdomen hitting the windscreen. The crack of my big toe. It felt safe; the car a shell with me the soft, squidgy mollusc inside.

When I was a kid and Mum and Dad were fighting, I'd lock myself in the car with the radio up full-blast, listening to The Cars. I'd get hungry and eat all the barley sugars from the glove box until my teeth hurt. Once, I slept in there all night with the cabin light on and a picnic blanket wrapped around my legs.

Right then, I had the same urge to sleep in the car. Anything was better than being inside while Randy pumped his sperm germs into Mum with his surgically enhanced member. I took off my sandals, climbed into the back seat and lay down with my feet dangling out the window. It was cool inside the garage and there was the same smell of petrol, grease and rusty toolboxes as when Dad used to tinker about drinking beer and listening to the cricket on his pocket radio. I took off my clothes and stretched out in my bra and undies, my body all limp and floppy. My muscles ached with fatigue but my head was still firing like a piston. I checked my mobile for the zillionth time. There were more missed calls from Hollie and she'd left a frantic message about Danny being missing. I thought about him being outside Scott's that morning and wondered if I should tell Hollie, even though I'd promised not to. What did Danny want with Scott anyway? It was weird, almost sinister. When Scott finally called me, I would ask him about their history. I had good vibes he'd ring me tomorrow. My legs had gone to sleep and it was pretty uncomfortable in the car, so I went inside.

Outside Mum's room, I knelt down to listen for any grotesque sex noises but all I could hear was the loud ticking of her bedside clock and Randy snoring. I crept down the hall to my bedroom, hid Scott's drugs in my undies drawer and stripped off naked for bed. Awake and horny, I lay in the dark for hours tracing figure eights across my stomach and tugging at my nipples, imagining the split-second before Scott's cock rammed up into me. I tried to wank myself with the end of my hairbrush but I was all bound up and edgy, and I couldn't fucking do it. It was like having the worse itch ever but with no arms to scratch it.

11

Four days went by and Scott still hadn't fucking called me. Extreme paranoia was kicking in, but I convinced myself that Mrs Greenwood had changed his sheets and that the note and choc had fallen down the crack between his bed and the wall. He can't have got the note or else he would have called about the drugs.

On Friday morning Mum was heading into town to buy a new outfit for a date that night with Randy. I dialled Scott's number as soon as she left the house.

Mrs Greenwood answered. 'Yes, love. He's sitting right here reading the paper.' She passed me over.

'Hi, babe.' He was munching on a piece of toast.

'Did you get my note?'

'Yeah, nah, I was meaning to give you a call but I've been a bit busy.'

'Did you like the chocolate?'

'Yeah, but it melted all over my pillow.'

There was a squirmy silence. I took a deep breath and went for it. 'Listen. Mum's gone shopping for the day and I thought you might like to come over,' I dropped my voice to a husky whisper, 'for some S.E.X.' As Trish said, there was no point in beating round the bush.

He laughed. 'Bomber's coming round to shoot hoops this arvo.' There was a long pause. 'But I can put him off. I'll be over after lunch.'

'Great. And I can give you the stuff from Trish.'

All morning, I ran around in a fluster: washing and blow-drying my hair; plucking the stray hairs from my porno-strip; painting my nails red to match my new half-cups and g-string; applying kissable lip-gloss and a butterfly sticker to my cheekbone. I took down his postcards in case he thought I was a psycho and I pulled out the fly screens in case he came to the window like he used to. Under my bed were the handcuffs and the leather whip I'd bought from a dodgy shop in the Valley. The thought of Scott coming round for sex and drugs really got me going. I grabbed the snap-lock from my undies drawer and opened it. I licked my finger, dipped it inside and rubbed all around my gums. My heartbeat quickened. Taking some deep breaths, I lay down on my sun-soaked bed, wriggling my fingers and toes like plant tendrils angling for the light. I focused, slitty-eyed, on the ruby sparkling in my belly-button. I hadn't had the opportunity to show it to Scott at the party and I couldn't wait for his reaction.

The phone rang. I answered in my drowsiest, sexiest voice. 'Hello?'

'Darling, it's me.' It was Hollie and I could tell, by the high pitch of her voice, that something was wrong. 'Why haven't you called me?'

'I was going to.' I felt bad. I was always letting her down. I should have called her back, but my mind had been on other things. 'Listen, there's something I should tell you about Danny.'

A shadow fell across my middle, blocking the sunlight like a sudden cloud. I sat up and there he was, right outside my window, grinning, in a pair of basketball shorts, no shirt.

'*Hollie*. I've gotta go, alright? I'll call you back later. I promise.'

'But what about—'

I hung up.

The sun blazed around him like an aura. Sick excitement ripped through me. It was just like old times when he used to come in the middle of the night. Even on the hottest night of the year, we'd sleep spooned together on my single bed, the sweaty sheets knotted around us. At first light, he'd wake up and drive home so that Mum didn't catch us. He hauled himself up and sprung, biceps flaring, onto the sill. I was propped up against my pillows, pretending to read, as if these days I always hung about the house reading novels in lacy lingerie and full makeup. He pounced onto my bed.

'You expecting someone?' he said, checking me out, his eyes roving up and down my legs, lingering on my belly - button ring, hovering over my wet-look lips.

'No one in particular,' I said, looking up from the page. His stare made me want to shed my skin but I'd spent a fortune on my bra and undies and didn't want to get naked just like that. I wanted him to kiss me all over like he used to, to build up slowly. I wanted him to discover my butterfly butt-tatt. But he sat at the end of the bed, his knees drawn up to his chest.

'Show us the gear, then,' he said.

'The gear? Yeah, cool, the gear.' I got it off the top of my dressing table.

We sat cross-legged on the bed with our knees not quite touching, the stuff between us, the sun streaming in through the window. He was perfect in every way. Even his shoulder-length hair and stubbly face turned me on. He was a man now, his jaw sharper, his Adam's apple fully formed. He unwrapped the elephants first, lining them up on the bed, same as Trish'd done. He counted them twice, up the row, down the row.

'How much do I owe you?'

'Don't worry. It's on me.'

He cocked his head to one side and looked at me. 'You sure, babe?'

'Positive.' I slapped him lightly on the leg. 'It's just great to have you back,' I said, realizing with a twinge in my gut that I sounded a bit wet. 'So, are you going to that rave?'

'Yeah. S'pose.' He was fingering the pills one by one, giving them the kind of attention I wished he'd been giving me. 'They've eroded a bit. You should have kept them in the fridge.'

'Yeah, but Mum'd find them.'

'You haven't changed one bit, have you? You're still the same girl I met that night at Café Neon.' He chuckled. I smiled. At least he was talking about us. 'You didn't even know it was a strip joint.'

'Yes, I did.' I lied. 'Remember that stripper.'

'Yeah, I thought you were a dyke, you were so into it.' He

opened the speed bag and peered inside.

'Stop it.' I wondered what he'd think of Hollie and I pashing.

'Babe, trust me, I'm not complaining. Two chicks are always better than one.' He stuck his nose into the bag and inhaled deeply like some kind of a speed connoisseur. 'Let's just say, if I had the opportunity, I wouldn't say no.' He nudged me with his big toe and handed me the speed bag. 'Rack us up a few lines while I hang a piss.' He stood up and pecked me on the cheek, his stubble thicker from a week's growth. 'You're so fucking sexy,' he whispered in my ear before disappearing down the hall.

I cleared the junk off my bedside table and tipped a fair amount of speed into the middle. He was acting like a real arsehole but I couldn't help myself, he looked so fucking good. I grabbed my credit card from my wallet and got to work carving out six straight and even lines.

One line for being dirty.

One line for being sexy.

One line for going wild.

One line for bad-girl want.

One line for Scott's hard cock.

One line for getting back together.

I licked my finger along the edge of the credit card and quickly rubbed it on my gums. Scott padded back down the hall, his feet slapping against the tiles.

'Your mum's still got that weird sign about washing your hands *vigorously*.' He was standing in the doorway. 'If it wasn't so fucking hilarious, it'd be really twisted.'

'She's got a new boyfriend called Randy Andy.'

'Sounds like a poof to me,' he said, flapping his wrists.

'He's got a massive dick.'

'Couldn't be bigger than mine.'

'It's huge.'

'How big?'

I estimated the length with my hands.

'Width?' he asked.

'Salami-size.'

'Bullshit.' He wrestled me onto the carpet and pinned my arms above my head. 'Mutai?' He was playing our mercy game, just like old times.

I shook my head, not giving in.

He flipped me over, twisting my wrists in Chinese burns behind my back. It hurt like shit.

'Mutai?'

'Mutai,' I conceded through clenched teeth. He released me and I rolled over. We lay side by side on our backs, close but not touching. I felt the heat radiating off his body and I could smell him – that salty, scalpy smell that made me so horny. He turned to me, his head propped up on his arm. I did the same so that only a thin slither of air separated us. We stared at each other for ages, each part of me burning under his gaze.

'Fuck, you look good.' He had goose bumps on his chest.

'I missed you, you know.' My ears throbbed hot and I had a sinking sensation in my chest like I'd said the wrong thing. He held a finger to my lips and shook his head.

'I know what *you* need.' He crawled over to the lines. I

rolled onto my back and stared at the ceiling. What the fuck was he playing at? I needed sex not drugs, but then, as Trish said, speed was meant to make fucking even better. I sat up and watched as he snorted two lines, back and forth, no fuss; then I had one. As he looked at me, Scott's pupils grew huge with lust. He pulled me to him and kissed me fiercely. Like eating the first strawberry of the summer, it was sweeter, juicier, more delicious than I'd remembered. His lips were so full, so ripe, I wanted to bite them off. He pulled back, turning around to the lines and polished off three more. I had the last one, feeling the stuff drip burning down my nasal cavity into my throat. When I looked up, he was gone.

'Scott!' No answer. I went searching for him. The speed was kicking in big-time now, firing my limbs, zipping through the twists and turns of the sausagey tunnels in my brain. I dashed from room to room. The house was bright and fresh. In the kitchen, there was the zing of lemon Pine-o-cleen in the air. I ran and skidded across the tiles, out through the sliding door to the courtyard. 'Ouch!' The pavers were hot. I nipped back inside. The cool hush of the lounge room with everything covered in plastic made me think of funeral parlours.

'Scott!'

'In here!'

He was lying on his back. Naked starfish on Mum's bed. The air-con was on full-blast and he'd tuned the alarm clock radio to Triple J. 'Suck My Kiss' by the Chilli Peppers was playing. His eyes were closed but his body writhed to the music. I stood there looking at his nakedness. His cock, smooth and thick, pointed straight at the ceiling in a massive erection. He'd always wanted to fuck on Mum's bed but I'd never had the guts before. It was just past three and I reckoned she wouldn't be home before five.

Scott opened one eye, lazily. 'Let's do it, babe.'

'One sec.' I dashed to my bedroom for the whip and the handcuffs.

We went wild. Scott ripped my g-string off with his teeth and threw my bra across the room. He pushed me face down on the bed and cuffed my wrists behind my back and tied my ankles together with the cord from Mum's chenille. He said he fucking loved my tatt. I screamed in ecstasy (and a bit of pain) as he lashed at my bare butt with the whip and talked dirty, calling me 'bitch' and 'whore' and 'slut'. He flipped me onto my back, my hands squashed beneath me in the cuffs. He straddled my face, forcing his cock into my mouth, ordering me to suck. I worked my tongue up and down it, careful not to snag with my teeth, mustering as much saliva as possible as he thrust back and forth, the friction hot against my lips. He grunted his enjoyment. All I could see were his balls, loose and dangling, as he hovered over me, his weight supported by one hand. I could feel my wetness mounting and I wanted him in me so bad. Drawing back, I said, 'Fuck me,' but he said, 'No,' and thrust back deep throat. I was choking but he didn't seem to notice.

'Is my cock big enough for you, babe?' he said, rubbing his hands all over my front, fondling my belly-button ring, pushing his fingers up into me. My mouth muscles were getting tired from the blowing, the cuffs were biting into my wrists. He went faster with his fingers, digging right up inside me like he thought I was going to come, even though he should've remembered that I'd never fucking ever been able to come off a finger-fuck. I drew back for a breather, but he barked, 'Don't fucking stop!' So I put him back in and went for gold. I could tell, from his groans and the way he stopped finger-fucking me, that he was close to the edge. He roared and hand-fulled my tits, 'Oh. Fuck.' His whole body went rigid and his cock stiffened in my mouth. 'Fuck,' he screamed, 'fuck, fuck,' each 'fuck' getting louder until his load hit the back of my throat. I gagged and gulped it down. I had never swallowed before, but Trish had told me that down the hatch was the only way. 'Before your taste buds know what's hit 'em,' she'd said. It left a gluey, grassy, Brussels-sprouty taste that made me want to spew.

'That was awesome, babe.' Scott collapsed beside me with a big grin on his face.

Although I was pissed we hadn't fucked, I figured there'd be heaps more times for that. While he snoozed, I sat up watching him. His cheeks were flushed from all the exertion, his hairless chest shiny with a light coating of sweat. His penis lay to one side, still full and luscious as an exotic fruit. I didn't want to disturb him because I didn't want him to leave. I wriggled down to lying position, as best I could with my hands cuffed and my ankles tied together, and rested my head on his chest. It was just past four. 'November Rain' by Guns 'n' Roses was playing on the radio. The Asian chick popped into my head. Those long pale limbs. That superior smile. I was tempted to ask him about her, but part of me didn't want to know. For now, it was enough just to be with him, inhaling his smell, listening to his booming heartbeat.

Scott jerked upright, tipping me off his chest. 'Someone's pulled into the drive.' Snapping off the radio, he leapt up and peered out the curtains. 'Shit. It's your mum.' He dashed around the room in a panic. 'Where're my shorts?

Fuck! The one time in her life she was early. I struggled with no arms to a sitting position. 'Quick. Get me the key. It's in a brown paper bag, under my bed.'

'But babe, she'll be walking in here any second.'

'You can't leave me like this!' With my ankles tied, I couldn't walk and, with my hands cuffed behind my back, I couldn't untie my ankles.

'There's no time,' Scott said, tugging on his shorts.

'Carry me into the bedroom. You can uncuff me and climb out the window.'

Mum's footsteps clacked across the porch. A second later, she was jiggling the key in the lock.

'Nah, I gotta split. Sorry. I'll call you later, OK?' He ran out of the room leaving me bound and naked on Mum's floral spread and I knew I'd never ever forgive him for it.

As the door creaked open and Mum clattered inside, shopping bags rustling about her, I burrowed, like an amputated rodent, under the covers. My voice weak and trembly, I called out, 'Mum, I'm in here. I'm really sick.'

In a flash, she was at my side, flinging her shopping on the floor, a look of tender concern on her face.

'Where do you feel sick?'

'Everywhere,' I said pathetically, moaning a little and shimmying down further in the bed, covers up to my chin. 'I was feeling hot and shivery so I came in here for the air-con.'

'You look flushed,' she said. 'Have you got a temperature?'

I rolled my head towards her on the pillow. She pressed her palm against my forehead.

'You're on fire.' She looked worried. 'Have you had a cold shower?'

'Yes,' I lied.

'What about fluids?'

'No.'

'I'll get you some lemonade.'

'Thanks,' I murmured, fluttering my eyelids closed, slackening my lips in pretend-suffering.

As soon as she was gone, I reared up like a vampire out of a coffin and surveyed the entire room, searching desperately for the whip. Maybe Scott had taken it with him. I fell forwards on to my stomach and dived under the sheets in case it had somehow ended up at the bottom of the bed. No luck. At the sound of Mum's heels, I fell back onto the pillows and resumed my sick-girl act, closing my eyes. Mum stopped halfway across the room. Her knee joints cracked as she bent down to pick something up off the floor. I peeked through slitted lids. She was inspecting the red bra and g-string which Scott had torn off me. She held the offending items at arm's length, as if some rampant infestation of STD germs might be lurking within the crotch of my knickers.

'Only prostitutes wear red underwear, Rosemary,' she said, all prim. She dropped the bra and knickers onto my face. 'Black's fine but red is for whores.' The lace was itchy. I opened my eyes and shook the lingerie off my face.

'Mum, I'm really sick, OK? Do we have to talk about this now?'

'So long as you know.'

'Fine,' I said, wondering how she could object to red undies, yet root a man she had known less than forty-eight hours.

'Here, sit up.' She held a big glass of lemonade with ice-cubes.

I didn't move a muscle, fearing a chink of the cuffs would give me away. 'I'm too weak.'

Mum held the drink to my lips. I sipped like an invalid, relieved to have the vile taste of cum washed away.

'You *do* look a bit green around the gills,' she murmured. I nodded and fluttered my lids closed. 'That's right. Have a little rest. I better get ready. Andy will be here soon.' She kissed me on the forehead and went to have a shower in her en suite.

As soon as I heard the water running, I kicked off the covers with my bound legs and manoeuvred myself out of bed. I hopped across Mum's room and was heading into the hallway when I heard scratching in the lock, then the front door squeaking open. I froze. A warm breeze wafted in against my whipped butt-cheeks. I turned my head to see Randy stepping across the threshold. Mum'd wasted as little time giving him a set of house keys as she had in screwing him. With a gargled intake of breath, he'd seen me.

'Oh, my goodness. Rosie. What happened?' His voice came out squeaky. 'Are you alright? Who did this to you?' He stepped towards me, shutting the door quietly behind him.

'Stay back. I'm fine,' I hissed. 'And get your beady eyes off my butt!'

'I wasn't looking. Promise.' He stared rod-straight at the ceiling, his neck going blotchy. He cleared his throat with a loud cough. 'Here, let me give you a hand.'

'Fuck off,' I said, hopping away, my tits bouncing all over the shop.

He held his hands up in surrender. 'Well, whoever he was, it's pretty rough of him to take off and leave you like that.'

'Rosemary!' Mum sang out from the bedroom.

'Fuck it. Untie me,' I said. 'Quick. Before Mum comes out. No perving.'

'What kind of bloke do you think I am?' He came over and dropped to his knees, his bald patch glowing red as embers. Licking his lips like crazy in concentration, he tugged and pulled at the dressing-gown cord around my ankles.

'Andy! Is that you?' Mum called from the bedroom.

I could feel the knot loosening.

'Yes, Janice!' Randy replied.

'I'll be out in a jiffy.'

'Take your time!'

The cord fell away and my legs were free but I was still cuffed. Mum's footsteps sounded across the entry.

'You've got to help me with these,' I rattled the cuffs at Randy before flying down the hallway to my room. I kicked the door shut and looked around. Despite Scott's big hurry, the pills and the speed bag were gone. He'd had time to grab his gear but no time to un-fucking-tie me. A few seconds later and Randy knocked.

'You ready?'

'Hold on.' I pressed my front against the wall, my tits crushed flat so that Randy couldn't perve. 'OK.'

He came in and wedged the door with a chair. 'Right, now where's this key?' he asked, all businesslike.

'Under the bed, in a paper bag.'

He fell to his knees and was scuffling around amongst shoe-boxes and last year's *Cosmopolitans* when there was a sharp rap on the door.

'Rosemary! Are you in there?'

'Fuck, it's Mum,' I cursed, but Randy had the key. He grabbed my hands in a rough, blokish way and fumbled with the cuff-lock.

It hit me that the situation was as awkward for Randy as it was for me. 'Hey, Randy,' I whispered. 'Thanks.'

'All part of the service,' he joked.

I sang out to Mum, 'I'm feeling a lot better now. Go on. You'll be late. Say hi to Randy for me.'

'No, I'd feel much happier if I checked your temperature again. You were really burning up before.' She jiggled the doorknob. 'Rosemary, open the door!'

The key turned. The cuffs fell away. I dived under the sheet. Randy stood frozen in the middle of my room, terror on his face. If Mum had barged in right then it would have looked mighty suspect.

'Randy, out the window,' I urged.

He jumped onto my bed, flying over the sill and crashing into the azalea bush with a stifled cry just as the chair tipped sideways with a crash. Mum burst in. Her eyes darted around for incriminating evidence, but there was none.

'I'm sure I heard a man's voice in here.' She opened the wardrobe and peered inside. 'What's with the chair?'

'In case Randy came in,' I said, lamely.

'Don't be silly.' Mum was all tarted up in a new red suit with big gold buttons and stiletto heels. It was evidently OK to wear prostitute-red on the outside.

'You look nice,' I said.

Her face softened. She sat down on the edge of the bed and pressed her palm to my forehead. 'Your temperature's gone down.' She kissed the top of my head. 'There's some spag bol in the freezer if you get hungry.'

With a feisty click of her heels, she turned and sashayed out of the room, as through my window I watched Randy slip across the courtyard and back inside the house.

'I'm in here, Janice!' He called from the lounge room, like he'd been there all along.

'Coming, possum!' shouted Mum, clickety-clacking down the hall towards him.

I sunk back against the pillows, rubbing my bruised

wrists. It was hot and scratchy in bed, my mattress warm from an afternoon roasting in the sun. I felt worn out, used and abused. A single mossie buzzed around my head. I squashed it dead against the wall and decided, once and for all, I was better off moving on, no matter how fucking sexy Scott was.

I woke in a sweat. From outside, there came a tapping sound. I snapped on the lamp and peered out. There was someone standing right outside my window calling my name. For a moment I thought it was Scott, come to say he was sorry. I shot up, sliding back the window to let him in.

It was Hollie. She stood white and bedraggled in a long cotton nightie, her face drawn, her dark hair limp and tangled.

'What's the matter? What are you doing here?' I asked, dazed. It was 2.11 on the digital and I'd been dead to the world. I helped her over the sill and she sat down, cross-legged at the foot of the bed. Her forearms were all scratched and her eyes were rabbit-pink from crying. I leant towards her, alarmed by the state she was in.

'Hollie. What's happened?'

'Why didn't you call me back?' Her eyes were wide, accusing. Her hands were scrunched in tiny fists, rooted into the mattress.

'I'm sorry, I've been meaning to.' It was half the truth but now, with Hollie sitting on my bed distraught and agitated,

I felt ashamed for neglecting her.

'You've been too busy with *him*.' She got up in a huff, crossing the room to the wicker chair, which was buried in a mountain of my dirty clothes. She chucked it all onto the floor and threw herself down. She closed her eyes and sat breathing heavily, her hands folded in her lap.

'Is it Danny? Is he still missing?' I implored.

Her eyes flashed open. 'I can't find him anywhere,' she said, agitated. 'All last week, he kept going off into the bush in that old, smelly coat of his. Every day he was up there. First he comes home with this dead wallaby, which I had to bury in the back garden.' She paused, studying her hands. 'And then, two nights ago, he didn't come home at all. I've been searching for him everywhere, up all the tracks, in the cave, but I can't find him. It's like he's just disappeared, and I kept calling you but you obviously don't care about me or Danny or anyone except that horrid... ' She grimaced at the mere thought of Scott.

'I saw him last Sunday morning,' I broke in. 'He was parked outside Scott's house but he made me promise not to tell you.'

She leapt out of the chair. 'Why didn't you tell me?' she fired. 'He's not well. He could be dead or anything.' She was pacing back and forth, like a little wind-up doll.

'He's not dead. Stop getting all worked up. C'mon, let's get some sleep. It's your party tomorrow. I bet he'll turn up in the morning.'

'And if he doesn't?'

'He will,' I said, 'I promise.'

Stumbling out of bed, I pulled her in beside me. I billowed the sheet up over us and stroked her forehead. She clung to me and murmured that she loved me. Her heart was racing a million miles per hour but, after a while, she settled down and went to sleep. I lay awake, listening to the geckoes squeaking inside the bricks, and wondering where the hell Danny was right at that moment.

12

The next morning, I woke to the sound of smashing pavers. Hollie was gone. She must have slipped out of the window without waking me. Sitting up in bed, I looked outside to the courtyard and there was Randy, pigeon-chested, in bright red stubbies, wielding a sledge-hammer.

'What are you doing?' I yelled above the din but he didn't hear me, so I chucked on an old T-shirt and I went outside. Mum sauntered across the courtyard, wearing a new lemon-silk dressing gown. She pashed Randy and handed him a mug of tea.

'What's going on?' I said to her. Randy continued his demolition frenzy, shattered bits of paver flying into the air and landing with a splash in the fishpond.

'Andy's building me an outdoor power shower.' She beamed across at him.

'What the hell for?' I stood, hands on hips.

'So he can scrub off all the bacteria germs before coming into the house,' she said as if it were the most logical thing on earth. 'It's my Christmas present.' She swung her hips around to Randy. 'Isn't it, possum?'

Randy stopped and turned around. 'What's that?'

'My Christmas present.'

'That's right.' He grinned back at Mum, wiping the sweat from his bald patch with a crumpled hankie.

'Where're you putting it?' I fired at Randy, eyeing the chalk boundary which had been marked up in a lopsided square beneath my bedroom window.

He flashed Mum a quick, nervy look. 'Well, Rosie,' he started but Mum cut him off.

'Andy's checked the pipes and there's really only one place for it. That is, without having to install a whole new plumbing system.'

'This way we can run the shower off the existing connection,' Randy added, 'and, so long as we don't use more than one shower at one time, there should be enough water pressure to activate the turbo-jets.'

'Great. Just fucking great.' I went inside, grabbed my car keys and pulled on my sneakers. I tore through the house and out the front door. Mum came flapping across the lawn, but I was already reversing down the drive. She tugged at the passenger door. It flung open and she managed to get her arse inside the car while it was still moving.

'Stop,' she said. 'There's something I want to tell you.'

I braked and gazed out the window, the engine idling, the sun crashing in through the windscreen, waiting for the inevitable lecture. But when I looked over at Mum, she was smiling like a loon.

'What?' I said.

She took a deep breath. 'Randy, I mean, Andy is moving in.'

I clenched the steering wheel. 'When?'

'Before Christmas.'

I stared straight ahead as Mum leaned across and hugged me, yelling in my ear, 'I'm so happy!' She pecked me on the cheek and leapt out of the car.

I swung backwards out onto the road and burnt rubber down the street, waking as many lazy burbanites as possible.

Lunchtime, I was meeting up with Dad. The thought of it filled me with dread. It only happened once a year at Christmas. We'd go the same coffee shop at the top end of the Queen Street Mall where he'd buy me a cappuccino (but not lunch) and give me a Christmas card with a crisp five-dollar note inside, enough to cover half the cost of parking in town. As I drove into town along the river, I planned my usual list of pleasant conversation starters: 'So, Dad, how're things in the life insurance business?' and 'Been playing any tennis lately?' and 'They reckon it'll be the hottest Christmas on record.' Work, sport and the weather; all safe territory outside of which it was best not to stray. But he always had to bring up Mum. And then came the tears – bleary, weeping tears; three-parts booze, one-part tear.

Dad was sitting at our usual outside table, overlooking the mall but close to the bar.

'Hi, Dad.' I was twenty minutes late.

He stood up as if I were royalty or something and I waved

at him to sit down. We didn't hug or kiss. I sat opposite him and ordered a cappuccino from the waiter. Dad looked at me blankly for a long time as if trying to figure out how he knew the daggily-dressed redhead sitting across from him.

'Hello, daughter,' he said, smiling with relief as if he'd just remembered.

'Sorry I'm late.'

'That's alright.' He gulped at his beer, wiped his mouth with the back of his hand, blinked. 'You made it in the end.'

'Yeah. Traffic wasn't too bad considering it's Christmas.'

'Yes. That's right. Christmas.' He grimaced and drank more beer as if to wash away the thought of it. I never bothered to ask how he spent Christmas. I imagined he spent it alone in front of the telly drinking tinnies and watching his old cricket videos until he passed out blotto in the chair. He probably didn't even eat.

My cappuccino arrived. I ate the chocolate off the top and pushed it aside to cool. Dad ordered himself another beer. On my way up the mall, I'd bought him a pair of Homer Simpson socks, which I thrust, still in the sock-shop bag, across the table.

'Happy Christmas,' I said.

Dad whipped the ever-predictable envelope out of his breast pocket. 'Merry Christmas, to my one and only daughter.' On occasions like these he spoke as he might write in a greeting card, stilted and formal. As I tore open the envelope, pretending that I didn't already know what was inside, he pulled the Homer socks out of the bag.

'Socks,' he said. 'I need socks.'

'Do you know who he is?' I said, pointing at Homer's giant, yellow face.

'Yeah,' he said, shaking his head.

'You don't, do you? He's a cartoon character that likes to drink a lot of beer.'

'Oh. Right. I get it.' He put the socks back in the bag. I should have got him sports ones instead.

I pulled out my card, which was from the same twenty-pack of identical Christmas cards Dad had been giving me for the past twelve years – an obese surfboarding Santa being towed along the crest of a wave by a fleet of flying reindeers with pink-zinced noses, their antlers poking through red and gold life-saver caps. I opened it and, miracle of miracles, a twenty-dollar note fluttered out. For Dad, twenty was a decent session at the pub.

'I wanted to get your mother a little something this year but I didn't know what to get her. So, I thought you could pick her out something nice from the twenty and keep the rest for yourself.' He was gripping his beer so hard I thought the glass would shatter in his hand, and his eyes had misted over. I knew what was coming next.

'Dad,' I said, under my breath, 'do you have to do this, again? The past is the past – you can't make up for it, it's too late.' He sculled his beer in one go and signalled to the waiter for another. I sipped at my coffee and tried to change the subject.

'Scott's back,' I said. After what Scott'd done to me the day before, I couldn't believe I was bringing him up, but then, it wasn't easy making light conversation with Dad.

'Who?

'Scott Greenwood. He's back from overseas.'

'Oh. That's good.' On the few occasions Scott had met Dad, the two of them had got on well, bonding over cricket or the footy, depending on the season.

'What about uni?' he asked, staring gloomily into the distance.

'Dad, I quit, remember?' I paused. 'Anyway, I'm thinking about going travelling.'

He grunted. 'What a load of bunkum.'

For a few long minutes we said nothing as Dad drifted back into his pickled past and drank his beer. I stared down at the bobbing heads of the shoppers, jostling up and down the mall; saggy-titted women, tired and flustered, overloaded with carry bags, who'd rather drop dead of exhaustion than return home without that final all-important item crossed off their Christmas list.

'You can't leave your mother alone.' It was like that with Dad. He'd stew on something for ages before short-circuiting back to an earlier conversation, like a fuse box with water damage. 'Forget this travelling palaver. Your mother needs you.' It was on the tip of my tongue to tell him about Randy but I held back, wary of his reaction. 'Listen to me, daughter.' Suddenly forceful, his words were lucid and direct, a man emerging from the haze. 'I know your mother better than anyone else.'

'But, Dad, I can't stay in Brisbane my whole life. It's not my fault she married an alcoholic.'

'She still blames me?' Tears were forming in tiny weirs at

the bottom of his eyeballs.

'She doesn't really talk about it,' I lied. There wasn't a day she didn't curse Dad for ruining the best years of her life.

'Do you think if I quit the grog she might have me back?' It was the same question every year and I was sick to death of it. I decided to spill the beans.

'Unlikely. She's got a new boyfriend. He's working on a cure for cancer and he's building her an outdoor power shower and he's got a great sense of humour and he treats Mum like gold... ' On and on I went, pumping Randy up to be some kind of superhero, while Dad's face contorted in a painful wince. I left out the bit about him being a bald, artificially enhanced geek who drives a rust-bucket, and finished with the clincher.

'... and he's moving in.'

Dad couldn't speak. His face was screwed up tight as a walnut. 'But she's mine,' he finally managed through clenched teeth. 'She's my woman.'

'She's not your woman. She divorced you, remember?'

'But I still love her.' He drained his beer. 'I've always loved her.'

'C'mon, Dad. Don't torture yourself.'

He pulled out a hundred-dollar bill from his wallet. 'Here. Get her something special. Jewellery. Gold jewellery.' I stared at the note lying on the table, slated that he'd rummaged a hundred for Mum when all I ever got were scummy fivers.

'She won't want it, Dad,' I said, huffily. 'Not from you.'

'Well, tell her it's from you.' He got up and shambled

towards the toilets on thick, stocky legs. Each year his shoulders got a bit more stooped, his shorts a bit saggier in the bum.

'Hey, I gotta go,' I called out to him.

He waved backwards, not turning around. I slipped the hundred in the card, next to the twenty, and headed down to the mall, relieved that it was over for another year.

Blondie's on the radio. I'm in my biggest, puffiest skirt and Dad's spinning me around and around. The lounge room's all blurry and I can't tell which way's up or down. The baked beans we had for dinner are all tumbly-jumbly in my tummy like I might vomit. I hope I don't vomit. Not on my nice pink skirt. Sooner or later, he'll let go. I'll fly through the air and crash land into Mum's new apricot leather lounge suite. She'd be so angry if she knew.

He lets go.

I'm flying through the air but the couch is out of range. I land with a thud on the floor but it doesn't hurt that much; just a bit of carpet burn on my knees. Dad rushes over to see if I'm alright.

'Must have lost my grip,' he says.

His face is huge and red and spinning. I struggle to sit up.

'Old noggin OK?' He rubs my head with his big, rough hand. I would have cried when I was younger but I'm five now. Besides, I don't want to stop the game. I pick myself up and hold my hands out for more.

'Give it a rest for a while, hey? I'm all out of puff.' He lies down on Mum's couch with his shoes up on the armrests, which he's not meant to do, and cracks open another bottle of beer. Watching Dad drink is boring so I start spinning around on my own. My skirt billows out, making a lovely cool breeze between my legs. Over and over, I keep spinning and crashing, spinning and crashing, until the baked beans come up in an orange puddle on the carpet. Dad's fiddling with the radio so he doesn't even notice when I hide the vomit under one of Mum's satiny cushions and sit on top.

'That's more like it,' he says, looking over at me all prim on the cushion. 'Since you're being such a good girl, let's go out for an ice-cream when I've finished this stubbie.'

Driving in the car, Dad lets me sit in the front as a special treat so long as I promise not to tell Mum. He turns the radio up really loud and we sing along to our favourite song about talking Japanese. I make my eyes go all slanty and Dad bursts out laughing. When the song finishes, he says, 'Bloody funny-looking bastards, those nips,' and we laugh at that, too.

We go to the drive-through bottle shop where Dad buys a carton of beer and a can of lemonade for me. Halfway home, I remind him about the ice-cream and we turn around and drive back to the corner shop where they sell Jelly-Tips. Dad gives me the money and I go inside. When I come out he is drinking a beer from the carton, even though the man at the bottle shop said they weren't cold. We sit in the car while I eat my Jelly-Tip; picking the chocolate shell off first, then sucking the jelly, then making the vanilla ice-cream last for as long as possible. Dad drinks another beer and tosses the empty can out the window.

'We'd better get back before Mum gets home,' he says.

'OK,' I say, wishing I could have another Jelly-Tip.

Dad pulls out from the kerb.

There's a screech-bang-crunch like in a Roadrunner cartoon.

I go flying through the air.

I hear the crack of my head against the windscreen.

Dad's screaming out my name. And then, everything goes black.

When I wake up, I'm in hospital and Mum's sitting beside me. She tells me how I nearly went to heaven. Every day she brings me presents: books and hair-clips and Freddo Frogs and felt-pens and puzzles and, one day, a pair of pink hippopotamus slippers. But Dad never comes. Maybe he's in a hospital for grown-ups. I ask Mum where he is but her mouth goes all twisted like a caterpillar and she says a bad word – *bastard* – under her breath. When I get home, Dad's not there either. His plastic Buddha's missing off the telly and his cricket movies from the bottom shelf of the bookcase have all gone, too.

13

It was just after eight when I arrived at Hollie's dead mum's party, wearing a black evening dress with diamanté straps. For Hollie's sake, I'd decided not to go to the rave. Besides, I'd convinced myself that, after his abysmal post-root behaviour, I was through with Scott for good. As I ran up the drive and down the side of the house to the back, my heels sinking into the pebbly path, I felt good and virtuous for the first time in ages. I prayed that Danny had turned up; if he hadn't, Hollie would be in a terrible state. Last I'd spoken to her, around five that afternoon, he was stil missing.

The backyard had been transformed into a Japanese-style garden complete with a meandering creek spanned in the middle by a red-lacquer bridge. In broad daylight, it would've looked a bit Disney but at night the effect was enchanting. Centre-stage, golden water tumbled from a jade sculpture, pooling in a circular pond glinting with black and orange koi-carp. *Madame Butterfly* blared from speakers set up on the deck. Manicured bonsai, especially imported for the occasion, stood as attentive as the kimono-clad waiters carrying silver trays of luminescent cocktails and black fish-spawn on ice. Red and yellow lanterns were strung up from the gum trees beyond which the bush loomed, a wall of solid black. From the dark, the crickets throbbed a backbeat to the hum of party chatter, opera and the chinking of crystal. Each year, I was always surprised by the odd and varied assortment Hollie cobbled together – distant relatives, university acquaintances and the odd scruffy English professor, most of whom only came for the French plonk and gourmet tucker. Whatever their thoughts about the Danny scandal, it didn't stop random neighbours flocking, too, all eager for a free piss-up in the name of dead Mrs Bailey. As I headed past the crowd of first arrivals, fidgeting in makeshift black-tie, guzzling pink champagne and spoofing over the scenery, I couldn't see Hollie or Danny anywhere. Mr Bailey didn't seem to be around either; some years he showed up, some years he was conspicuously absent, not that Hollie seemed to care.

I made it to the spiral staircase, decked out in fairy lights, and climbed up to the house. Helping myself to a glass of champagne, I roamed from the kitchen to the lounge room, the dining room, the piano room, the parlour, even peeking behind the oak-panelled door to Mr Bailey's study, but there was no one around. I tramped upstairs and, as I proceeded down the thickly carpeted hall, nipping into each bedroom, the noise of the party became muffled and distant. I called out to Hollie but there was no reply. It wasn't like her to neglect her guests. At parties gone by, she'd flit around, topping up drinks, bringing around tray after tray of delicacies, laughing theatrically. She'd even stand up on the deck and say a few words, just like Mrs Bailey used to do. The number of times I heard someone remark, 'She's the spitting image of Lesley, isn't she?'

I came to Mrs Bailey's bedroom door. After a few deep breaths for my jangles, I turned the cut-crystal doorknob and pushed inside. The room was cloaked in dark shadows, the air chilly. No Hollie here either. Walking up to the mirrored wardrobes, I took the opportunity to check myself out. I dropped my hands, letting them wander, slipping smooth down the slinky front of my top, over my breasts, my stomach, my hips. I lifted the hem of my dress up to admire my pins; the way my thighs sliced without touching, the way my butt sat firm and pert with one nice crease underneath.

Someone giggled.

I spun around, tugging down my dress. Hollie was lying sideways on the bed in a full-length geisha dress in blue silk. She'd been hiding in the shadows. Her face was painted white and seemed to hover in mid-air, immaculate as a mask. Her lips were shaped into a perfect cupid's bow and her hair was pulled into a severe bun, so tight it tugged at the corners of her eyes. She held an open bottle of Moët by the neck.

'Hey, I've been looking everywhere for you,' I said, plonking down on the bed. 'What're you doing in here?'

'Waiting for you.' She took a swig from the bottle and stared at me. 'You're late.'

'Sorry. It's been a crazy kind of day. First Mum tells me her new squeeze is moving in, then Dad has his annual

Christmas breakdown on me. I've had enough of both of them.'

In a blink, Hollie's face was transformed and she beamed a hundred-watts. 'You can come and live with me.' Like she hadn't tried that one before. She wriggled towards me, her silky dress sliding against the satin coverlet. 'We could have so much fun together, don't you think?'

'Maybe. What about Danny?'

'Oh, he won't mind.'

'No. Have you seen him?'

'He's late, late for a very important date.' She laughed, rolling around on the bed.

'You're pissed.'

'Am not,' she slurred.

I grabbed the bottle off her and had a go. There was only a mouthful left.

'C'mon,' I said, pushing off the bed. 'Maybe Danny's downstairs.'

'No. You've got to dress up, too.' She ran after me, pulling me back by the waist.

'But, Hollie, there's isn't time. Your guests are waiting.' I sighed, relenting, 'Alright, then.'

Hollie shuffled geisha-style across the room. She flung open the mirrored doors to Mrs Bailey's dressing chamber, a treasure trove of lace and chiffon, satin and organza, hoop skirts and netted bustles, frills and sparkles and ribboned hems. Mrs Bailey had loved to dress up. She had gear from almost every epoch imaginable – Egyptian, Roman, Medieval, Regency, Elizabethan, French Renaissance, 1920s

Flapper, Sixties Mod. The floor was littered with shoes; brass-buckled pixie and Victorian lace-up boots, platforms, red glittery pumps, crystal-beaded mules, fluffy kitten heels, black patent knee-highs and silver stilettos. Accessories spewed from boxes lining the shelves above the costumes: tiaras and cowboy hats; pink and purple and lime green boas; wigs of all shapes and colours; a magic wand with a sequinned star; a life-sized pair of lilac-feathered wings.

Hollie shut the door, killing the noise of the party, and switched on a lamp. It was dark and stuffy, the air thick with the smell of moth-balls and old lace. 'Here.' She threw a dress at me. It was exactly the same as hers – embroidered silk with covered buttons running all the way down the side – except red. I stripped off to my daks and tried to pull the dress over my head.

'It won't fit.' I looked up. Hollie was checking out my tits. 'What?' I crossed my arms over my chest.

'Nothing.' She glanced down. 'Unbutton it first.'

I slipped my arms into the sleeves and pulled the edges together but the material was too slippery.

'Let me do it,' Hollie said.

I turned around to face her. In heels, she was the same height as me. She crouched between me and the wall. With light, nimble fingers she started buttoning me up from the hem, pulling the satin tight, smoothing the fabric over my chest. My heart quickened. Although we'd been dressing up like this since we were kids, it felt different this time.

'Now your face.' Hollie smeared white goo all over my

cheeks and painted on lips. She brushed my hair and pinned it up with bobby pins and chopsticks, which dug into my scalp. When she'd finished, she stood back with a strange little smile. She bowed, her dainty hands pressed together, and said, 'You look beautiful.' She held a hand-mirror up to me. I looked like a total freak but I nodded and bowed.

Hollie dragged me back into the bedroom and dived on the bed. She rolled onto her side, her head propped against the fluffy cushions, her body rocking with the gentle motion of the waterbed.

'I saw you,' she said, coyly.

'When?' I was perched at the foot of the bed.

'Before. You were doing this.' Laughing, Hollie ran a hand down the front of her flat chest. 'You looked sexy.' She slid down against the pillows, shimmying her dress up her thighs.

'I wasn't doing anything.' I crossed over to the window and looked down at the party, which had degenerated into a full-on backyard piss-up. Boxes of Domino's pizza and Big Rooster chicken were being passed around. The men had ditched their jackets and bowties. *Madame Butterfly* had been swapped for *Abba's Greatest Hits* and the women were jigging around barefoot on the grass to 'Mamma Mia'.

'Pack of bevans,' I said. 'They'll be pissing in the fishpond next.' I turned to Hollie. 'We'd better get down there.' She was kneeling on the waterbed. As the surface dipped and bobbed, she swayed from side to side, her dress ruched so high I could see the white crotch of her knickers showing through her pantyhose. She beckoned to me.

'Come here.' She stood up shakily, her dress bunched around her waist. 'I want to tell you a secret.' She lost her balance and lurched for the wall. 'A secret about Danny and me.' She started undoing her buttons, popping them open one by one. Her bodice undone to the waist, she slipped her arms out of the sleeves and pulled the dress down over her hips. The skin on her stomach and her chest was as white as her geisha-ed face and she was the skinniest I'd ever seen her. She stepped out of the crumpled dress and kicked it across the room towards me.

'Kiss me,' she purred, flinging herself backwards onto the bed. 'Kiss me like we're lovers. Kiss me on my dead mum's bed.' She sighed theatrically and closed her eyes.

I stood, watching her wriggle and squirm on the satin, her back arched like a vixen. It was just like all the other times, except this Hollie was more confident, more alluring, and the change in her was exhilarating. For a moment, it caught me off guard but then we'd been playing this game since we were ten years old. I climbed onto the bed and crawled towards her head. She sank back, a faint smile curling her lips. I sat up on my heels next to her head. Her face was porcelain perfect, like I could have crushed it in my hands. I reached out and stroked her cheek. White powder came off on my fingers. With her eyes still closed, she held out her hand. I pressed my lips to her palm, then all the way up her arm, leaving a red-lipstick trail, like bites on her skin. She stretched and sighed, tossing her head from side to side on the pillow like Cathy in her death fever.

'Hollie. Look at me,' I said.

Her eyes flashed open. I leant in and pashed her. She clasped my face in her hands and she looked so serious that I laughed and tipped sideways onto the bed. Lying back, I stared at the ceiling, which was littered in glow-in-the-dark stars I'd never noticed before. There was the Southern Cross and the Saucepan and the Milky Way.

'Rosie?' Hollie sat up on one elbow and looked at me, her eyes crazy-bright. Something cold brushed against my stomach. I jerked up. My skirt was up around my hips and Hollie's fingers were hooked under the waistband of my undies.

'What are you doing?' My heart raced and I felt breathless. Hollie stared at me, all white face and smudged red lips.

'I want to touch you,' she said, evenly. 'Please. Let me.' She tried to push me down by the shoulders, but horrified, I shot off the bed. The faint sound of breaking glass came from downstairs. A cheer went up. A chorus of men shouting, 'Taxi!' followed by raucous laughter.

'I've got to go,' I said, sharply.

'Where?' She came after me.

'Out.' I decided, in that moment, to go to the rave after all.

'You can't leave me!' she screamed, grabbing me by the chopsticks in my hair and pulling me back towards the bed.

'Let go. You're hurting me.' She was acting like a total psycho.

'I won't let you leave me.' She tugged hard at my hair but

I bit her on the arm. She cried out as I ran towards the door.

'Where are you going?' she demanded.

'To a rave.'

'With *him*,' she spat.

'Maybe.'

Her eyes shone hot with outrage and confusion, her lips twisted and furrowed like a kabuki mask.

'What the fuck's wrong with you, Hollie?' I stood in the doorway, glaring at her.

'Just go!' she screamed.

'Fine,' I said, and walked out, slamming the door behind me.

Downstairs, the party had deteriorated into further bogan chaos. *Midnight Oil* was on the stereo and men were head-banging or playing air guitar on the deck, singing tunelessly into empty beer cans. Two women sat big-bottomed on the jade sculpture, shovelling great slabs of chocolate gateau into their gobs. The waiters had shed their kimonos and were splashing about the fishpond in their undies. Danny wasn't anywhere. As I pushed through the crowd, I was relieved to be getting away from the party and from Hollie. It was just like her to take things too far. Sure, she was drunk but she'd never been like that with me before and it felt strange. We'd crossed some kind of line. The way she'd looked at me, the way she'd slipped her fingers inside my knickers, it wasn't just our usual fantasy act. It was like she was serious

I jogged down the drive, as best as I could in the geisha get-up, towards my car. The party hubbub faded to a muted hum, drowned out by the crickets pulsing around me like a force field. There was a full moon and the track up the side of Mount Coot-tha shone luminescent-white as a fresh scar. Bats swooped low over my head, blotting out the night sky. The bush was black, faceless, throbbing, as I hurried across the cul-de-sac. Eager to be inside the car, I fumbled and dropped my keys in the darkness and, as I bent down to pick them up, something hard and sharp pressed against my back. My heart turned cold. There was a foul stench and the touch of hot breath on my neck. I didn't dare look around and my throat went too dry to scream.

'Where you going?' There was something familiar about the gruff male voice but I couldn't place it.

'What do you want?' I said, trembling.

'Turn around.' He pulled the blade away from my back. I spun around and gasped. Drenched in moonlight was a tall, dark-skinned man. His hair was black and matted with dirt. His teeth shone bone white. He was naked with orange and white markings all over his chest and arms. At his side, he carried a long thin stick, at one end the sharp point I'd felt against my back. The carcass of a small animal was draped over his left shoulder. Apart from his nose, which was thin and narrow, he looked like an aborigine.

'Me, Danny-Dilly.' He took a step backwards and lunged at me with the spear.

184

'Danny?'

'You, Rosie-Maroo,' he said.

'Fucking hell.' I tried to wrench the spear from his grip but he was too strong. 'You scared the crap out of me. Where the hell have you been? Hollie's going nuts.'

'Me hunting,' he said, his face stern, his black eyes glinting like mica. 'You roast yams.'

'Stop talking like that,' I said, checking him over. 'You're filthy. You mustn't have eaten for days.' He was so skinny that each time he breathed it looked as though ribs would poke right through his mud-caked skin. 'Go inside and have a shower. Not through the backyard or you'll freak everyone out.' I wagged my finger at him. 'And get rid of that dead animal. It stinks.' I slid inside the car and slammed the door, but he just stood there, on one leg, leaning against his spear-stick. I wound down the window. 'Go on. Get. I'm already late.'

In one swift movement, he stuck his head inside the car. The white teeth and the bulging eye-whites in that big dark head of his were frightening and I had to keep reminding myself it was only Danny.

'Where are you going?' This time he spoke normally.

'To a rave in the Valley. Now pack it in, Danny. Get that mud off you, then go see your sister.' I revved the car but still he wouldn't budge.

'Who are you going with?' he persisted.

'None of your business.' I placed my palm against his filthy forehead and pushed his head out of the car. Releasing the handbrake, I rolled the car backwards down the hill. For a while he jogged beside me with his spear, shouting out all sort of bullshit about death and evil spirits and bloody revenge. I switched the radio on for some hardcore to drown him out. At the bottom of the hill, I did a slick three-point turn and looked back up the road, but he'd disappeared. I called Trish to tell her I was coming after all and she screamed down the mobile:

'We're gonna rave our tits off, Rosebud, rave our tits right fucking off!'

14

When I got to Trish's, we snorted some whiz and she said I looked real sexy in my geisha-girl gear. She told me to leave my makeup on for effect and, with a pair of kitchen scissors, she hacked a metre or more off the bottom of my dress until it was so short you could see my undies when I bent over. Trish was dressed like the devil with her hair dyed traffic-light red and gelled into horns on top of her head. Her face sparkled with red glitter and she wore red PVC fuck-me boots that reached mid-thigh. In her satin hot pants and sequinned bra-top, she could have been a trannie. There was not a skerrick of fat on her tummy, and her tits, tight and firm as tennis balls, were more pec than boob.

The devil and the geisha-girl – what a pair of weirdo freaks!

Before we left, I used Dad's one hundred and twenty smacks to buy two green elephants off Trish. I dropped one and kept the other for later. Trish took her second for the night. She reckoned fast driving brought them on quicker so we sped into the Valley, running red lights and doing eighty along Coro Drive. We turned the hardcore up so loud the car bolts rattled and my jaw shook.

When we got to Arena, we had to queue outside. Across the road, in their usual Valley posse, were the local aborigines, propped up against the wall, sucking booze wrapped in brown paper. They were all wearing flannelette shirts and filthy trousers; not like schizo Danny at all, naked with his spear and his bush kill and his tribal body markings. Dad reckoned aborigines were all dole-bludgers who couldn't handle their booze. Mum'd told me how once, when he was maggot from an all-day session at the pub, Dad and one of his mates, Bill Simmons, got to calling them names down the bar. Egged on by their women, the aborigines led it outside. Bill, reserves rugby player for Queensland, loved a fight but Dad jumped the fence as soon as he got the chance, leaving his mate surrounded. Looking across at the aborigines now, there was something about them that made me uncomfortable, a bit scared even. Perhaps it was the way they looked right through me with sad, dead eyes. I had no idea what they were thinking.

Trish had moved along the line so I caught up to her. Everyone was checking each other out as if it was a big competition to wear the most freaked-out shit. I could tell the other bunnies, with their boring tiny-tees, tartan minis and pig-tails, were wishing they'd come as a sexy devil like Trish. It felt good being with someone so hardcore. No one could tell I'd never been raving. Scott would be impressed. I was getting that bad, sexy feeling in my stomach, which probably meant the elephant was brewing up. Soon as I spotted Scott, I'd go right up and roast him for bailing and then, once I'd made him grovel, I'd pash him all hot and sexy with my thigh wedged between his legs. Yeah, he was a prick but I still wanted him.

Trish was dancing on the spot. Her feet were glued to the pavement, her arms taut and pumping at her sides. Her eyes were huge and bulging with no white around the edges. She grinned at me. 'I'm fucking rank, Rosebud.'

'Yeah, I think it's kicking in. My legs feel all tingly.'

'I'm so fucking rank,' she repeated, as the queue surged forwards and we crossed the threshold. We paid the twenty smacks cover and got a fluoro wrist-band with **Oblivion** stamped round it. Trish was body-searched but they waved me through. I walked down a dark tunnel and waited for her at the end, feeling the bass was coming up through my toes, itching to get into it. Trish rocked up, saying that everything was sweet and that they hadn't got the gear because, as she told me, 'I shoved it up my fanny.' We pushed through a black curtain and I was hit by the hugeness of it. Arena had five or six levels, stretching upwards into the swirling clouds of dry-ice, banded with neon pink and yellow and orange lasers. DJs were playing different types of techno on each floor – hardcore, trance, trip-hop, ambient and acid-house. Around us, ravers cut through the haze, quick-limbed and bug-eyed under the strobes, drinking bottled water, their eyes shining white and huge in set-jaw faces. I saw lips blurring, mouths opening, but no sound came out. It was like being in a silent movie; the hardcore drowned out everything.

I tagged along behind Trish, all the time scanning for Scott through the haze. We skirted around the hardcore dancefloor, where the guys wore baggy pants with their undies poking out the top, no shirts and fluoro whistles strung around chicken necks. They all had shaved heads and their pale skins glowed sickly green under the lights. The hardcore chicks looked pretty much like Trish, short and runty with spiked hair and snappable arms. It didn't look much like Scott's scene, though. I was busting to go and find him but Trish wanted the loos. She yanked me into a cubicle and locked the door. Lickety-split, she had the gear out of her undies. She kicked down the loo-lid and shoved the eckys, wrapped in tin-foil, down her bra-top. She tipped a small pyramid of the speed onto the lid, re-sealed the bag and handed it to me. I stood in the corner watching as she racked up lines and crouched down over the toilet.

'Fucked a guy in here once,' she said, sniffing.

'Really?' The place stank and there was hardly any room.

'Yep. He snorted off my arse then did me doggy. There was a massive queue, chicks were yelling at us to get out but we were so fucked we didn't give a shit. Some stupid bitch tried to crawl in under the door but I stuck my boot in her face.'

'Did you ever see him again?'

'Who?'

'The guy.'

'Nah. Maybe. He was German or something. We didn't speak much. He had these big, hard hands and he kept spanking me on the butt, over and over, until he shot his load. It hurt like fuck.' She grinned. 'Want the last line?'

'Yeah. Alright,' I said, trying not to think about all the nasty herpes and hepatitis germs wriggling around on top of the loo-lid. I snorted. Pronto my heart beat faster. Trish took the eckys from her bra-top, swallowed another one and offered me my second.

'Nah.' I couldn't stop smiling. 'I'll save it.'

'After a while, you get immune like me,' she laughed. 'I'm coming down already.'

Handing me the speed bag and the eckys, she flicked up the loo-lid with the toe of her boot, pulled down her daks and squatted for a piss.

'I'm keen to hook up with Scott and the guys,' I said, looking the other way.

'Yeah, alright babe,' she said, 'but when I start peaking we gotta be raving, OK?'

I nodded, wondering what level Scott might be on. I reckoned he'd be in the chill-out room. Trish dried off, grabbed the gear off me and shoved it back down her undies. From her bra-top, she pulled a packet of spearmint chewy and handed me a stick. 'Stop you getting lock-jaw.' As soon as I put the gum in my mouth, I couldn't stop chewing. I was a fucking crazy chewing machine. I grinned some more at Trish and we headed back out.

I wasn't too into the hardcore crowd, a pack of zealy-eyed, weaselly-faced speed freaks, but Trish pushed her way right into the middle and started psycho-raving. I hung back on the edge, watching her dance – her jaw clenched, her fists churning like pistons – until she disappeared into the mists of dry-ice. I slipped away, following a group of ravers through a velvet curtain in the wall, vibing Scott to be on the other side.

The first thing was the moon. It hung bright as a floodlight in the inky sky, illuminating a sea of bobbing faces fixed with rapturous smiles and unblinking eyes. My heart slowed as if falling under its command, its calming gaze, and I felt normal again. I took a deep breath and looked around. The area, about the size of a basketball court, was covered in fake grass and enclosed on all sides by a six-foot wire fence over which a few freeloaders were scrambling. At one end, around an open stage, ravers danced in loose and fluid movements, spinning and twirling. The music was tribal trance, ambient techno mixed with native Afro beats. Centre-stage was a giant black DJ in a sarong. To the side, three smaller African guys played bongo drums of varying size. There was no artificial smoke or flashing strobes, just the moonlight coating everything in silver.

The beat came to me in waves, washing over me. It was hypnotic. I found myself drifting further and further into the crowd, as if pulled by a magnetic force towards the stage. There was no resistance, the bodies around me parting to let me through. I danced, a warm glow suffusing my limbs. Unlike the hardcore freaks inside, ravers swayed and chanted, mellow and non-threatening. As each track slid into the other, the DJ didn't speak. The moon seemed to smile down on me with love and god-like benevolence. I opened my eyes as wide as possible to take in its every blemish, it shadowy cracks and crevices. I was filled with a painful longing. And I knew that all around me everyone felt the same as, arms above our heads, we reached for the moon's embrace, blissfully ensnared. I felt the ecky in me, lumbering through my veins, thick and viscousy, soaking into my brain. Across every inch of my body, I could feel my pores expanding, widening, getting wet. I wanted to be fucked by the moon, fucked by the music. Scott flashed through my mind but he was small and distant, a tiny speck compared with my new lunar lover.

Strange how just then, I spotted him. He was dancing right in front of me, Bomber and Muzza on either side. A bolt of excitement ripped through me. He'd probably been there all along. He was wearing a navy-blue Bonds singlet, tight checked pants and his old Converse. His hair was pulled back into a ponytail, revealing the nape of his neck glistening with sweat. He was wearing a necklace of amber beads. I sidled up behind him and covered his eyes with my hands.

'Guess who?' The smell of his sweat got me bad with want.

For a few seconds, he kept dancing with my hands over his eyes. Then he pulled my hands away and spun around. His face was pale as if the moon had soaked right through his skin and his eyes were huge purple marbles in his head. I could tell from his vacant stare that he didn't recognize me and for an awful moment I thought that maybe, dressed up as a geisha-girl, I looked like *her*. But then he grinned and

I knew he was remembering yesterday's fucking on Mum's bed.

'Hi, babe,' he said. 'You spooked me.' The guys turned around. Muzza waved, Bomber blanked me. 'What's that white shit all over your face?'

'I'm a geisha-girl,' I whispered in his ear. 'Slave to men's deepest, darkest desires.'

'OK.' He gave me a strange look. 'Whatever turns you on.'

'Hey, thanks for bailing on me, yesterday.' I jabbed him hard in the ribs. 'That was so fucking shit of you.'

He shrugged, still dancing. A second earlier, I'd been half-kidding, playing sexy-angry, but his arrogance and lack of remorse got me riled.

'No. Fuck off. I couldn't believe it. You even went to get the stuff.'

'OK,' he softened. 'I'm sorry.'

'No. Not good enough.' I crossed my arms, enjoying the moment. 'I'm fucking serious. I couldn't believe you just took off like that.'

He looked me in the eye. 'I panicked. Babe, I'm really, really sorry. Honest.'

I shouldn't have let him off so easy. I should have walked but I was starting to peak and he looked so heavenly in the moonlight. As the music crested and fell lusciously away, he brushed my arm lightly and the warm pads of his fingers sent shock-waves through my body.

'Come with me,' he said. 'I'll make it up to you.'

We sat cross-legged amongst all the other raver-lovers, who were pashing against the cool, black walls of the chill-out room. It was dim, the odd lava lamp lighting small patches of darkness with a murky glow, the rest of the room writhing with shady silhouettes; faceless legs, arms, bodies. From the blackest corners, girls whimpered and guys grunted like animals to syncopated beats set to random, spacey sounds; shooting stars, the crash of a water droplet magnified a million times, alien babble. This was where you went to fuck.

We sat on large, velvet cushions still not touching. From downstairs, hardcore beats vibrated up through the floor and into me, sparking the last of the ecky which sat like silt in my pussy, driving me wild and crazy for some Scott-sex. I reached out and stroked his silky biceps.

'How 'bout yesterday, hey?'

He grinned. His teeth glowed neon. 'Yeah.' He was digging around inside his Converse for something. He pulled a small square of alfoil from his shoe and hid it in the triangle between his crossed legs. He focused, his head bowed in concentration, his shoulders broad and glossy in the blue-ish light.

'Scott?' I wiggled closer so that our kneecaps were touching. All my resolve had vanished. I felt rank enough to tear off my dress and fuck him right there, in front of everyone. So what if he was a bastard? It made no drop of difference.

'Scott?'

'Yep.' He didn't look up.

'I'm so rank for you.'

'Rank? You mean, horny?' He glanced to his left and right, then quick as a flash brought a pill to his mouth and swallowed. 'It's the ecky,' he said. 'Another one and you'll want to fuck the universe.' I was about to tell him it was more than just the drugs when he held a finger to my lips and popped another pill. He grabbed the back of my neck and pulled me towards him. He opened his mouth so I could see the green elephant, perched on his tongue. Then he pashed me and my whole world collapsed to just me and him. The hard, bitter edge of the pill thrust upon my tongue.

'That was for yesterday,' he whispered, his lips brushing against my ear. I took a gulp from my water bottle and swallowed. I opened my eyes. Everything was sharp and bright and perfectly clear as if the pill had taken instant effect. I leant forwards and wrapped my arms around Scott's neck, squeezing so tight my brain shuddered in its cavity.

'I better get back to the boys,' he said, pulling away.

He slipped the alfoil down his sock and put his Converse back on. I traced my fingers, soft as spider's legs, up and down his arm.

'Scott, there's something I want to ask you.'

He went to get up but I jerked him back down by the wrist.

'You've got to tell me.'

'Tell you what?'

'Is there someone else?' I paused, my heartbeat speeding

out of control. 'Some Asian-looking chick?'

'Hey, not now, OK?'

He got up. I got up. We stood, side by side, not saying anything, peering into the shadows. Less than a metre away, a girl orgasmed hysterically, her bare legs viced around the naked torso of a scrawny guy.

'Don't go,' I said.

He lifted his head. His mouth was smudged red with my geisha lipstick. His eyes flitted over my face but he didn't look me in the eye.

'Babe,' he said, rubbing his fingers back and forth across the shiny glass beads of his necklace. 'I've gotta go.'

'What about yesterday?'

'You said it was casual. Remember?'

I went cold and clammy. 'Yeah, but I thought you—'

'Fuck, babe. You're doing my head in.' He turned to go.

'Wait.' I stepped in front of him.

'I'm going back outside.'

'Please, tell me.' My head swam with a million hacked-up pieces of the Asian chick; her pearly limbs, her superior smile.

'There's nothing to tell,' he said, pushing past me. 'Take it easy, babe.'

He disappeared behind the black curtain.

I slid down the wall. I could feel tiny explosions in my head, like the pop of soap bubbles, and my stomach cramped with a hollow, aching emptiness. I pulled my knees up to my chest and chewed on a piece of my hair. To my left, a guy and girl were masturbating for each other, their hands twitching like gerbils in their undies. I looked away, rankness clinging to me like dirt. I sat on my foot, pressing my heel into my crotch, sucking on my water bottle. The full force of sex and lust and badness sizzled in me. It wasn't fair. I slipped my hand inside my undies, touched the dampness, sunk my teeth into my arm.

'He no good fella.'

Startled, I looked up, whipping my hand out of my knickers.

It was Danny.

Still naked and mud-smeared, he crouched down besides me, penis dangling. The lingering stench of the dead wallaby on his skin was unbearable. And yet, I was strangely happy to see him.

I leapt up. 'What are you doing here?' He must have climbed the outdoor fence.

'Me spear him?' Danny jabbed at the air with the sharp end of his spear.

'Danny, cool it, alright?' I glanced around but everyone was either too fucked, or too busy fucking, to notice him. 'I thought I told you to go home.'

'I'm here for a reason.' He stood up, brandishing the spear above his head. Across the room, a line of chilling ravers looked up.

'Don't worry. He won't hurt you,' I said, but they didn't seemed too bothered. They probably thought he was just in some kind of extreme rave kit. I needed to get him out of the place before someone not so wasted got suspicious. I turned to Danny. 'For fuck's sake, what are you doing?'

He lunged forwards as if sparring with an imaginary enemy. Taking him by the hand, I bee-lined across the room but Bomber and Muzza were coming through the curtain. I tried to push past them with Danny, hoping they wouldn't recognize him, but they both stopped dead in front of us.

'Man, either I'm having a really ripped trip or that's Danny Bailey,' said Muzza, his face glowing blue-green in the eerie light.

For once, Bomber was quiet. He looked Danny up and down, lingering over his cock and the white markings on his chest.

'What a nutter!' said Muzza.

'Fuck me,' muttered Bomber. 'Woody said he was out.'

'Hey, Danny, what did they do to you in there?' Muzza was in fits.

'A bit of anal therapy, I reckon,' said Bomber, slipping back into wanker mode. 'He's off his fucking dial.'

'Fuck off, Bomber,' I said.

'Where is he?' said Danny, stabbing the air with his spear.

'Who's he talking about?' said Muzza, stepping back out of Danny's range.

'He doesn't know what he's doing,' I said to Bomber and Muzza. 'Why can't you just leave him alone?'

I turned to lead Danny away but he was scampering down the stairs.

I was searching for Danny on the ground floor when I ran into Trish. She'd taken off her top and was hardcoring, sweat running in rivers between her breasts. Her left tit was pierced with a silver hoop ring which spangled under the strobe.

'You ripped, babe?' she grinned.

I asked her if she'd seen a guy with a spear but she threw back her head and laughed at me, a wild, crazy cackle, and dragged me onto the dancefloor. My second ecky was mounting, all these crazy pulses zooming around in me. I breathed deep and zoned into the music, my heart sparking. The beat was infectious and I started to rave.

A digitally altered voice boomed like the Wizard of Oz.

COME WITH ME.

The ravers screamed. A born-again vibe filled the air. Trish was raving so hard I thought she might explode. Her jaw rippled under skin, her stick arms whipped into a white blur. Her face glowed with radiation intensity. The bass felt injected as if each note was riding, piggybacked, on my blood cells, gliding through my veins.

ON A JOURNEY INTO YOUR DEEPEST SOUL.

The ravers were primed and charged, their legs and arms and fingers rigid as steel. Under the strobe, everyone was green – a sea of supplicating aliens worshipping their DJ god. My heart was pounding so hard it hurt, but I couldn't stop raving.

TO DARK MAGICAL PLACES YOU HAVE NEVER BEEN BEFORE.

I was stuck fast to the floor, my molars chomping chewy

like crazy, my cheeks sore from grinning. Trish went ape-shit, her body tight and writhing like a wind-up toy, beads of sweat like diamonds flying off her into the air. God chanted in his robot voice.

REACH UP AND PICK THE FRUIT.

SINK YOUR TEETH DEEP INTO ITS SKIN.

I pressed my hand against my chest, willing my heart to slow down, but it was full to bursting, its curvaceous sides hard-walled with excess blood. Around me ravers thrashed and heaved. I turned to Trish but she was head-massaging some girl-raver with blonde pig-tails.

FALL DOWN, MY BEAUTIFUL THINGS.

FALL DOWN DEEP INTO THE EARTH.

FILL YOUR SOULS WITH DECADENCE.

I felt the peak building inside me like an orgasm, taking me over. I needed Scott so I could fuck him. His smooth, hard cock rammed up me for ever. That's all I wanted. The speakers boomed.

THIS IS DJ-MEGATRON FROM SWEDEN.

TAKING YOU TO THE LIMITS.

TAKING YOU TO THE EXTREMES OF REALITY.

Trish was transfixed, her eyes closed, her lips parted like she was coming. I felt heavy, drowning, my body slick and tight and vibing as an eel. From the corner of my eye, I saw Danny, prowling the edges of the dancefloor, spear poised as if for attack. No one seemed to notice him. It had to be some sort of fucked-up hallucination. To kill the demons, I turned back to Trish and grinned. She grabbed me by the back of my head and clamped my mouth down on to her unpierced tit. 'Suck me, babe.' I sucked hard on her erect nipple. It felt awesome. I hoped Scott was watching. She wrenched me onto the other tit. I put the hoop nipple-ring between my teeth and tugged, licking all the while with tongue. She scratched her fingernails back and forth along the base of my scalp, getting faster and faster, as the beat accelerated towards the bomb.

'Suck harder, bitch,' Trish screamed, and I sucked harder, biting down on the tight bud with my front teeth. The climax was close. DJ-Megatron was teasing and squeezing us out like sponges, our brains ripped and frazzled. Inside me something softly exploded and I felt a wet oozing in my groin. It was heaven; the sweet and salty taste of Trish's skin and the swirling heat of bodies, intimate and intense. My mind was sharp, colours surreally bright, the music infinitely textured, but my body had turned to mush. I took a breath, raising my head like I'd been underwater.

Across the dancefloor, Scott was staring at us. He'd taken off his singlet and his chest gleamed wet. Our eyes snared and he raved over to us. I turned to Trish and shouted in her ear, 'Pash me.' Our tongues collided, writhing inside one another's mouths. Scott came up behind me, biting into my neck, lifting my geisha-girl dress up high around my waist, wedging his cock hard against my undies.

Nothing mattered now, nothing, except the glorious dripping of skin; the sharp tang of adrenaline; a soft sinking into blood-soaked oblivion; a gentle dipping into other people's bodies. We all felt it; our hearts wound tight as fuck, on the brink of the bomb. God was playing us, making us scream and ooze and melt and blaze with rankness. I could have ripped my scalp right off my head and slithered out through the top, freshly born and bloody, pulsing and glistening with new life. I was cocooned; Trish in front, Scott behind. He tore off my dress and unhooked my bra so that I was naked, except for my undies and my shoes.

Again, I saw Danny hovering on the edge, jabbing at the air with his spear. I imagined him striking his prey, blood spilling on the dancefloor. Powerless, I closed my eyes and sank back against Scott's hardbody while Trish licked and bit and sucked at my nipples.

CAN I TAKE YOU FURTHER?

Just when I thought it was all going to finally explode, DJ-Megatron ramped it up one more notch.

My skin was sliding in great sheaths off my body.

Scott put his hand down the front of my undies and strummed on my clit.

The ceiling whirled and spun rainbow colours overhead.

Danny's spear floated through the air in a slow, graceful arc.

DJ-Megatron dropped the bomb.

My heart burst into a trillion tiny pieces and everything went black.

15

The first thing I heard was their fighting. It was the same fight they'd been having for the past fourteen years. I lay still with my eyes closed listening to them bicker, trying to figure out where I was. If they were in the same room, it had to be serious.

'Brings back memories being here, doesn't it, Trevor?' Mum was saying. 'God knows I'll never forgive you. It's a wonder she even speaks to you.'

'She could have died last Sunday bloody morning but where were you? Busy with some fella.'

'That's none of your business.'

I opened my eyes to a white ceiling. Dust motes drifted in broad beams of sunlight which slanted over my head. There were bleeping sounds and the distant rattle of a metal trolley. I turned my head in the direction of Mum's voice. The pillow scrunched, crisp and starchy in my ear.

'She's awake!' Mum rushed to my side and kissed me wetly on the forehead. 'Oh, Rosemary. I've been worried to death.' I blearily took her in. She looked different. She was wearing dangly earrings and her hair had been re-styled into a smart bob.

'Nice hair.' My voice was hoarse and squeaky.

'You like?' she said, fingering the blunt ends. From the other side of the bed, I felt a big, rough hand squeezing mine and I turned my head.

'Hi, Dad.' The sun blazed in through a large streaky window, making it hard for me to see him.

'You're going to be alright, daughter.'

I smiled at him, then fixed back on the ceiling, exhausted by the glare and all the head-turning. It felt like mid-afternoon. I was in a single bed, the top sheet tucked in tight as a straitjacket around my chest. A long, cotton nightie rasped against my skin. A small telly with fuzzy reception, no volume, hung from the ceiling. *The Days of Our Lives* was on so I chanted the corny intro in my head – '*like sands through the hourglass; these are the days of our lives.*' As Mum leant in to fluff my pillows, I noticed a needle sticking into the back of my left hand, strapped down with a piece of transparent tape. On my other arm, there was a fluorescent orange bracelet made of plastic which I figured was my hospital ID. I held my wrist close enough to read '**vion*Oblivion*Oblivion*Oblivion*Oblivion*Oblivion*Oblivion* Oblivion*Obli**' stamped in bold typeface. It meant nothing to me.

'Let me get that awful thing off you,' said Mum, grabbing my wrist. She tried to pull the band over my hand but it was too tight. She bent over and bit the plastic between her teeth but still it wouldn't give. Dad shuffled forwards.

'Give it here.' He whipped a Swiss army knife from his trouser pocket, flicked out the blade and slit the bracelet from my wrist. It rolled down my chest and I picked it up, trying hard to twig what '**Oblivion**' meant, but my head was light and swimmy.

'What happened?' I said.

'You're lucky you're not brain damaged!' Mum wailed.

'For Christ's sake, Janice, calm down.' Dad patted my hand.

Mum huffed. 'Don't you pretend like you're a part of this family.'

'For god's sake, just tell me what happened!' I looked from Dad to Mum and back to Dad.

Mum got up and paced around the bed. 'What the hell were you doing, Rosemary? Taking ecstasy tablets! You used to be such a clever girl. What's got into you?' She shook the bracelet at me, then flung it in the bin. A bubble burst in my brain.

Pop! The taste of something hard and bitter cushioned on a satiny tongue.

'Shut up, Janice,' Dad said. 'We're in a bloody hospital.'

Yeah, I was in hospital but why or how I had no clue. The sun shifted and I could see other beds around me. Next to me, there was a woman, about twenty-five, with one of her legs in traction. Opposite, there was a man with his whole head wrapped in bandages.

'You collapsed at a nightclub in the Valley,' said Dad, matter-of-factly.

Pop! Suck me, Rosie. Suck me. A nipple-ring hard between my teeth. Soft licking with tongue.

I turned to Dad, 'What day is it?'

'Two days before Christmas,' said Dad. 'You've been in

and out of unconsciousness for a day or so now.'

'You could have died,' cried Mum.

My head whirred. I looked up and there at the foot of my bed was a young doctor with a pink carnation stuck in the breast pocket of his shiny, pin-striped suit. With a deep frown, he inspected my chart, then proceeded, with sharp, efficient steps, up the bed and perched on the side.

'You've had a close shave, Rosemary.' He was peering into my eyes with a bright light. He had oily hair and his breath reeked of black coffee and fags. 'You've suffered a minor respiratory arrest and severe dehydration. When you came in, you weren't even breathing.' He slipped the cold disc of a stethoscope down the neck of my nightie. 'We've been monitoring your heart and other major organs for damage and,' he paused to listen to my ticker, 'it all seems to be OK. You've been lucky.' He withdrew the stethoscope and smiled at me like I was three years old. 'Now, would you like to go home for Christmas?'

Christmas. Christmas with Mum and Randy. I was busting out of my pants.

'Yes, Doctor. It would be lovely to have her home for Christmas,' Mum chirped, and fluttered her eyelashes just because he was a doctor.

He took a fancy gold pen from his suit pocket, scribbled something on my chart and hooked it back on the end of the bed.

'One of our psychiatric consultants will be around in the morning to have a little chat with you,' he said.

'Don't worry. She'll be alright, Doc,' said Dad, patting me

on the head. 'She's a tough old boot.'

As soon as the doctor was gone, Mum was at Dad's throat. 'You're such an embarrassment.'

'What?' said Dad.

'Since when do you talk to a doctor like that? Calling your daughter a tough old boot.'

'It was a joke.'

'The only joke was marrying you.'

They were giving me a headache so I found the remote attached to a retractable cord and turned up the volume on *Days,* which was just finishing. That shut them up. Dad got up and stood at the windows, hands deep in his pockets, looking down at the heavy, silent traffic lumbering along some major arterial.

Mum sat on the bed. She glanced around the room and whispered, 'Hollie's brother attacked a young man at the Arena nightclub, the same night you were there. The police have been up here already, asking all sorts of questions. They want to know if you were involved, Rosemary. If there's anything you know, you better tell me, now.'

Pop! Danny's spear floated through the air in a slow, graceful arc.

In a flash, I was wide awake. Scott. Danny had speared Scott. That's why he'd been stalking him all along. Dad pivoted from the window.

'It's been all over the papers. I didn't realize it was the Bailey boy. Thought he'd been locked up years ago. Didn't he bump off some kid?'

'Rosemary, please try hard to remember,' Mum insisted.

'The last thing I want is you getting in some kind of trouble.'

'Mum, I can't remember anything.'

'They reckon he was dressed up like some kind of abo,' Dad added. 'He stabbed the guy with a spear. Then he just disappears. The cops are everywhere trying to find him.'

'Did they say who he was? The guy Danny attacked?' I asked, trying to sound casual.

'No, not yet,' said Dad.

'Is he alright?' I asked, praying like fuck Danny hadn't killed Scott.

'Yes,' Mum jumped in. 'They said on the news he was in a stable condition.'

I sat up in bed, busting to know if it really *was* Scott. I needed to call the Greenwoods and then Hollie to find out more about Danny but I couldn't do anything while Mum and Dad were still in the room. Visiting hours were nearly over so I waited it out, chewing at my nails and channel-surfing while Mum probed my drug-fucked memory and Dad went back to staring out the window. Once they'd said their goodbyes, walking out together like a normal married couple, I grabbed the phone off the nightstand and dialled the Greenwoods but there was no answer. They were probably all at the hospital. No doubt in a room just around the corner. Next I tried Hollie's house. Mr Bailey picked up.

'Yes?' He sounded strained, overwrought. He wasn't due home from the States until Christmas but he must've flown in early because of Danny. 'Who is this?' he demanded. The gruffness in his voice made me panic and I hung up straight away. I tried Hollie's mobile but it was switched off. As a last resort, I called Trish at work. She'd know what'd happened. Fat Helen answered the phone and said Trish'd called in sick. Smelling a lie, I rang her place. She answered in a croaky voice.

'Are you really sick?' I snapped.

'Hey, Rosebud, I thought you were someone from work.' There was a pause as she lit a cigarette and inhaled down the line. 'Have the cops been up there yet?' Her voice was suddenly normal, if a little wired.

'No. I don't know. Why?' I said, cagily.

'I was gonna come up to see you and Bomber but I've been so fucked.'

'Bomber?'

'Yeah, didn't you know? Right when you collapsed, some weirdo pretending to be a coon came at him with this spear thingy and punctured his kidney.' Trish snorted.

'Is he alright?' I asked, relieved it was Bomber, not Scott.

'Yeah. Scotty came by yesterday and said he was doing OK.'

Scotty? 'But you don't even know Scott.'

'He was there when you collapsed. He gave you mouth to mouth while I called the ambulance.'

'Oh.'

'Anyway, Rosebud,' she said, in a changing-the-subject tone, 'the whole night was pretty insane. You were having a spastic fit and Bomber was on the floor, blood gushing everywhere. The ambulance guys came in and took you both to hospital. The cops were all over the place but the

210

abo-freak got away. Scotty tells me that it was Hollie's brother. It's all over the telly. What a psycho.' I tried to interrupt but Trish was talking too fast. 'Anyway, Scotty and me, we got a cab up to the hospital but they told us to go home but fuck, we were still beaming off our tits, so we went back to the rave.'

'*You what?*' Across the room, the guy in the mummy bandages grumbled at me to keep it quiet. Lowering my voice, I hissed, 'I can't believe you did that.'

'Did what?' she said, all innocent.

'I was in some kind of coma and you and Scott went back to the rave? Whose idea was that?'

Trish sucked on her cig. She had a wheeze in her chest. 'I think it was Scotty's,' she said, unfazed.

'Then what did you do?'

'Oh, nothing much. We came back here for a bit. Played some tunes, smoked some hash, crashed out on the couch. Serious, we were gonna come up but we reckoned your mum'd tear strips.'

They'd fucked, I was sure of it. I wished that Danny *had* got Scott. He fucking deserved it. I was too angry, too hurt to speak, so I hung up and shoved my head under the pillow so the other inmates couldn't hear me crying. I tried Hollie's mobile again, desperate now to hear her voice. It was still switched off but this time I left a message:

'Please call me. I need to speak to you.'

Later that night, Hollie came by to visit. As soon as she saw me, she hurried over, flinging a bunch of white lilies on the bed, and kissed me on the lips.

'Oh, my darling,' she said. 'I've been so worried about you.' She looked paler than usual, with black shadows under her eyes and she was wearing one of her costumes – a Medieval-style dress in crushed purple velvet with a large jewel-encrusted crucifix around her neck. After all the shit with Scott and Trish, it was like oceans of sunshine to see her, and when she leant in and kissed me again, I held her close.

Hollie tugged off her boots and wriggled into bed with me. Her fingers, usually cold to the touch, were warm as she pulled the sheet up over our heads. She pressed her lips against my ear and whispered, 'Let me tell you a secret.' Her eyes were bright with excitement like she wasn't upset or worried at all. I was sure she was going to tell me that Danny was OK and where he was hiding.

'What is it?' I urged.

Hollie hesitated, her cheeks flushed. 'I've been dying to tell you since it happened but I was worried what you would think.'

'What are you talking about?' I whispered. 'Tell me about Danny.'

'This *is* about Danny, darling.' She squeezed my hand under the covers.

'Hey, visiting hours are over!' A butch peroxided nurse

ripped back the sheet and stood glowering over us. 'That means you gotta leave, princess,' she barked at Hollie, who scampered out from under the covers.

'C'mon,' I said. We headed down the corridor, out of the ward, and took the lift down to the cafeteria on the ground floor. After two days in bed, my legs felt weak and papery, but it was good to be walking again. Hollie got two hot chocolates out of a machine and we sat facing each other at a corner table. Apart from a woman mopping the floor and a man with his head buried in his arms, the place was deserted.

'Where is he?' I started, but Hollie shook her head and kicked me hard in the shin with her boot under the table. From her bag, she pulled a leather-bound notebook and tore a small square of the thick, creamy paper from the middle. She scribbled something with her fountain pen and pushed it across the table.

'*He's in the cave.*'

I grabbed Hollie's pen and wrote on the paper: '*What about the cops?*'

She nodded and wrote: '*I said nothing.*'

Hollie scrunched the paper up into a tiny ball and swallowed it down with a big gulp of hot chocolate. I almost laughed. We walked out to the main entrance and sat down on a plastic bench. No one was around.

'So, what's the big secret?' I said, remembering how excited Hollie had been back in the ward.

She broke into a broad grin. 'Well, I'm not sure what you're' She paused, looking down at her lap. 'Oh, God.'

'C'mon, Hols. Just tell me.'

'No, it's nothing.' She shook her head. 'Forget it, OK? I'll tell you another time.' I was too buggered to argue so we said nothing for a while. Hollie swung her legs back and forth impatiently. I had no energy left in me but I didn't want Hollie to go yet.

'You know, for some reason I thought he'd got Scott,' I said. 'It sounds bad but I was kind of relieved when I heard it was Bomber.'

Hollie turned to me, a sudden hardness in her eyes. 'Bomber?'

'Yeah, you know, Scott's mate. But then, it could've been anyone, couldn't it? The police know Danny didn't mean it, right? They know he's ill?' I was testing her. Deep down I knew Danny had been after Scott. Why else had he been stalking him the past week? He must have got Bomber by accident. But I wanted to know what Hollie knew. If there was something she wasn't telling me.

She searched my eyes as if she knew I was bluffing. Then, jumping up from the bench, she headed for the exit. I called after her, bewildered by her reaction. Too late, she was gone through the automatic doors, her purple skirts billowing upon a sudden hot gust of summer wind. As she ran across the road and into the night, my instinct was to go after her, but I turned and went back to the ward, exhausted.

16

It was Christmas Eve morning and I was on my way to the hospital shop to scrounge up some kind of present for Mum and Randy, when I ran into Bomber. He was shuffling down the corridor in a pair of rubber thongs and a white dressing gown. By his side was one of those metal wheelie contraptions carrying a bag of bright yellow piss. It was for this, and the look of sheer misery on his face, that I stopped to speak to him.

'Hi, Bomber.'

He stared at his feet and mumbled, 'Heard *you* were in here.' Out of his rapper gear, he seemed smaller, kind of deflated.

'How are you?' It felt mighty strange being nice to Bomber.

'Fucked. Thanks to that fucking faggot weirdo, my kidney's fucked, man.'

'I'm sorry.' What else could I say? 'He didn't mean it.'

'Like fuck he didn't,' Bomber seethed. 'I was there when he killed Matty Taylor.' He pounded his fist into his palm. 'Bam! Smashed right into his skull. Scrawny little cocksucker. Like fuck he didn't mean it. He meant it then and he means it now. Man, I can't wait to get my hands on him as soon as I'm out of here.'

'He's not gay, Bomber. Just because he doesn't pump weights and jerk off to porno all day.'

Bomber snorted. 'Nah, man. Don't tell me the fucker's not bent. It's so fucking obvious.' He flapped his hands in imitation of Danny. 'Just ask Woody. Oh yeah, man, Woody knows.'

'What does Scott know?'

Bomber ignored my question. 'You're mates with his sister, right?'

'So?'

'Well, you tell whatever-her-name-is that I'll be coming to beat the crap out of him. He's dead meat, man.'

'Aren't you a bit old to still be playing the school bully?'

'Nah, you listen to me.' His voice dropped to a whisper. 'I've got a good idea where the fucker's got to. You see, way back, before he turned butt-poker, we were all mates, Danny, Woody, Muzz and me. *Real* good mates.' He drummed two thick fingers against his temple. 'He thinks he can outsmart the cops, well, I reckon I can smoke the cunt out of his hole.'

'You're so full of it, Bomber.' I said, walking away. 'You've always been full of it.'

But the rest of the morning in the ward Bomber's threat played on my mind. Sure, he was a first-class shit-stirrer but there'd been genuine menace in his voice and I was worried he knew something about the cave. His cryptic line kept resurfacing – *Just ask Woody. Oh yeah, man, Woody knows* – until the shrink came by and asked me to describe how I felt about my parents' divorce.

That afternoon, Randy picked me up from hospital in my car. Mum was waiting for her Christmas cake to come out of the oven so she'd sent him instead. Randy carried my overnight bag as we walked across the carpark. After being cooped up for so long, the sun-glare off the tarmac gave me an instant headache. I slumped back in the seat with my feet up on the dash and wound down the window. I was in no mood for chit-chat but as soon as we were on the road, Randy started.

'So, how're you feeling? We've been worried about you,' he said, as we chugged down the overpass past Suncorp Stadium. 'Janice, your mother, she thinks you need a change.'

I stared out the window at the Fourex brewery, sniffing at the rich, yeasty air blowing in soft around me. 'What? Like a sex change.'

'No,' Randy chortled. 'A change of direction.'

'Oh. I see.' We were stopped at the lights. In front of us was a supermodel couple in an open-top beamer. They were eating soft-serve ice-creams and laughing. I hated them. 'But I am changing direction.'

'Great. A positive attitude is the first step.' Randy thumped the steering wheel and grinned across at me. 'So, you've been thinking about going back to university?'

'No.'

'Oh.' His smile faded. That shut him up for a while. I

zoned out the window, watching the khaki blur of eucalypts skid by as we puttered through Auchenflower, then Toowong. Going past Shoppingtown, Randy turned to me, one hand on the wheel.

'I know what you need.' He was beaming like a born-again. 'Inspiration. Don't you get excited just thinking about all the wonder out there, waiting to be discovered? I mean, how could anyone get bored when you can learn how stars are made or dream about fourth dimensions or imagine life on other planets or decode your own DNA or contemplate the awesome possibilities of string theory?' He blinked, excitedly. 'Don't you think?'

'I dunno.'

'Just look at all the beauty in the world.' Randy waved his hand out the window as we skirted around the concrete monolith of the Green Hill Reservoir. 'The millions of different colours of coral in the ocean, the velvet touch of a rose petal, the fascinating lives of ants, the unsolved mysteries of the human mind, that deep midnight blue of the sky on a winter's night, the lovely squeak of sand between your toes at the beach.'

'Whatever you reckon, Randy.' We were turning right into Fleming, the old rollercoaster road. Randy took it slow.

'But, that's all there is,' he said. 'The here and now. The proverbial bug in amber. You've got to live it to the full because there's probably not much afterwards except a few of your old molecules zipping around in outer space. C'mon, Rosie. What do you think? What's the point? What's it all about, hey?'

I thought hard for a decent comeback. 'Oblivion.'

Randy pulled into the drive and yanked the handbrake. He undid his seat-belt and pivoted around to face me. 'You mean, just being? Not thinking about the past or the future?'

'Yeah, I s'pose.' I got out of the car. 'Thanks for the lift.'

'No problem, Rosie. Hey, let's talk about this more later, OK?'

While Randy parked my car in the garage, I went inside. Mum was in the kitchen licking cake mixture out of the bowl. She rushed over and hugged me. I stood stiff in her embrace, annoyed that she'd set Randy up to brainwash me.

'Are you alright? How are you feeling? Do you want something to eat? How 'bout a nice cup of tea or some Christmas crackle?' She was being way too nice.

'I want to go to bed.'

'OK,' she said. 'Why don't you go lie down in my bedroom with the air-con on? It'll be quieter in there.'

I spent the rest of the afternoon dozing on Mum's floral spread, despite the muffled sound of drilling coming from the courtyard. Around six, Mum came in and woke me in a flap. The cops had dropped by to ask a few questions. I went out in Mum's chenille to find them drinking tea in the courtyard. Mum hovered about offering them Christmas cake and smiling her head off. For once, Randy stayed out of it.

They'd read my hospital records so it was easy to act like I didn't remember anything. They asked me about Danny – how long we'd been friends, when I'd last seen him, if he'd mentioned anything about Bomber. I lied, saying I couldn't remember when I'd last seen him. They asked me if I had any idea where Danny might be hiding and I shook my head and said, 'Sorry, I haven't the slightest.'

After they left, I went back to bed in my own room. I got thinking about Bomber's threat again. There was no use telling Hollie. With Mr Bailey back at the ranch and the cops no doubt tracking her every move, she'd have no way of getting to him. More than that, I didn't want to frighten her because she'd probably just lose it. She'd been acting so bizarre lately. I had to warn Danny myself, but I'd do it later, in the middle of the night when all the burbans were dead to the world. I set the alarm for midnight and tried to get some shut-eye.

I snapped on the lamp and slipped out of bed. One minute past midnight on Christmas Day. I chucked on a T-shirt and a pair of shorts, and tied my hair back in a ponytail. After so much snoozing, I felt fresh and sparky. I crept through the darkened house. As I passed Mum's new fibre-optic Christmas tree, glowing red to purple to orange in the dark, I didn't even stop to check out my presents.

Outside, the air was thick and muggy, not a murmur of a breeze through the tree-tops. It was like the earth had stopped breathing to listen for life on other planets. I ducked across the lawn and in through the side door of the garage. Not wanting to wake Mum and Randy with the car, I grabbed a torch off the shelf and my old kid's bike and wheeled it out onto the drive. I hopped on and pedalled away through the moon-washed streets to Hollie's place. As I rocketed down Fleming, I threw my head back to the sky, which was deep and black as old blood. My T-shirt billowed out behind me and my hair lashed about my face. I was flying – the wicked witch on her broomstick. On my way up the last hill, sweating and pumping at the pedals, I looked across at the ascending row of slumbering houses which lined Hollie's street. In each front window was a plastic Christmas tree, multi-coloured lights blinking on and off, out of sync with each other. The only real tree was Hollie's. I could just see it, tall and erect in the front casement window at the very end of the street. It was decorated with nothing but fairy lights which didn't foxtrot or do the rumba, but shone cold and bright as stars.

A car was parked outside Hollie's house. From its shape and size, it wasn't Mr Bailey's Lexus. My spine tingled as I dismounted and dropped down into a ditch hidden from the road. I dumped the bike and scurried along the eroded trench. To my right, the bush throbbed and pulsed. When I was abreast with the parked car, I popped my head up over the verge. Inside, the cabin was in darkness but I could just make out a silhouette. I clambered up the incline and hauled myself onto the bitumen. With my heart thumping like crazy, I cut across the corner of the cul-de-sac and hid behind a lantana bush. From this position, I could see there were two men inside the car. The cabin light came on and they bent their heads over something. They had to be the cops, on the prowl for

Danny. I turned and scrambled up the track, under a cover of thick scrub, towards the cave. Above the tree-line, the red lights from the TV towers blinked like a warning to go home, but I pelted up the steep incline, fumbling through the dark, until I reached the cave. I stepped up to the entrance, rubbing my hands against the rough surface of the rock, feeling my way. Quiet as a bug, I dropped to my knees and crawled inside. It was so black I couldn't see my hands in front of me, but I could feel the earth cool and smooth between my fingers as I headed deeper into the cave. At the egg rock, I sat up and switched on the torch. A pair of eyes, red and glistening, swooped down upon me. I screamed. There was a flurry of wings beating about my ears, hissing and flapping. I folded my arms around my head and crouched into a ball, burying myself small and hard as a stone, digging my toes into the earth.

'Rosie-Maroo?'

'Danny?' I stood up, swinging the torch towards the back of the cave. He was leaning against the far wall, wearing a grubby T-shirt. The light shone hard against his thin arms and his wiry legs. His skin was streaked with mud. Slowly, I walked up to him and pressed my palm against his hollow cheek. I exhaled, my muscles softening with relief. He grinned his wide white-toothed smile and touched me the same, rubbing his dirty hand over my face.

'Rosie-Maroo,' he repeated.

'Danny-Dilly.' I smiled. 'Are you OK?' He was close enough for me to inhale the dank, grassy smell of his skin, the stink of his unwashed hair.

'The spirits of the cave are looking after me.' He was speaking in his weird pseudo-aboriginal way and it made me nervous.

'Danny, listen to me.' I looked into his eyes and felt this strange sensation like drowning. Anxious to say what I had to say and get out of there, I squeezed his hand, then let go. 'I came to warn you about Bomber.'

'What about him?'

'I think he knows about the cave. He's coming up here.'

Danny nodded and walked to the middle of the cave. He lit a candle. In the centre was a pile of ash and twigs, the remnants of an open fire. Peering closely, I saw what looked like the charred remains of a small animal; a blackened head, a white flash of bone exposed here and there along its body. Danny crouched down and fished a chunk of fleshy bone out of the embers. He tore strips off it with his teeth.

'What is it?' I said, disgusted.

'Bandicoot.' He chewed away. 'Want some?' He offered me a bit of grizzled meat.

'No, thanks.' He shrugged and continued munching. 'Danny, there's something I want to ask you.' He looked at me, eyes possum-bright, quizzical. I took a deep breath. 'What happened between you and Scott?'

Danny scowled and kicked his toe in the dirt. 'Why don't you ask him? He's *your* boyfriend, isn't he?'

'No. Not any more.'

'Oh.' His eyes flickered over my face. 'I thought he was. Hollie told me he was.'

I heard the rustle of the trees outside. Inside the cave the air became lighter, less oppressive, and I felt a chill as the earth edged closer to dawn. Danny threw the stripped bone to the ground and wiped his mouth on his T-shirt. He knelt down and bundled sticks and dry leaves together to re-build the fire.

'OK,' he said, lighting the kindling with the burning candle. 'You want to know about Scott? I'll tell you.'

I nodded and perched on the egg rock. Our shadows reared up around us as the flames stretched higher. I pulled my T-shirt over my knees. Danny paced back and forth across the cave, his profile a giant hunchback against the wall. It took him ages to settle down but then he crouched near the fire and began.

'It was the summer holidays and I'd just turned fourteen. You and Hollie were up here, playing your Shakespeare games. It was really hot and sticky and I was bored. There was jack all to do. All my mates except Scott were away so I called him to see if he wanted to hang out.' Danny paused and stared into the fire. He scratched at his belly. His neck muscles were strained, his shoulders tense. A tangled lock of hair hung over the left side of his face. He brushed it away and continued. 'So, Mrs Greenwood drops him over and, as soon as he's inside, he pulls this porn video out of his backpack. He's nicked it from his brother's room and is raring to watch it so I get us some wine from Dad's cellar and we put it on in the billiards room. It's mostly lesbian stuff. Scott's really into it. He rewinds it five or six times. He keeps looking over at me like he wants to make sure I'm into it, too.'

'You weren't?'

'Yeah, sure, but not as much as him.' Colour rose beneath Danny's muddy cheeks. He reached for a stick and prodded at the bandicoot carcass. 'Next thing he gets his dick out and starts jerking off. Don't ask me why, but seeing him do it so casual gives me an instant hard-on. He glances over, sees my boner and grins. "Just whack it out," he says to me. I scull more wine and stare at the porno. By this time, I'm fairly wasted. Scott's batting away. His eyes are closed, head back against the couch, frowning like this.' Danny mimicked Scott's expression in a way that was startlingly familiar.

'So I slide off the couch and onto the floor. I unzip my shorts, hoping Scott keeps his eyes shut, and whip it out. I'm going for it when he looks over. "Yeah, boy," he goes. "That's it." Scott's dick is still out, erect, in full view, and I watch my hand drift over and touch it like it's not my hand but someone else's. I give it a squeeze. Scott sighs and slumps back in the couch. He's got his eyes closed and he doesn't say anything. I edge in closer for a better grip and wank him, slow at first, then faster till he comes. For a few seconds, he just lies there, not moving a muscle, but then he sits up and says, "Thanks, mate" like I've just bought him a beer or something. He doesn't seem the least bit embarrassed but my face is burning up. I go upstairs for a towel but when I come back he's gone.'

Danny's story didn't surprise me. It was just Scott's style to sit back and take whatever was on offer. What slated me was knowing what must come next. Danny stood up,

225

shaking his head. He went back to his pacing.

'The rest of the holidays we spent a fair bit of time hanging out, playing video games and cricket in the backyard, smoking pot. He told me about all the stuff he'd done with chicks and how he liked to spy on his older brother having sex. Each time he came over, I'd jerk him off but we never talked about it and he never touched me. I started having feelings, you know, weird feelings, but everything changed when school went back. The other guys still came over to watch porno, drink and do cones, but not Scott. Never Scott. Then, they all stopped coming over. At school, they completely ignored me. Then this rumour started going round that I was gay.'

'But you're not, are you?'

'No. Maybe. I don't know. I like women alright.' Danny padded back and forth across the cave floor, getting more and more agitated. 'Anyway, the rumour gets around and then they all start laying into me after footy.'

'Who's they?'

'Bomber. Muzza. Matty.' Danny stopped, his head bowed to the ground. 'Scott.'

'Scott?' I looked up and Danny was leaning against the wall, his hands clenched at his side.

'Yeah.'

'But he told me he wasn't in on it.'

'The other guys in school, they all turned a blind eye. They didn't want to be seen siding with faggot-boy. I put up with it for ages. Who was I gonna tell? Dad? A teacher? One night, I just lost it. They had me up against the wall, kicking me in the shins. I guess I fought back and wrestled free. Then Matty comes charging at me. I swung at him and caught him on the side of the head and he flew back against the lockers, this stunned look in his eyes, and slid down onto the cement. He slumped sideways and there was this awful silence. Everyone was watching, saying nothing. I was praying for him to get up. Scott tried to pull him up, but his head just lolled to one side and blood was coming out of his mouth. Bomber threw a bucket of cold water on him. I had this sick feeling spreading through me. I knew I'd done something bad. The rest of the guys from the team came over in their socks and undies and someone went to call an ambulance. Scott stood up and screamed at me, his eyeballs popping out of his head, "You fucking faggot bastard, you've fucking killed him." Muzza was saying, "Fuck, man. He's fucked" over and over, and I remember Matty just lying there with his eyes all glassy.'

Danny sunk down on his haunches, his filthy arms wrapped around his knees, his head hung low. He tipped over onto his side and rolled around in the dirt. I lay down next to him and hugged him to me for a long time, inhaling the soil, the trees, the scent of blood and fur and flesh which clung to him. After a while, he drifted off and I crawled out of the cave into the first glimmer of dawn. The gum trees were slicked with gold and the air was fresh and humming with the new day. I ran down the hill, sneaking past the cops who were asleep, chins to their chests, and rode home.

17

We stood on the front lawn in the blistering sun. It was Christmas Day. Randy was wearing dick togs and a Santa hat. Mum was sporting a skimpy, red bikini, which revealed every last shaking inch of her middle-aged flesh. I stood as far apart from them as possible, in the lime-green bikini which Mum had given me, just a few minutes before, as my Christmas present.

'Now, put these on,' said Randy, handing a blindfold each to Mum and I. 'Keep your eyes closed until I say.'

I reluctantly put it on. If only I could have been having a normal Christmas with a normal family like the Greenwoods. I pictured Mr and Mrs Greenwood and all Scott's rellies sitting around the tree in their pyjamas, opening the presents. Randy manoeuvred us into a chain; himself at the lead, Mum holding onto his waist, me bringing up the rear. I felt like a complete tosser but Mum was spoofing.

'Isn't this exciting?'

'This is stupid,' I grumbled.

'No talking,' said Randy. 'Just follow me.' We headed around the side of the house, through the side gate, click-clack, and along the bark path. As we crossed the fishpond, Randy took a deep breath.

'OK, girls. On the count of three. One.' There was a high-pitched squeal of pipes groaning into action. 'Two.' A spluttering sound and water splashing against tile. Mum whimpered in anticipation.

'C'mon,' I said, fed up with the palaver.

'Three!'

And there, in all its hideous glory, was the Decontamination Chamber, pastel pink (Mum's favourite colour) and gleaming in the sunshine. It was enormous. It took up more than half of the courtyard. It reached flush against the eaves and stood at least two metres wide. Bursting with pride, Randy pulled back the retractable frosted glass door to reveal a glittering confusion of nozzles, jets and flexy hoses, each one firing a relentless trajectory of shooting water. On one side was a full-length mirror; on the other, a set of metal racks equipped with every kind of anti-bacterial liquid, soap, shower gel and body wash as well as various scrubbing brushes, sponges, pumices and loofahs-on-sticks.

Mum was in raptures. 'It's so beautiful.' She smothered Randy in sloppy kisses. Dragging him with her, she leapt into the shower and began sudsing herself into a decontaminating frenzy. Then she started on Randy, tearing off his Santa hat, and working up a thick lather all over him. I couldn't stand it any longer. I went to my room and shut the door. The back of the Chamber was right against my window, blocking out most of the light. I stumbled towards my bed and sunk down onto it, pulling the sheet over me. Closing my eyes, I pictured a pale and distracted Hollie, sitting down with Mr Bailey for their usual Christmas lunch at the Marriott; and poor Danny, alone in the cave with nothing to eat except chargrilled bandicoot. I racked my brains for some way I could help him, but I'd done all I could – the cops were bound to get him sooner or later. From above the rumble of the power shower, there came raised voices and the sound of a scuffle. Mum was shrieking. I got out of bed and went outside to see what was causing all the racket.

Mum was in the middle of the courtyard, jumping up and down, her face contorted in horror. Christmas lunch lay splattered across the ground. There were broken plates everywhere and the table and chairs had been tipped over. Inside the shower, Dad had Randy in a mean headlock up against the pastel tiles. Turbo-strength jets of water fired into Randy's face as he kicked and squirmed and flapped his arms about. Dad stood rigid with his arm around Randy's neck, soaked through to the skin in a pair of striped pyjamas and his old Volleys.

He shouted in Randy's ear, 'Who the hell do you think yar screwing around with my sheila!'

Mum rushed forwards into the shower, trying in vain to pull Dad off her new lover. 'Call the police!' she shouted back at me, her face streaming with water.

I stood rooted to the spot. No way was I calling the cops. For once, I was on Dad's side.

'Rosemary! For god's sake! *Do something!*'

'Like what?'

'Call Mr Greenwood! He's a policeman, isn't he?' I wasn't

calling the Greenwoods. Scott might've answered the phone and he was the last person on earth I wanted to talk to right now.

'He's retired, Mum,' I said. 'And it's Christmas.'

'This is an emergency!' Mum raced inside to the phone. I watched from the other side of the courtyard as Randy struggled to fight back. He managed to slip out of Dad's hold and they fell into a sloppy tackle, punches misfiring, legs flailing this way and that. Above the strangled snorts and groans, I could hear Mum inside on the phone to Mr Greenwood. Dad got Randy pinned again.

'She's mine, y'know,' he shouted. 'My woman. Say it and I'll let yer go. Just this time, mind. And if I ever, ever catch your hairy mitts on her again, there'll be trouble, y'hear. Big trouble.' Randy shook his head in defiance. He shouted something back at Dad but I couldn't hear it above the torrents. 'I wanna hear you say it,' roared Dad. 'My woman. Trevor's woman.' Funny how he'd had fourteen years to get Mum back but it was only now she'd gone and got herself a new bloke that he was taking action. It was obvious he'd been on the turps all morning. His eyes were glazed and bloodshot from the half-dozen or so tinnies he'd probably knocked back since breakfast. Like Nan used to say, it was the devil in the drink that tipped him over. Sober, Dad'd never hurt a cockroach. He was a pacifist at heart. Perhaps it was my fault for telling him about Randy, who, right at that moment, wasn't getting off too lightly. Dad had the hose looped around his neck like a noose and was pulling tight. But Randy stood firm. 'C'mon, mate,'

Dad barked in his ear. 'Spit it out and I'll let yer go. Fair deal.'

Mum threw herself into the shower, pummelling Dad with her fists. 'Let him go! Let him go!'

'Stand back, Janice,' said Dad. 'Let me handle this.' It was obvious that neither man was going to back down: too much pride on one side; too much grog on the other.

A car screeched to a stop outside. I rushed to the front door. Scott was sprinting across the lawn, shirtless in a pair of boxers. Why the hell had he come? I did my best to snub him. Behind Scott came ex-cop Mr Greenwood, armed with a riot baton and a spray can of tear gas. I led them through to the courtyard where they jumped on Dad and wrestled him off a dazed and saturated Randy. Dad, the nifty codger, slipped out of their clutches, shouting, 'I wasn't trying to hurt the bugger, just stop him mucking around with my wife!'

'You can run but you can't hide, Trevor,' said Mr Greenwood, trying with Scott to corner him. 'You can't escape the law.'

'But I can bloody well have a go,' rallied Dad. They'd never met before but I'd always thought that Mr Greenwood and Dad would have got on well; both men were passionate about beer, cricket and Buddy Holly.

Meanwhile, Mum'd nipped into her bedroom, returning with the handcuffs, which Randy, the frisky bugger, had never given back to me. She slipped them to Mr Greenwood, who took them with a solicitous nod of his head. Quick as a pro, he clamped the cuffs on Dad.

I caught Mum smiling at the sight of Dad being dragged away like a crim as she cooed over beaten-up Randy. 'Poor possum. My poor, brave possum.'

Leaving Mum to nurse Randy, I went outside to the men. Mr Greenwood was already at the wheel of the Falcon, engine idling. Dad was restrained in the back, head hung low. His anger had ebbed away, leaving him shamefaced and melancholy. I tapped on the window but he wouldn't even look up at me.

'Hey, Rosie.' Scott's head popped up on the other side of the Falcon. His tanned arms rested on the rooftop. 'You want to lead the way to your old man's place?'

'I think Dad'll manage that,' I said, real curt. 'Why are you here anyway?'

'The old man needed a back-up.' He grinned. 'You wanna come with me?'

What was he playing at? Did he want to apologize? Un-bloody-likely. I knew him for what he was now and I despised him – for rooting Trish and for what he'd done to Danny. This was my chance to tell him what a piece of scum I thought he was.

'Yeah. Fine,' I said. 'I'll get my car.'

Scott got in and we took off, the Falcon tailing. Being Christmas, the roads were eerily empty. For the first few minutes, we didn't speak. Scott stared out the window. I planned my attack, trying not to inhale the sexy smell of him, sitting bare-chested so close to me. I was still in my bikini. Scott leant forward and pumped the air-con.

'Do you mind?' I snapped. 'It's freezing.'

'It's fucking boiling.' He jabbed it off. 'What's up your bum?'

'Nothing's up my bum.'

As the temperature rose around us, we sped along in frosty silence up the hill, past my old primary school and the used car yards, shooting the lights on orange. I simmered, waiting for the right moment to let rip. Scott turned to me and smiled.

'I've been thinking about us a lot lately,' he said. 'About the good times we had before I went away.'

'Have you now?' I said, thinking about him rooting Trish and not bothering to visit me at the hospital.

'Yeah. We had something special, didn't we?'

'Maybe. Maybe not.' He'd fucked Trish. He'd fucked Danny over.

We pulled up on the side of the road. I cut the engine and sat looking out the window at Dad's shabby block of brick units. Scott's lips brushed my bare shoulder. His hands were in my hair.

'Don't,' I said, pushing him away.

We got out of the car and waited on the pavement for Mr Greenwood and Dad. From the house across the road, I could hear a kid singing 'The Twelve Days of Christmas' accompanied by the tinny tape recording. As soon as the song finished, there was loud clapping and adult laughter.

'Rosie... ' Scott started.

'What?'

'Merry Christmas.'

'Yeah, whatever,' I said, wondering why he was being so

nice. He started humming the carol we'd just heard. 'Stop that, would you?' I said, prodding him with a stick. 'It's really annoying.'

'Sorry,' he said, sheepishly.

A second later the Falcon turned the corner and glided to a halt. Mr Greenwood bounded out of the car and opened the back door. He pointed at Dad, cop-style. 'Nice and slow out of the vehicle, Trevor. No funny business now.'

Dad scowled at him. 'I'm not budging till you take these bloody handcuffs off me. You can't treat a bloke like this!'

'I think you can take them off him now,' I said to Mr Greenwood.

'The offender should be confined before removal of restraint,' he prattled.

'Give it up, Dad,' said Scott. 'It's Rosie's old man, not Hannibal fucking Lecter.'

'Language, boy,' said Mr Greenwood, but he removed the handcuffs anyway.

'Go easy on me, big fella. You're not a copper any more,' Dad slurred, getting out of the car and tripping over the gutter. I took him by the arm. 'Thanks, daughter,' he said, quietly.

Dad's bedsit was at the top of a three-storey block, but I'd never been inside before. For a long time after the accident, Mum wouldn't let me near him and then, when I was older, we'd always meet up on neutral territory. As we trooped up the stairwell, the air was damp and musty, and I dreaded to see what his place was like. We stopped outside the front door; 13b with the paint peeling off. I turned back to Dad for the keys. He fumbled in his pockets, his hands unsteady and his eyes watering, then he passed me a single grubby key tied to a loop of string. I unlocked the door and pushed inside.

It was the smell which hit me first; the smell of damp and moth-balls, stewed prunes and stale beer. It hung thick in the air, clinging to my skin like Mum's invisible germs. As I checked out the place, I thought how much she'd hate it. How disgusted she'd be at the unwashed plates stacked high in the sink, the litter of crunched-up tinnies scattering the carpet, the uneven matchstick blinds cloaked in a decade of dust. It was embarrassing to have Scott and Mr Greenwood see it. I pictured all the lonely nights, weekends, years Dad had spent in this dive. He had an alright job selling life insurance, so I couldn't understand why he didn't get somewhere decent. There was little, if any, decoration, except for his trusty, plastic Buddha, which sat on top of the telly, and, on the back wall, my old favourite, the vegetable poster which used to cover one of Dad's kicking holes in the hallway. I went up to it and stared at the smiling carrot and couch potato and the peas in their cosy pod. It was like seeing old friends again.

Dad had opened a fresh beer and was loading one of his beloved cricket videos into the machine. Scott and Mr Greenwood were standing around looking uncomfortable and sipping on Fourex tinnies which Dad must've given them. I glanced over at Scott and he winked at me like we were all sweet and rosy again. I still had no clue as to why he'd come, what he was trying to prove.

'What've you got there?' Mr Greenwood asked as the telly buzzed with snow.

'Most legendary Test of all time. Centenary Test, 1977. Me and my mates, Keith Tillney and Dicky Coombes, went down to Melbourne on the Greyhound. Still reckon it was the best day of my life. You were only a couple of weeks old,' he said pivoting around to me. Typical. Mum's got post-natal depression and Dad runs off to watch cricket with his beer buddies.

'The Poms were alright then,' quipped Mr Greenwood. 'They put up a decent fight.'

'Yeah. S'pose. That fidgety 174 from Randall.' He jabbed fast-forward on the remote, lifting his finger at exactly the right spot. 'Greig bowling to Hookesy. Take a look at this cameo knock-fest.' They were spellbound as the Aussie batsman slogged five fours in one over. Each time Hookes hit a four, Dad leapt up, sloshing beer on the carpet. By the end of the over, Mr Greenwood and even Scott were doing the same. 'And then there's Marshy's golden century.' Dad pressed pause and dashed across to the bar fridge for more beers. I followed him into the kitchenette.

'Don't you think you should slow down a bit?' I said, standing in front of the fridge.

He made one of his awful scrunched-up grimaces. 'Arrghhh, Jesus, yer sound just like your mother. Can't a bloke have a few on Christmas Day?' He pulled the beers out of the fridge and replaced them with warm ones from a carton on the floor, before padding back to the telly. I decided to do the washing-up. There was no detergent, so I used coal tar shampoo from the bathroom. I fished the crud-encrusted plates out of the sink, filled it with scalding water and set to work picking the gunk off with my fingernails, squirting the coal tar at the grime while Dad dragged Scott and Mr Greenwood down his memory lane. The next time he got up for more beers, he came over to the sink to see what I was doing. He picked up one of the freshly washed plates and stared at it for a long time, turning it over and over, inspecting it from every angle.

'Good work,' he said, pulling three more cans out of the fridge.

Mr Greenwood's mobile went off. 'Yes, love, we're on the way.' He hung up and turned to Scott. 'You'd better come, too, boy. Now that your mother's got over the shock of your big announcement, she'll be wanting to celebrate.'

My guts slurried. Celebrate? Celebrate what? I waited for Scott's response. I lowered the plate into the sink and listened, my ears grown elephant-sized.

'Tell them I'll be home soon. Rosie'll give me a lift.' Scott raised his voice and shouted, 'Won't you, babe?'

'What?' I shouted back, like I hadn't been eavesdropping.

'Give me a lift home?'

'Yeah, alright.' Perhaps he wanted to apologize for not coming to see me in hospital after all. Or come clean about Trish. One thing was for sure, I'd find out what he had to celebrate. Mr Greenwood headed for the door.

'Thanks for the beers, Trev. You watch yourself, now. Next time I won't be so easy on you.' He took the cuffs out of his pocket and shook them at him, grinning. 'I'm warning you, mate.'

'Arrhhh, shut ya gob, Bill,' said Dad.

'Don't be too long now, boy,' Mr Greenwood nodded at Scott. 'Sooner or later you've got to face up to your new responsibilities.'

I stepped out of the kitchenette. 'Merry Christmas, Mr Greenwood.'

'Yeah, you too, Rosie.' He winked at me and disappeared out the door.

I stood for a while in the lounge room. Lillee was bowling. Dad was sitting forward in his chair and Scott was leaning against the armrest, riveted to the telly. It gave me a warm feeling, seeing them together. I headed back into the kitchenette to finish the dishes, but within a few minutes there were raised voices coming from the lounge room.

'But everyone reckons the Aussies are better than ever,' argued Scott.

'You don't know what you're talking about, son. The new breed may be pretty slick on the one-dayers but they haven't earned their Test stripes yet. Not in my book, anyway.'

Scott wasn't backing down. 'Nah, Mr Williams, you're behind the times.'

'Hey, now you listen here, you little twerp. You bloody watch what you're saying.' I recognized the switch in Dad's voice, the menacing rumble which foreshadowed a violent outburst. A plate I'd been drying slipped out of my hands and smashed on the floor. My ears burned hot and my neck stiffened. Dad came storming in, his rage quickly transferred from Scott to me.

'What do you think you're doing?'

'It was an accident,' I stammered, kneeling down to retrieve the broken pieces. He loomed over me, his fists clenching in and out by his side. Beyond him, I could see Scott, hovering in the background, not knowing what to do. Dad took a step closer, a piece of plate crunching beneath his soaked tennis shoe. I bowed my head and continued collecting the bits of broken plate into a pile.

'Leave that!' he boomed at me. 'Look at me!' He kicked the pile of bits out of the way and dug into my shoulder with iron fingers.

'That hurts!'

'Look at me!'

I forced my head up. His rough hand moved over my face like a blind man's. I closed my eyes and prayed that he wouldn't hurt me. He twisted back my fringe, pulling the hair off my forehead.

'Rosie, are you alright?' Scott called out.

'Mind your own bloody business!' Dad roared.

I stood up. Dad was tracing one thick finger up and down the ridge of the scar. Not daring to open my eyes, I let him stroke away until my whole head was suffused with a cool, tranquil calm.

I opened my eyes. 'Dad?'

He looked away, shielding his face with one big hand, as if ashamed of his emotions.

'It's OK,' I said, not sure if I should hug him.

He let out a huge groan. I reached across, my fingers resting lightly on his forearm. He turned to me with bloodshot eyes.

'It was an accident,' I said, patting my fringe back into place.

'No, it wasn't,' he said. 'It was my stupid bloody fault. I could have killed you.'

I tried to imagine living with that guilt for all those years. 'Dad, stop it. There's no point.' I took his big hand in mine and gave it a little squeeze. I wanted so bad to make him smile.

'Just don't... don't waste your life like me.'

'Come off it, Dad. You're not dead yet. Maybe you could try and meet someone?'

'What, like your mother?'

'At least she's happy.'

'Happy? Do you think she's happy? With that poofter?'

'Yeah, she seems to be.'

'Did she like her present?'

I'd used the money to buy eckys off Trish. 'You mean the one from me but really from you?'

'Yeah. Did you get her something nice?'

'Yeah, a lovely gold bracelet from Oroton.'

'Good,' he said, nodding his approval. 'At least that's something.'

18

Dad stood at the window, waving down at us, a fresh tinnie to his lips. I couldn't believe, after all the years, that he'd said sorry. As I gripped the steering wheel and sped off down the hill, I wondered if things would change between us now or if it was too late for that. His words had left me with a light, expanding feeling in my chest, but my initial high ebbed away and my mind turned to Scott, who was sitting beside me, fiddling with the hem of his boxer shorts. Although he'd wanted to drive, I'd insisted on taking control. My anger was back on track and no amount of sweet talk was going to put me off this time. I had more than a few things to say to him about screwing Trish, and I wanted to know what his big announcement was, too. I settled back into the driver's seat, still in my bikini, speeding along the deserted streets.

'What was all that about?' said Scott.

'Nothing.'

'Did he used to hit you?'

'No.'

Scott pointed at my scar. 'I thought you got that falling off a bike.'

'We were in a car accident when I was five. Dad was

driving maggot. My head smashed through the windscreen. I was in hospital for three weeks.' We stopped at the lights. Water mirages shimmered crazy above the bitumen.

'How come you never told me?' Scott said.

'I dunno.' I shrugged impatiently, thinking about the stuff *he* hadn't told *me*. 'You fucked her, didn't you?'

'Who?'

'Trish.'

'No, I didn't.' He was smiling.

'There's no point lying. I know for a fact.' I was pushing eighty in a sixty zone.

'I didn't fuck her.' Scott ran his fingers through his hair and clicked his tongue. 'She's hardly my type.' He glanced at the speedo. 'Slow down, hey.'

But I pressed my foot harder, hooning bevan-style around the Denmac Ford roundabout. 'What is your type?'

'Fiery redheads,' he grinned.

'Ha!' I threw my head back and laughed. 'Yeah, right. I heard you were banging some Asian chick overseas.' An image of them fucking crammed my head.

'Who told you that?' Scott looked out the window.

'Why didn't you come and see me in hospital?'

'Because your psycho mother would've killed me.'

'I bet you went and saw Bomber.'

'He's my best mate.'

'And what am I? Just some slut you used to fuck? You're such a prick.' I did a u-ey at the lights and sped back the way we'd just come.

'What are you doing? I've gotta get home,' Scott said. 'For

fuck's sake, ease off, alright?' He swiped at the wheel. I swerved, narrowly missing a road island, and accelerated along Moggill Road, through Toowong. Turning off at the cemetery, I flew up the hill, past the botanical gardens and the derelict quarry, veering left at the sign which said '**Mount Coot-tha Lookout 1 km ahead**'. I wound down the window and my hair went flying wild in the hot, dusty breeze.

'You've really fucking lost it, haven't you?' Scott shouted.

As I raced further up the mountain, Brisbane fell away below us like a futuristic wasteland. I pictured all the burbans below, sleeping off their Christmas bellies, floating like overweight corpses on the surface of a thousand backyard pools. About halfway to the top, there was a dirt embankment overlooking the view. At night, lovers parked their cars along the siding to pash and root, but, at 5 p.m. on Christmas Day, there was no one within coo-ee. I pulled over, the tyres skidding on the loose gravel.

'What are you doing now?' said Scott.

I cut the ignition, cranked the handbrake, killed the radio.

'What's your big announcement?'

'I don't know what you're talking about.' He was lying. I could see it in his eyes and in the way the top of his ears went a bit pink, same as when he'd said he hadn't rooted Trish.

'Tell me!' I grabbed his arm, digging my fingernails into his skin. He yelped, jerking away.

'Bitch!' he said, inspecting his arm.

I glowered at him, my tongue hot with venom. 'Fuck you.'

We sat, steaming in silence. The engine ticked and expanded. The heat rolled in around us, thick and suffocating, pressing me into the seat. Sweat beads rolled from the roots of my hair, down the back of my neck and my spine. I smiled across at him.

'I know a secret.'

Scott turned and looked at me. 'What secret?' His eyes roamed my tits and I could tell he had sex on his mind. Danny's name was on the tip of my tongue but I didn't want it to ruin the moment. Scott crawled over the brake-stick towards me.

'Just shut up and fuck me, alright? I know you want me.'

But I pushed him off and flung open the door. I leapt out of the car and stuck my head back through the window. 'I know about your little secret.' I turned and bolted, gripping the car keys tight in my hand. I crossed the road and hurried down the embankment into the bush, skidding on the gravel. The undergrowth was thick and spiky, lashing at my bare legs. Sharp stones bit into the soles of my feet. I had no idea where I was going; I just wanted Scott to chase me. I could hear him thrashing after me, swearing and calling out for me to come back, and I kept running in no particular direction, my vision smudging in the heat-haze. Everything was a blur of brown and silvery-green, as if the friction of my body against the world could have set the bush on fire.

Scott was gaining on me. I could hear him panting, the

snap of fallen branches underfoot. He kept yelling, 'I'm gonna get you, Rosie. I'm gonna get you real bad,' in a voice that got me half-frightened, half-rank. I couldn't wait for him to catch me but I wasn't giving in easy. Blood fired in my veins as I jumped over rocks and fallen logs and ducked under low-lying boughs. I squeezed the car keys tighter in my hand and looked out across the valley. The sun was a huge, red disc. The horizon was streaked with wisps of blood-coloured cloud, bathing the city in an eerie, pinkish haze.

'Gotcha!'

Scott tackled me around the waist. We fell hard to the ground. The keys flew out of my hand. My shoulder grazed against a flat slab of granite. He had me trapped, his legs straddling my waist. He was laughing cruelly, his mouth wide open.

'Mutai?' he said.

I squirmed and shook my head. 'No way. Not until you tell me.' I flung my arms back against the rock. The granite was hot beneath me. Its warmth made me horny. He watched me, his hands resting loose on his thighs. I could see his cock rising steadily against the satiny material of his boxers, slipping through the fly, the head smooth, pink and glossy. He swallowed, audibly, visibly. I laughed, my voice low and strange, my nipples so tight and bursting they could have rolled off from my chest. He lay down flat on top of me, the weight of his body pressing me into the rock. His face was close to mine, his breath sweet and beery against my cheek. Stretching up, he roughly prised open my fists, pulling back the fingers, one by one. 'Where're the keys?'

'You'll have to strip-search me,' I said.

'That won't take long.' He grabbed both my wrists, pinning me to the ground, and pashed me, deep with tongue. Next thing, his shorts were off and his fingers, hot and insistent, shoved the crotch of my bikini bottoms to one side. Planting his arms against my hips, his cock nudged and bumped at my pussy. I ached with rankness. He thrust hard up into me. I yelped. I hadn't done it in two years and for a second it hurt, but then it felt awesome. I swung my legs around his back, my fingers twisting in his hair. Dusky sunlight spangled and burned around him like an aura. We rocked back and forth. Gold light flitted in and out of the eucalyptus overhead. I felt myself rising, teetering on the edge.

'Call me a slut,' I hissed.

'You fucking slut,' he said. 'You filthy fucking whore.' His neck was strained with one thick, pulsing vein. We went for it, riding hard and fast, my thighs slick and foamy as a racehorse's. My eyes were shut tight. The granite rasped at my skin but I was nearly there. I was so fucking bad, such a bad, bad, bad, bad, bad girl. Oh fuck. Oh fucking fuck. I saw my orgasm shimmering ahead and I galloped towards it, my legs viced around Scott's torso, my butt-muscles clenched and pumping, my fingers looped and gripped in his hair. 'You dirty cunt,' Scott growled, as I bucked and reared beneath him, biting into his chest, my whole body convulsing, and then there was nothing but the softest blackness raining down on me and I slumped back onto the rock. It was the best orgasm I've ever had. Scott came soon after but I was dead, or as good as, drugged with the sweetest post-coital nectar. Save his breathing, all was silent.

Scott slid off me, his chest wet with sweat. I opened my eyes and sat up, feeling weak and giddy. The bad-girl sizzle ebbed away, retreating inside me. My crotch was hot and damp; my back grazed and stinging. Scott crawled away from me, his bum up in the air. Between his legs, his balls hung loose in the heat. A few metres away to the left of the granite rock, a frilly-neck froze, reared its collar and hissed, its forked tongue flashing in and out. Scott turned and stared at it, mimicking its throaty gargle, his hands splayed around his neck. The frilly got all in a tizz. It whipped around in circles, hopping on its tiny clawed feet, its beady eyes bright with fear and anger. Scott pegged a stick at it. Its tail pitched upwards and it darted away, scuttling across the dirt, and I thought how gutless Scott was and how much I hated him.

'I know the truth about you,' I said, searching for the car keys in the fading light while Scott stood by not helping.

'Yeah?' he said. 'That I'm a fucking awesome root.'

'No.' I paused, waiting for him to look at me. 'I know about you and Danny.'

A muscle spasmed in Scott's cheek and everything froze like in a Western. Those tiny seconds after a gun goes off. Then thwump, thwump, the bodies start hitting the dirt. I opened my mouth to eat back the words but it was too late. I'd triggered something now. Scott came up behind me and grabbed my wrists, squeezing hard.

He whispered, close in my ear, his spit hitting my cheek. 'That fucking faggot cunt! I know he's been after me.' I bet he'd liked it too much, the feel of Danny's hand on his dick. It must've fucked with part of his head. The part that teetered, wavered, wondered if. So he'd crushed and tortured it, clubbed and stomped and killed it before it took him over.

Letting go of my wrists, he pushed me roughly up the hill and I stumbled forwards onto my knees. 'You think you know me?' he said, 'C'mon then. I want to show you something.' He strode off ahead, not once looking back at me as I followed him up to the car. As we drove down the mountain in silence, I felt numb. BrisVegas lay sprawled, a great expanse of dirty green studded with a million rooftops burnished orange as the sun collapsed into the valley.

I pulled up under the leopard tree.

Scott burst out of the car, slamming the door so hard it shuddered up my spine. His head filled the open window. 'Get out.' His voice was steady.

I sat in the driver's seat, not knowing whether to obey him or take off.

The Greenwood house was ablaze with light. Upstairs, the Christmas tree winked in the window and the front door was wide open to catch the breeze. Silhouettes, adult- and kid-sized, zipped back and forth like shadow puppets. Downstairs, the men were playing pool. I caught the whiff of barbie-meat. Mr Greenwood's favourite Buddy Holly track, 'True Love Ways', drifted out across the lawn.

'Get outta the fucking car!'

I jumped. Scott was on my side, hauling me out of my seat. He dragged me across the lawn and up the front steps, two at a time. The door was open but the fly-screen was locked. He rang the bell. His eyes shone manic.

'Coming!' Mrs Greenwood sang out from the kitchen. She came clattering down the hall. The lock clicked and she swung back the screen. 'About bloody time!' She was wearing a bright-red belted dress and green bauble earrings with bells which tinkled when she moved her head. She saw me and stopped, her over-powdered face creasing into a sharp frown. 'Rosie!' she said, forcing her lips into a fake smile. 'What are you doing here?'

'Outta the way, Mum,' Scott ordered.

Mrs Greenwood stood firm, blocking the doorway, her arms folded across her bust. 'Do you think that's such a good idea?' she said to Scott, then turning to me, 'I mean, Rosie dear, haven't you just got out of hospital?'

'No, she's fine.' Scott barged past her, tugging me inside and down the hall.

I tried to wrench my arm free but he pulled me through to the living room where Mrs Greenwood's tribe of sisters were sipping sherry and Scott's young cousins were playing with their new Barbies. We stood under the artificial arch. The women looked up from their gossip and then, clocking me in my lime-green bikini, exchanged raised eyebrows. I felt naked, a mollusc with no shell, my back still stinging from our root on the granite. I wished to god I had some clothes on.

Mrs Greenwood slipped between us. 'Look, everyone. You remember Rosie, don't you?'

'What's *she* doing here?' Auntie Beth hissed.

'You've got a bit of a cheek, haven't you, luvvie?' Auntie Marge squawked.

'Where is she?' demanded Scott.

Mrs Greenwood shook her head and pursed her lips. Scott grabbed my hand and stormed through the kitchen, down the stairs and through the rumpus. Mrs Greenwood and her sisters followed behind like a flock of geese, carrying their sherry glasses with them. The kids, sensing drama in the air, charged like excited goslings in their wake.

As we crossed the lawn, the grass was cool and lush beneath my feet. The Grubs were warming up for a set. Coloured lightbulbs were strung up from the fence, drenching the lawn in red, purple, orange. Mr Greenwood was on the barbie, which was alive with popping sausages and smoking squares of beef. He looked up as we went past and shouted, half-cut, 'For goodness' sake, Rosie, put some bloody clothes on, why don't ya?' Near the band, I spotted Muzza, and Bomber just out of hospital, sitting on folding stools. Kirstie was there, too. They were all talking to a woman with jet-black hair. Scott strode across the lawn towards them, ripping me along, Mrs Greenwood and her sisters still behind us.

As we got closer, I could see it was her. She was sitting

sideways to Bomber and Muzza. Her legs were stretched out in front, her bare feet up on a chair. Scott ditched my hand. She swivelled around, awkwardly. It was her. Almond eyes. Creamy skin and long limbs. Her stomach was huge. The ground rocked beneath me and my legs bowed. I told my knees to lock.

'You alright, babe?' she asked Scott with a pommie accent, smiling as she smoothed her slender hands over her swollen belly. My ears burned hot and bile rose in my throat.

'I'd like you to meet an old friend.' Scott nodded at me and Bomber tittered as she struggled to stand up. She was wearing dark jeans, slung below her bump, and a loose peasant-style blouse. She was taller and more beautiful than the photo, softer in the face. Around her neck, she wore a string of amber beads the same as Scott had been wearing at the rave. I swam in her beautiful, calm face.

'Amber, Rosie. Rosie, Amber,' Scott said. 'Rosie and I went out for a while, when we were kids.'

'Lovely to meet you,' said Amber. She smiled at me, but I couldn't speak. Wrapping his arms around her shoulders, Scott looked at me over the top of her head.

'Can you believe it? I'm going to be a dad.'

But last week I swallowed your cum on Mum's bed and today, less than an hour ago, we rooted like crazy fucking rodents. I felt like my insides had been scooped out with a hunting knife. Bomber and Muzza sat back, revelling. Scott bent his head and whispered something in her ear to which she laughed, clapping her hands together girlishly. Edging away from

252

the scene, I watched them, blackest envy rising like sludge in my chest. I wanted to be somewhere far, far away.

'Are you alright, Rosie?' Mrs Greenwood came up behind me. 'I kept telling Scott to tell you but—'

'I'm fine.' I stared at a patch of grass over her shoulder.

'Course it wasn't planned, but they get along so well. And the nice thing is they've decided to get married. Before the baby, mind. It's the proper thing to do, don't you think? Only a small do. Just the rellies and a few close friends. Bill's going to set up a marquee here in the backyard.'

Nice. After rooting me and Trish and probably a million other bitches behind her back, the bastard was fucking hitching her. I almost felt sorry for her, but then she was welcome to him.

19

After that I don't remember thinking, just doing. I had this overwhelming need to see Hollie. She'd been right about Scott all along. It was beautifully clear to me now.

I accelerated hard up the hill and parked on the side of the road. There were no cop cars but that didn't mean they weren't up there. After all, Danny was armed and dangerous, a convicted murderer on the loose, a threat to happy, burban lives. Expecting Hollie to be in her bedroom or Mrs Bailey's, I went in the side, through the parlour and up the stairs. I heard footsteps from the darkened hall and looked up to see Mr Bailey leaning over the balustrade. It was ages since I'd seen him and, as he came towards me out of the shadows and down the stairs, I panicked.

'Rosemary, what are you doing here?' He was wearing a dark suit and a silver tie. His face was ashen and his hair, too, newly greying at the temples.

'Nothing,' I stammered. 'I just came to see Hollie.'

'She's not here,' he said, sharply. He stopped, halfway down the staircase, and, as if needing the support, gripped the banister. I noticed how he still wore his wedding ring. 'She's gone for a walk.'

His eyes skimmed over me but it was like he was seeing

something else, some memory from the past. I wanted to get out of there as fast as possible, but I had to say something.

'Is she alright?' I asked.

He glared at me. 'Why wouldn't she be?'

'It's just that with Danny and everything.' I was retreating down the staircase one step at a time.

'The police have everything under control,' he said, smoothing a hand down his tie. 'And we are doing all we can to assist them.' I couldn't tell if it was an act or if he was genuine. Since I could remember, he'd been cold, humourless and distant, but there was something crumbling about him, like he was just holding onto reality. He cleared his throat. 'Perhaps it would be best if you stayed away from the house, at least for the time being. I'll tell Hollie you came by.' He smiled, icily. Nodding, I turned and strode back through the house, knowing exactly where Hollie would be.

The night was deep and still, the finest slither of a moon in the sky. The police could have been lurking anywhere so I kept alert as my legs carried me up the track. Around me, the bush was oddly silent. I tried my hardest to be quiet but every tread seemed to echo around the mountainside. About halfway to the cave, I spotted a distinct beam from a flashlight slicing through the trees less than a hundred metres up the hill. Someone was heading in my direction. I ducked behind a bush and waited, my scalp shrinking with fear. Every few seconds, the light-beam swept across the track. From the heaviness of the footsteps, I could tell it was a man and, as he came closer, I saw that he was wearing dark combat trousers and a black T-shirt. I tried to get a glimpse of his face but I couldn't get a clear view through the bush without being seen. I squeezed my eyes shut and crouched tighter, but whoever it was had back-tracked and was heading east, away from me. I pelted, light as a fairy, to the cave.

Breathless, I sank to my knees and crawled in through the overhanging vines. It was dark, my eyes straining to adjust, but there was a weak, flickering light coming from the deepest corner of the cave. A giant shadow shifted back and forth across the ceiling and I became aware of little, soft cries and whimpers, echoing around the walls. A nervous dread skittered through me. I edged to my left, my shoulder knocking against the crumbly wall. The dank smell of old dirt and limestone filled my nostrils. I crawled in further, crouching behind the egg rock to get a better view.

Hollie was lying down, her hair spilling across the earth. Stark white against the red soil. Around her throat a high, stiff collar of French lace from which her long thin neck, whiter still, strained. Her chin jutted up towards the roof, her cheekbones pinched and flushed. A film of dust coated her lips and her eyes were closed, lids fluttering.

Danny lay naked on top of her, running his blackened fingers through her hair, fucking her. Mud from his skin dirtied the stiff, white peaks of her skirt. With a gentle sigh, Hollie's back arched against the ground and she wrapped her long, skinny legs around his torso. Diffused light, coming from a small gas lamp in the corner, hung in a golden cloud around them. They looked like delicate, exotic creatures from another world but my insides rioted with revulsion and horror and there was a bitter, metallic taste in my mouth.

Danny thrust into her, his shoulder tense and flared, and Hollie sighed. If they'd looked up they would have seen me but they were too engrossed in each other. I felt like bits of me were fading away, becoming invisible. I stayed a few moments longer, wretched and trembling but unable to pull myself away. Danny was falling, his lips sinking onto Hollie's mouth. I blinked and retreated.

It was only when I was outside, the silence of the bush pressing in on me, that the tears came hot and fast, and I fled, not caring if the cops caught me, back down the mountainside.

I got in my car and drove, as if by driving I could clear my head of what I had just seen. But there was no denying the truth of it and, as the cool night air whipped in around me, it sledged me hard – a whole, secret world they'd kept from me. I wondered how long it had been going on and why Hollie hadn't told me. Crossing the Captain Cook bridge, I got onto the freeway. For over an hour, the road unfurled black and empty in front of me and I followed it, numb and blind and unthinking.

Somehow, I ended up at Main Beach. I parked under a

buggy fluoro and went down to the beach. The grains squeaked between my toes and my hair flapped in the breeze. I inhaled deeply, the air fresh and salty with the whiff of fish and chips. I fell to my knees in the sand, lulled by the vast plain of ink-black water, stretching out in front of me. A middle-aged couple walked past in the shallows splashing each other, their laughter hitting my ears in windy bursts. They were heading south, towards Surfers'. Not far off, the golden city of high-rises clung to the edge of the beach, shimmering in its own dreamy halo. I watched until the couple became tiny specks against the nightscape and then I pelted into the surf, my thighs thrusting through the still-warm water, diving over the foamy crests.

Lying back, I surrendered to the rips and currents, my limbs hither-thither, seaweed tentacles squirming beneath me. I had no one now. All Hollie and Danny needed was each other: two snakes eating each other to death in the dirt, locked in an endless embrace. The night sky rocked above me and I let the waves enfold me, filling my mouth, my nose, my eyes. A huge wave picked me up and carried me up to its crest, then dragged me headlong under the water. I let the undercurrents take me as I tumbled and rolled and floundered, my knees grazing on the rough sand below. If this was the end, I was happy enough to be taken.

With an indifferent heave, the sea spat me out and I was dumped hard and spluttering on the shore. I lay breathless, the wet grains catching on my face, coating my arms. A dog came up and sniffed at my crotch. I sat up and shooed it away, then tramped back up the dunes to my car, the sea in my ears, the tang of salt on my tongue.

When I got home, the love-birds were snuggled on the plasticated couch, watching *The Sound of Music*. Randy's head was wrapped turban-style in bandages and his right eye was a nasty shade of eggplant. Mum shot me a 'where do you think you've been' look, but didn't say anything. I sat on the poof and watched the rest of it with them, my brain jam-packed with the vision of Hollie in the cave, all white with muddy streaks.

20

I woke to Mum in the Chamber singing the song where Julie
Andrews tells Christopher Plummer she must have done
something good despite her wicked childhood and her
miserable youth. I got up and went to work. After all the
craziness, it was a relief to be back flicking doilies in the air-
con. We had hardly any customers, just a few oldies from
the gerry home across the road. BrisVegas was like a ghost
town, like the whole burban lot of them had racked off to
the beach to escape the psycho heat. Forty-three max today,
it'd said on the radio.

Trish was on my shift but we hadn't spoken since the
night of the phone call. The first couple of hours, we avoided
each other: she hung out back smoking joints; I stayed
behind the counter, serving the odd customer. Hollie kept
ringing my mobile but I put it on silent. I'd had sixteen
missed calls from her already that morning. I felt bad not
answering, but I didn't know what to say to her. I knew I had
to speak to her, to tell her what I'd seen, but I felt vague and
trembly and I'd lost my appetite. I told myself I would call her
later, after my shift, once I'd got things straight in my head. I
went back to the old flick and peel, staring up at the box. The
first day of the third Test had been on all morning but there

was a break for the midday news. The news-girl came on, her fake-tanned face filling the screen like a giant orange:

'Police are still searching for a twenty-three-year-old white male who, dressed to look like an indigenous aborigine, attacked a man with a spear last Sunday morning at Arena nightclub in Fortitude Valley.'

A prison mug shot of Danny, looking thin and gaunt.

'As the hunt continues in bushland near his home in the western suburbs, police are still refusing to comment on possible motives for the attack. But a spokesperson for the aboriginal community has expressed outrage, calling it a calculated act of race crime against their people.'

'That loon with the spear still on the rampage?' Trish was standing beside me, sucking the devil out of a joint. I nodded, hoping that Danny was safe in the cave and not roaming about the place.

'You know where he is, don't you?'

'No.' In my paranoia, I imagined her as Scott's secret informer.

Out of nowhere, Uncle Slob appeared. He stood glowering behind Trish who spliffed on oblivious.

'Is he in the bush?'

'Behind you,' I whispered.

Trish turned around. Slob shot forwards, snatching the joint out of her hand.

'Out the back, now!' he ordered, giving her a sharp shove, adding to me, 'Keep an eye on things out here.'

But I couldn't help spying on them through the crack between the swing doors. Trish stood in the corner of the dingy back office while Slob paced up and down. I wondered if she would snitch on me for being in on the skimming. After what she'd done with Scott, I didn't put it past her.

'I should have known you'd go bad,' Slob snarled, showering Trish's face with spit, 'just like your scumbag father.'

Trish's dad had run off with another woman when Slob's sister was pregnant with Trish. Although she'd never met her dad, Slob was forever saying how he'd grill his balls if he set eyes on him again.

'Ever since you started here, profits have been going down and yet we've never been busier. I couldn't work it out.' He took out a hanky and wiped the sweat off his forehead.

Trish had her hands on her hips, looking bored and tapping her right foot to some imaginary techno beat. Slob pumped his meaty arms.

'And then, when the scotch kept going missing, I knew it was you.' He struck at his chest with a fist. 'The wife thought I was troppo. But I knew any daughter of that lousy prick had to turn out rotten.' He paused to let the full force of his insult sink in. 'So, what've you done with it, Trisha?' His face was so red I thought he was going to have a coronary. 'Where's all the cash? It must be about two grand by now, hey?' He grabbed her chin in his pudgy fingers and shook it. Trish jerked back from him. I didn't know Trish had nicked that much, I'd only scored a couple of hundred.

Trish smiled. 'I've spent it.'

Slob raised his fist, like he was going to punch her in the

face, but forced it down, his arm rigid with unspent fury. 'You've got till tomorrow morning to pay it back, all of it, or else I'm calling the cops.' His chest was heaving. 'After tomorrow, I never want to see you lousy piece of shit again. Now get out of here!'

Trish sashayed out of the office, winking at me as she went past. I raced back behind the counter, relieved she hadn't dumped me in it. Slob blustered out, red-faced and swearing.

'Get the fuck outta my sight!' he roared at Trish, oblivious to the blue-rinse biddies drinking tea in the corner.

Trish calmly took off her apron and chucked it in the bin. 'You coming, Rosebud?' she shouted to me as she stepped out into the hazy, mid-afternoon sunshine.

'Yeah, alright,' I said, thinking fuck it. I was sick of Slob's perving and waiting on beardies and making bloody cappuccinos. Besides, working at Temptations would be misery without her.

That night Trish and I went feral. We went to the R.E. and drank Johnnie blue label in the beer garden while chatting up rugger-buggers in RMs and plaited belts. Their total lack of brains and style didn't stop Trish dragging one of them behind the loos for a quick root in the bushes. She was in top form, we both were, high on booze and freedom. Late in the afternoon we stumbled over the road to Flight Centre to book Trish's ticket to India. As soon as I was in there, surrounded by all the glossy mags and that whiff of travel bugginess, it came to me as clear as fucking crystal.

'I'm going, too,' I said, realizing how long I'd dreamed of escape.

Trish cheered. 'Yeah, baby, let's go rank together!'

'Nah,' I said. 'I'm going to London. Like I said I would.' The first flight available was on New Year's Day. I paid my deposit and we left. Outside, Trish did some cartwheels on the pavement. I felt like stripping off and running down the road naked. It was the best feeling ever. At last, I was free. No more Temptations! No more BrisVegas! No more Scott Greenwood!

Back at Trish's bedsit, we snorted lines and ate some tabs. We turned the hardcore up full blast and danced until the sweat was pouring off us. To cool down, we took a shower. Trish dyed my hair Kermit-green and we shaved each other's pubes right off. We did more lines until we were rolling around on the floor laughing. We couldn't stop. I actually pissed myself. Afterwards, we chucked *Bad Boy Bubby* in the video and watched Bubby glad-wrap his pet cat over and over again on continuous replay. Then, we went speeding on the Western freeway and I stuck my head out of the window and screamed, my green hair flapping like the wings of some exotic bird from the Amazon. I turned to Trish, my face squashed back like in a centrifuge, and shouted, 'I love you!'

'I fucking love you, too!' she yelled back.

We were still beaming as we drove to the Toowong public pool and climbed the fence for a late-night skinny-dip. It felt like we were there for yonks, ducking and diving in the silky, black water. Afterwards, we lay flat and panting on the grass, gazing up at the stars. The night was sweet and muggy. I turned to Trish, my head propped up on my wrist, too ripped to care I was starkers.

'I know you rooted Scott,' I said.

Trish ran her fingers through her spiky, green hair. She looked child-like, almost innocent. Perhaps it was because she had no pubes.

'But I don't think we did,' she said, eyes wide, her eyelashes clumped into cute, little points.

'It's cool, you know,' I said. 'You don't have to lie about it. I don't give a shit any more.'

'Nah, it's not that. I can't remember if we did or not. It's all muddled up. Did he say we did?'

'He denied it, but I could tell he was lying.'

'Then, maybe we did. Fuck knows. My head's a pile of mush.'

'I know you, babe, and I bet you did.'

'Probably.' She pulled up a handful of grass and stuffed it in her mouth. 'Sorry, Rosebud.'

I watched as the stars tumbled out of the sky, pinging cold and bright as diamonds along my naked body. 'You know what?' He's having a kid with this chick called Amber. Can you believe it? I thought he loved me.'

I had a bit of a cry. Trish hugged me. We clung to each other, our bodies warm and damp. I lay back on the grass and reached for Trish's hand, wanting her to know I'd forgiven her. She rolled over and kissed me on the lips, then sprung up, whooping like a wild beast, and bomb-dived into the pool.

By the time we got back to Trish's, the sun was coming up. The sky glowed bright pink and the morning chorus was kicking in. I can't remember going to bed but when I woke up, it was mid-afternoon and Trish had gone. She'd left a note stuck to the fridge with chewy:

See ya, Rosebud,
Plane to catch. Thanks for a crazy fucking night.
Trish x
P.S. Can you drop the keys into the estate agent and tell them I've gone? There's a box of my stuff in the lounge room – clothes and crap. Take what you want, chuck the rest. Don't think I'll be coming back to this shithole!

I spent the rest of the week at home, packing and planning my escape. I'd already decided not to tell Mum or Randy about going, just to disappear, leave them all wondering, scratching their sun-softened heads. The only person I had to tell was Hollie. I still hadn't called her yet. The image of her and Danny rooting in the cave filled my head like a porno vid. So, now I knew what Hollie had wanted to tell me at the hospital. Most people would think a brother and sister doing it was sick but I didn't know what to think. I wasn't angry. If anything I felt kind of sad for them, not having anyone but each other, and a bit sorry for myself, being so far outside their secret world.

Apart from packing, I kept a vigilant eye on the news. Each day the cops made out they were closing in on Danny. They showed footage of the brigade thrashing through the bush, swaggering under the weight of their holsters. It was a joke. Senior Constable Pitts would come on saying, 'We're pretty bloody certain he's out 'ere somewhere and we won't give up till we get 'im. Don't you worry about that. He can't just escape into thin air.'

Towards the end of the week, I got the guts to call Hollie. Time was running out and I needed to tell her I was leaving, and that I'd seen her in the cave with Danny. She answered on the first ring.

'Rosie?'

'Do you want to go for a chocollo in the air-con?'

Exactly ten minutes later, Hollie pulled up outside in the Lexus. I went running out in cut-offs. She was wearing the same white muslin dress, freshly washed, that she'd had on in the cave. She eyed my green hair but didn't say anything. We drove to Shoppingtown in silence, in case of, as Hollie scribbled on a scrap of paper: '*Bugs.*'

With the sales on, it was a bitch finding a park but eventually we got one up near the food court. Arm in arm, we marched across the carpark, anticipating the cool blast of air-con and soothing musak. Once inside, we made straight for Wendy's, great purveyor of chocollo. I bought us two extra-large cones and we sat down on plastic swivel stools, licking away and watching the shoppers scurry past us. It took me a few minutes to psych myself up.

'Hollie,' I said, touching her wrist. 'I saw you. In the cave.' I took a deep breath. 'With Danny.'

She pretended not to hear.

'Hollie, look at me.'

She brushed my hand away. There was a long silence. She refused to look at me. I got up from the stool and stood facing her. Her lips were set. She crushed the chocollo cone in her hands. I hugged her but she was wooden in my arms.

'I don't think anything bad,' I whispered in her ear.

She pushed me back and spun around on the swivel, facing the blank wall. I sat beside her and put my arm around her.

'Please. Don't be like this. I understand. Really. Other people might think it's weird but I don't. You love each other.'

She raised her head and stared at me. 'We're freaks,' she spat.

'No, you're not. I don't think that.'

'Yes, you do. Deep down, you think it.'

'You're wrong.' I brushed away a stray hair which had got caught in her lip gloss. 'You... you both looked... ' my heart was beating wild, 'beautiful.'

Her eyes glistened. Her cheeks coloured. 'Really?'

'Yes.' I slipped my fingers into hers. She lifted my hand to her mouth and kissed it. The Wendy's man was staring at us over the counter.

'Hey, you girlies, if you've finished, move along.'

'C'mon, Hollie,' I said. 'Let's get out of here.'

We walked back slowly, hand in hand, to the car, talking it all through and telling each other everything.

21

Mum and Randy were going ballroom dancing at the Hilton for New Year's Eve. They stood in the doorway: Mum in a daring strapless number she'd bought in the sales; Randy in black tie. When they asked what I was doing I told them I was staying in with a vid and a delivery pizza. Randy gave me a sympathetic nod but Mum smiled.

'Good,' she said. 'It's about time you took it easy.'

As soon as they were gone, I leapt off the couch and started getting ready. Hollie had invited me to the cave for a New Year's Eve party, just the three of us – Hollie and me and Danny. It was my last night in BrisVegas and I had this feeling, like something major was going to happen. Everything I'd thought about Hollie and Danny had changed and I didn't quite know how I was going to act around them. I wasn't sure what to expect, what part I had to play. I wondered if Hollie had even told Danny that I'd seen them in the cave. I was nervous, but excited, too, as if I was about to do something illicit or forbidden. Like the first night I went clubbing and met Scott.

I dyed my hair black from Kermit-green and set it in hot rollers. I painted my fingernails and toenails purple, and slid my silver serpent armband up my arm. I rubbed coconut oil over my body until my skin shone, honey-coloured. As I dressed, a moth brushed its wings against my sticky skin. I pulled on a pair of Bonds, no bra. Then, a skirt, falling in soft, filmy folds, and my white-lace camisole, its edges curled and scalloped against my stomach. As night fell, I unravelled the rollers and shook out my hair. It cascaded in loops and bangs down my chest. The contrast turned my face pale and my scar seemed to glow in the dusky light. It shone back at me, a jagged crescent-moon. I painted my lips blood-red and my eyelashes thick with heavy mascara, liquid liner around the eyes. I looked like a goth-freak but it was all for Hollie. I grabbed some of Trish's hardcore CDs, put on my strappies and headed outside. The night-sky held its breath, a vast swathe of indigo arched over me, heavy, as they say in Shakespeare, with portent. I had that scoopy hollowness in my gut. It wasn't dread or excitement, but a teetering, falling feeling, like a premonition, as if the gods had already decided our fates that night. I got on my bike and sped away to Hollie and Danny.

So much for intensifying the search. That evening, there were no cop cars outside Hollie's house. The lazy buggers had probably racked off home to New Year's piss-ups, like the ones going on up and down Hollie's street. Bevan music blared out into the night. Meaty smells filled the air. I rode up to the top of the hill and dumped my bike in the ditch. Hollie's house loomed black and hushed as a mausoleum, except for the Christmas tree, still lit up in the casement, and for a moment I thought I saw Mr Bailey standing next to it in the window. I turned and started up the track. There was no moon at all. I couldn't see my toes. As I ran through the bush to the cave, I felt jittery, like on a first date, but buzzy with anticipation, too.

Hollie was setting out the food. Orange fish-spawn glowed fluorescent in the soft light. There were silver trays piled with fleshy oysters and Moreton Bay bugs, their clawed legs splayed at obscene angles. A giant poached salmon lay bloated, and its huge, dead eye seemed to follow me as I entered inside. There was an ice-bucket with three bottles of pink champagne and three large satin cushions for us to sit on. Purple candles flickered out from rocky crannies, filling the cave with an overblown, musky scent. Opera was playing low. It was the same Wagner stuff Danny'd had in the Lexus, the night he drove me home from Scott's. As I crawled in, my shadow loomed against the back wall. Startled, Hollie spun around. She was alone.

'You gave me a fright.' She flung her arms around me, then, stepping back, said, 'You look *ravishing*.' The word, *ravishing*, and the way she said it, rolling the 'r' and pouting her lips, took me back to the night of her party when she'd acted so strangely with me. She was wearing a black evening gown and patent heels which had both been her mother's. Around her neck, she wore a diamond choker, which threw droplets of purplish-red light across the hand paintings on the wall. Her face was radiant.

'Would you like some champagne, darling?' Her eyes lingered over the exposed strip of my stomach, my rubied belly-button.

'Sure.' I felt ill at ease around this new, sexually experienced Hollie. She pulled a bottle from the ice, wiping down its sides with a linen napkin, and popped the cork with an expert twist. And all the time, my mind was flicking between the Hollie I was seeing and the Hollie I had seen on the floor of the cave, muslin skirts gathered to her waist, long legs twisted around his muddied body.

'Where's Danny?' I asked as she poured into two crystal flutes.

'He'll be here soon.' She handed me a glass. I took a sip. Hollie looked at me, her head to one side. 'What are you thinking?'

'Nothing.' I smiled. A single bead of sweat slipped down my spine. 'Just how lovely you look.' And she did, but once I'd said it I felt myself falling again, like Alice chasing the white rabbit down the hole. And, here I was in the cave, with my head nearly touching the ceiling, a grown-up Alice with strange new desires stirring inside me.

Blushing, Hollie held her glass aloft. 'To my noble Oberon.'

'To my darling Titania, Queen of the Fairies,' I said, adding, 'and to Danny.'

'Yes.' Her eyes darted towards the entrance of the cave, then back to me. 'To Lord Danny, Bravest Warrior of the Night.'

We chinked. Hollie sipped daintily, holding the stem of

the glass in her fingers. I guzzled mine down and lowered my head, taking in the rich, lurid colours of the food. For dessert, there were three bowls of sugar-dusted strawberries, cherries and plums and a turret of whipped cream. I bent down and stole a strawberry.

'Put that back.' Hollie shook a finger at me, but I popped the strawberry in my mouth. 'They're meant for later,' she said, coming up behind me, wrapping her arms around my waist. She was wearing a new perfume which made me at once light-headed and aroused. I turned around and kissed her. Her lips were cool and cherry-scented. She pressed herself to me and I cupped her face and held it, the fragile jaw, the smooth polished cheeks.

'What's that?' Hollie drew back from me. The sound of male voices was coming from outside. The taste of strawberry soured on my tongue. They were coming closer, their voices clear on the windless night. There were two of them.

'Where the fuck is it?' one was saying.

'Don't ask me.'

'This is shit. It's too dark. Here, give us the lighter.'

'You've got it.'

'No, I don't, dickhead.'

'The police,' whispered Hollie. She was shaking, her eyes wide with terror.

'Yeah. The bastards.' There was no point in telling her the truth of who it was. Scott and Bomber. They sounded drunk and stoned shitless. Before, I'd thought it was just stupid macho talk, but now I knew it wasn't. Before, I could have done something, warned someone, but not now. Seconds passed, Hollie tense and clinging to me. From outside, came the whiff of pot. Their voices drifted away until there was silence, except the distant rumble of burban parties. Now, there was nothing I could do but wait and pray they didn't find him. It was nine-thirty and Danny still hadn't showed. I poured us two more glasses and stared at the untouched oysters. Hollie nibbled on some fish-spawn. I sculled my drink, set the glass down and crawled towards the entrance of the cave. I couldn't stand it any longer. Perhaps Scott would listen to me. Perhaps I could talk him out of it.

'Where are you going?' Hollie looked up in alarm.

'Outside,' I said. 'For some fresh air.'

'I'll come, too.'

'No. You wait here.'

But before Hollie could protest there were footsteps coming closer again, then stopping right outside the cave. They must have heard us, our voices carrying on the still night air. A giant shadow fell across the entrance. I clutched Hollie's hand and pulled her with me behind the egg rock where we crouched rigid. They were crawling inside and there was a scraping sound, like a stick being dragged over rock. Hollie whimpered. I pressed my hand to her mouth and peered out from the rock. Danny was clambering towards us with his spear. Its bloodied tip gleamed in the candlelight and a dead possum hung around his neck.

'It's alright. It's Danny,' I said, amazed that he hadn't run into Scott and Bomber. Hollie leapt up, ecstatic to see he had evaded the cops. He was in full aborigine mode, his naked body covered head to toe with mud and decorated with chalk markings. He wore bush turkey feathers around his wrists and ankles. When he saw us, standing like two glamour pusses with our glasses of bubbly, he grinned, the whites of his eyes luminous in the shadows, and stood up straight, letting the dead animal slump in a heap. Hollie nudged it away from the food with the toe of her stiletto.

'We've been so worried about you.' She ruffled his filthy hair and kissed him on the lips. Danny swung her about in his arms and pashed her. I looked away, not sure how to behave in front of them. Hollie laughed, her face aglow as he set her down.

'Look, Danny,' she said. 'Rosie has joined us.'

I waved, feeling a bit third leg.

'Me hunting,' Danny boomed, and thumped his blood-streaked chest. He stood with the spear by his side, one leg bent with the sole of his foot resting against his kneecap.

Hollie chided, suddenly sombre, 'You know the police have just been here, right outside.'

Danny scampered over to the dead possum. 'Revenge is sweet for those with innocent hearts but for souls tarnished with bitterness, revenge is doomed to fail.' I looked up and he caught my eye. He knew Bomber and Scott were out there, waiting for him, but Hollie had no idea what he was talking about.

'I'll put on some hardcore,' I said. It was coming up to ten, time to get our strange little party revved. I whipped out the Wagner and put on one of Trish's CDs, low so that the cops – so that Scott and Bomber – wouldn't hear.

Danny was crouched, intent over his kill. Lulled by the

hardcore vibing up through the floor, I lay belly down on the sheet, my heels kicking to the beats. Hollie sat on a cushion, sipping her champagne, as I watched Danny go to work, tipsily engrossed by his antics. Using a small blade, he skinned the possum carcass. Then he slit the belly, stuck his hand inside and scooped out the glistening guts. It made my stomach flip but I was fascinated by the deftness of his hands. I took a slug to calm my squeamishness while he rammed his spear, arse to neck, skewering the carcass like a pig on a spit. He built a tepee of twigs and dried leaves, and twirled a stick between his palms, the end drilled into another horizontal stick, until it smouldered. He blew on it, gently and then, a few minutes later, there was a fire. Cradling the spear in y-shaped branches at either end, Danny suspended the possum over the flames.

'What about Hollie's food?' I said.

'It's no good,' he said, scrunching up his face.

'I heard that!' exclaimed Hollie, pretending to be offended, as Danny and I laughed. It wasn't long before Danny lifted the spear from the fire and began tearing off stringy sections of the blackened meat with his fingers, ripping into the carcass like he hadn't eaten in weeks, stuffing it greedily into his mouth.

'What's it taste like?' I asked.

'Delicious,' he said, gob full. He passed over a strip of charred flesh. I grabbed the meat from his grubby fingers and took a small bite. The overriding taste was of charcoal but it wasn't bad – a greasy, slightly stringy version of crispy duck. I polished off my bit, washing it down with some champagne.

'More?' said Danny-Dilly, offering me another bit.

'Nah, I'm OK.'

'You're both disgusting!' Hollie stood over us, appalled.

Danny hooted. I laughed. She looked so funny when she was angry. I slugged some more champers, spilling it down the front of my top. Danny snatched the bottle and choked it back. The hardcore was quietly peaking. The rocks softly boomed, the walls gently shook with bass. I crawled over and turned it up, one more incy notch.

'They'll hear us,' Hollie hissed.

'Fuck 'em!' I screamed. The drink fired in my veins. I jumped up and raved around the fire.

'Yeah, fuck 'em,' said Danny. He leapt to his feet and joined me, kicking up dirt and stamping, waving his arms around, chanting and clapping just like when we were kids playing aborigines.

'C'mon, Hollie! Dance with us!' I yelled.

I grabbed her by the waist, spinning her around and pashing her so deep and luscious with tongue she forgot about being haughty and joined in the corroboree. Danny wore the bloody possum skin on his head. We all held hands and danced around the fire, singing and chanting and drinking. After a while, it got so hot I had to strip off to my undies. Hollie did the same, getting down to her white bra and knickers. Mixing some bottled water with orangey dirt, I painted Hollie's legs and arms and tummy with tribal stripes and zig-zags. She did the same for me; cool, pasty fingers spiralling my breasts, wriggly lines across my stomach, dots and dashes up the fronts of my thighs. God, it felt nice.

It seemed like hours went by as our shadows grew long and skinny. The candles burned low and the light dimmed to an eerie yellow, but still we didn't stop. Our bodies ran with sweat. Our tribal markings melted away. The mud which had covered Danny from head to foot dissolved leaving streaky patches on his pale skin. As the hardcore ended, we could hear the whiz-bang of New Year's fireworks exploding on top of Mount Coot-tha, echoing back and forth across the valley, and closer, down in burbia, BrisVegans hooting and carrying on.

'It's midnight!' I screamed.

I scrambled over to crank the tunes but when I turned back, Danny had Hollie pinned against the hand-painting wall and they were pashing like lovers. He pressed into her, his hands clamped around her shoulders, his dark hair shrouding her face. Hollie's body shuddered with desire. I swallowed hard. Crouched in the lengthening shadows, I watched them. A sharp yearning flared in me and I wanted to go to them, to be a part of it. It had always been a game with Hollie and me. Made-up names. Fantasy scenarios. Lord and ladies and pink champagne. But this wasn't a game. Hollie's undies were smeared with mud from Danny rubbing against her. Out of the corner of her eye, she saw me and understood. She beckoned me over with a little tilt of her head. Danny was looking across at me, too. They were waiting for me. But something held me back. I slid down against the cool rock, pressing my palms into the soft ochre.

Hollie blinked and turned back to Danny. They sank, their bodies melting into the earth. She lay on the ground, her lids lightly closed, her hair fanned out behind her while he roamed over her, peeling off her underwear, rubbing his grubby hands over her small breasts, down her ribcage, clasping her feet, kissing her toes. My eyes ached with it all: her paper-white skin; his body, taut and bony, stained with the blood of his kill.

And when he entered her, I gasped. Rankness kicked in me but I banished it away, ashamed. I stared into the fire. But when, a few seconds later, she cried out, her toes scrunched in the dirt, my resistance crumbled and I crawled over, slithering up between them. I clung to her, biting at her lips, her tongue. She kissed me, while, with soft, muddy fingers, Danny pulled off my undies. I rolled over to face him and twined my fingers in his hair. He pulled me closer and our mouths locked. Hollie nestled along the length of my spine, kissing the back of my neck. I lay down flat in the dirt. Danny climbed on top of me. His body was warm, dank-smelling of charcoal and leaves and old earth. I closed my eyes and inhaled him, drawing him deep into me, and then I was falling and coming, falling and coming, as the ground beneath me dissolved away to nothing.

Afterwards, we lay in the dirt. My head rested on Danny's

stomach. Hollie was beside me, our legs entwined, her cheek pressed against my breast. From the gentle rise and fall of her breathing, I could tell she was sleeping. The last candle died and the embers from Danny's fire cast a deep, red glow.

'Danny?' I whispered. 'Are you awake?'

'Yes.'

'Are we bad?'

'No.' He was rubbing his fingers up and down the ridge of my scar. It felt nice, the warmth from his fingertips spreading through my body. We lay in silence. I listened to the gurgling of Danny's belly, digesting possum.

'It wasn't your fault, you know, what happened to Matty Taylor.'

Danny stiffened. I sat up, lifting Hollie's head off my chest. She stirred, a little murmur, and rolled away, into the pinkish dust. Danny sat up on his haunches. He closed his eyes and let his head snap back. The skin under his chin was pure white. He levelled me with his gaze, his eyes black and cold and bottomless.

'Sorry,' I said.

The fire flickered, then ebbed away. Darkness seeped in around us. The embers sat heavy, silent, listening. I looked up at the roof of the cave and imagined a million evil eyes staring down at me from the crevices.

'Danny-Dilly,' I whispered.

'What?'

'I'm scared.'

'There's nothing to be scared of.'

In the darkness, I could hardly see him when his voice came to me: small, disembodied, strange. 'Let me tell you a story.'

'What story?'

'A story the spirits told me,' he said, solemnly. He paused, poking his spear amongst the dying coals. 'One day the three youngest children of the tribe were playing in the cave when some evil spirits came and sniffed them out. The evil spirits had the power to imitate voices and they started calling out in the voices of their mothers and grandmothers, saying they should go home because the hunters had returned with a big kill. But the good spirits, who lived in the rocks of the cave, realized the children were in great danger and warned them to stay put until the evil spirits went away. Night fell and the children lay down and slept together on the floor of the cave. Although they were frightened they trusted the good spirits to keep them safe.

'By the third day the children were thirsty and hungry and yet the evil spirits still lingered outside the cave. That night, the rocks trembled as the good spirits called out for help across the land. But, sensing a battle, the evil spirits did the same. Weak and starving, the children could hear the hum of the evil spirits buzzing around outside the cave. They clung to each other with fear. If they opened their eyes, they could see the yellow eyes of the evil spirits peering through the cracks in the cave. No matter what the good spirits said to soothe them, they were terrified. The children had a bad feeling that the good spirits would be outnumbered. So, they made a secret pact. If the good spirits were losing, they would hold their breath until they died. Anything was better than being ripped apart by evil spirits who would gobble their livers and munch their bones and use their teeth for decoration.

'All night the children stayed awake listening to the battle raging around them. At first, it sounded like the good spirits were winning but then the evil spirits fought back with roars and snarls and the sounds of ripping flesh. As dawn broke, the good spirits' powers were weakening. The roar of the evil spirits was deafening and the children decided it was time to hold their breath. So, the three children held their breath and died.'

Danny stopped. I could hear him breathing. The slightest breeze blew from outside, tickling my shoulders. Hollie stirred. She sat up on her elbows, rubbing her eyes.

'But less than a second after they died, the heavens opened and the rain came down washing the evil spirits away. The children had mistaken the roar of thunder for the sound of the evil spirits winning. When the good spirits returned to the rocks of the cave, they looked down upon the children and thought they were just sleeping. "Wake up, children," they said. "The evil spirits have been washed away by the storm we called for you." But the children were dead and the rocks of the cave shook and heaved as the good spirits mourned their parting, imitating the wails of their mothers and their grandmothers.'

I felt like crying. It was a beautiful story.

Hollie whispered in my ear, 'It's not true. He made it up.'

She sighed and went back to sleep. Danny came towards me. He was holding something cradled in both hands which he then set on top of the egg rock. He knelt before it, tears carving white streaks down his dirty face. It was the baby skull.

'Danny?' I said. 'What's the matter?'

'They're calling me.'

'Who?'

'The spirits. They want me. Can't you hear them?'

'You're imagining things. Come to sleep.'

But he stood up and paced around the cave.

'Don't go outside,' I mumbled, only half-aware in my sleepiness of a vague dread, a muted fear. 'It's dark.' I rolled onto my side with my arms tucked up for a pillow and watched Danny, stomping through the dead embers, back and forth, back and forth, chanting under his breath. I called out once more for him to lie down with us, but he didn't seem to hear me.

I woke with a start, bolt upright. I didn't know where I was but then I looked down and there was Hollie, asleep, her arms around my middle. We were both naked. My head was pounding and my mouth was dry as dirt. I checked my watch. It was seven thirty-two on New Year's Day morning. In less than six hours I was meant to be on a plane to London. I glanced around for Danny but he wasn't in the cave.

'Hollie.' I shook her by the shoulders. 'Wake up.'

She mumbled something, snuggling closer to me.

'Hollie,' I said, a little louder. 'Get up.'

She yawned and opened her eyes, a clear startling blue. 'We're in the cave.'

'Yeah, we're in the cave,' I said.

'We've got no clothes on!' With a cheeky, childish grin, Hollie folded her arms across her chest. She was acting like the old Hollie, all girly innocence like nothing had happened, but I could remember it all, especially the sex.

'Where's Danny?' Hollie asked, bum-wriggling into her daks.

'Don't know.' I snatched my Bonds out of the dirt and put them on. Something gnawed at the edge of my brain like rats in the roof but I couldn't think straight. Thin light seeped through the entrance and there was a lingering smell of smoke. Clutching my head with one hand, I stumbled out of the cave for some fresh air.

I was choking even before I got outside. The further I went, the more difficult it was to see. My eyes were smarting, and when I stood up in the clearing, the red roof of Hollie's house was obscured by a white mist. But it was the silence of the bush, usually teeming with the trills and whips of the morning chorus, which got me freaked. I listened for the tiniest sign of life but there was nothing, nothing except a deep, low rumble. Then, from behind me, further up the hill, came the frantic scurry of bush animals through the undergrowth – and birds, wings flapping and whirring above me, bursting through the tree-tops. I spun around and was hit by a hot blast of air. Thick, grey smoke smothered me. A raging wall of orange and yellow flame was descending from about two hundred metres up the mountain. It could only be a few minutes before the inferno reached the cave. Already, I could feel the air temperature rising around me and it was harder to breath, but the ground beneath my feet was soft and strangely cool. Dizzy and gasping, I rushed back inside the cave, now hazy with smoke.

'Hollie! There's a fire!'

She jumped up, her eyes wide with panic. 'Where's Danny?'

I peered around the cave but there was still no sign of him.

'We have to find him.' Hollie raced outside.

'We don't have time,' I shouted, scampering after her.

She disappeared into the smoke and I could hear her screaming, 'Danny! Where are you? Danny!'

'Hollie!' I shouted in the direction of her voice. 'We won't find him. It's too thick.'

'Danny!' she screamed, running towards the flames. 'Danny-Dilly!'

I took off after her up the hill. The fire roared above us. 'Hollie, come back!' I raced around, my arms thrashing about for her, yelling and tripping over rocks in the white fog until I stumbled into her. Her eyes blazed blue with terror. She was crying.

'He's not here, Hollie!' I heard the crackling of burning scrub, the whoosh of bushes exploding into flame. I could hardly breathe. Black spots appeared like gnats before my eyes. 'We've got to go!' I yelled at her.

'No!' She kicked and spat and scratched at me. She beat her fists against my breasts, but I grabbed her hand and turned, pelting blind, dragging her with me, through the billowing smoke. The fire chased us like a rampant dragon devouring everything in its path, a great flaming mouth of destruction. A blazing gum tree tumbled from the sky and ash rained down upon us. Branches lashed at our arms. Our heels singed. The tips of our hair caught alight, scorching our naked backs. A huge black crow rose like a phoenix out of the tree-tops, its feathers aflame, as we screamed *Danny-Dilly, Danny-Dilly, Danny-Dilly* all the way down the mountain.

22

The police hounded us. They came around to Mum's, where Hollie and I were recuperating, and interrogated us in bed. They thought we'd started the fire. They wanted to know where Danny was and what we'd been doing in the bush that night, if we'd been drinking or taking drugs. I wondered what they would have said if we'd told them the truth – that we'd danced around the fire and ate roast possum and sculled pink champagne and lay down in the dirt and had sex. God knows what I said to them; I was still in shock. The top of my left ear had got burnt and it was sore and throbbing. I was on heaps of painkillers and I had the shakes real bad. When they asked me if we'd lit a fire, I said I couldn't remember. When they asked me where exactly we were, I muttered something vague. I didn't say a word about the cave. Even though they took us into separate rooms, neither of us mentioned the cave. I was sure they'd nail us for something but in the end they buggered off.

We were at Mum's for a couple of days and then we moved back to Hollie's. There was more room for us there and Mr Bailey pretty much left us alone. It seemed like the right thing to do and I was relieved to get away from the

Mum and Randy love-nest. We watched the bushfires, which were still raging only a couple of hundred metres from the living-room window, and when a man from the fire brigade ordered us to evacuate, Mr Bailey refused to budge. It took them more than a week to control the blaze. By then, the bush was devastated, not a single blade of grass was left. It was a picture of hell; blackened stumps, smouldering ash, rising clouds of grey vapour and, every now and then, the splitting sound of a charred tree-trunk crashing to the ground.

Once the fire had died down, the forensic cops went up to search for Danny's body. They reckoned it was arson. They figured that if they could find his body, it would give them some clue as to who'd started it. But, after a week tramping around in the ashes, they didn't find anything. The police issued a statement, saying it was a stray spark from the Mount Coot-tha fireworks that was to blame – not arsonists after all – and that Danny was presumed dead. But I knew that Bomber and Scott had something to do with it.

For a whole month, Hollie didn't speak to anyone. Not to me. Not to Mr Bailey. She locked herself in Mrs Bailey's bedroom and didn't eat a thing. She was adamant Danny was still alive. She took the fact that they hadn't found a body as proof he was still up there roaming about, hunting possum with his spear. One night, soon after the cops had cleared out and the media had gone home, we went up to the cave to look for him. Inside, everything was just how it'd been on New Year's Eve. All perfectly preserved. Like the fire hadn't touched it. We found the possum bones and the stereo and the empty bottles of champagne and our clothes draped over rocks and the satin cushions and the wicker basket, the food rank and rotting inside. The baby skull was still sitting on top of the egg rock where Danny had put it – except there was no Danny. From then on, Hollie spent her days wandering about in the bush or sitting for hours at a time in the cave. I tried to reason with her, to explain how it would have been impossible for him to escape, but she'd scream and stick her fingers in her ears, streaking up the track in her muslin skirts, filthy with soot.

That's why I still haven't told her about Scott and Bomber being up there. The last time I spoke to Scott was on the phone, a few weeks ago. I wanted him to know that I knew he and Bomber had been up in the bush the night of the fire. He answered on the second ring, laughter in his voice. Mrs Greenwood was in the background, humming.

'It's me.' We hadn't spoken since Christmas.

'Oh.' His laughter faded. 'Hi.'

'How're things?'

'Fine.'

'How's Amber?'

'Yeah. Good.'

I paused. 'It was you guys, wasn't it?'

'What?'

'Danny.'

'Yeah, what about him?' He sounded impatient to get off the phone. 'He's dead. It was on the news.'

'Bomber said he was gonna kill him.'

'He was just talking shit.'

'But I heard you. That night. You and Bomber were up there.'

I heard his knuckles tightening around the receiver.

'Breakfast's ready!' Mrs Greenwood sung out.

Scott cut to a whisper. 'Listen. I know what you're thinking but you're wrong, OK? Bomber and me had nothing to do with it. Alright, we gave him a hard time at school and I feel bad enough about that, but you've got it wrong if you think us guys had anything to do with it.' He coughed. 'I've gotta go.' He hung up but I knew then for sure that it was Scott and Bomber who'd lit the fire. I was going to tell the cops but for some reason I haven't – at least, not yet. I guess it's harder for me to go through with it now Scott's a father. And with no body found, I wonder how they could prove that Scott and Bomber did it anyway.

In February, Mr Bailey reluctantly organized a memorial service at Pinnaro Lawn Cemetery. Hollie reacted badly, spitting in her father's face, threatening to kill herself. She said it was like burying him alive. I stayed out of it, shutting myself in Hollie's bedroom.

The day of the service, the drought broke. It was the first skerrick of rain since September and it didn't just rain, it chucked it down so hard the heels of my black strappies sank in the mud. It was a small gathering, mostly relatives. Randy went on behalf of Mum, who couldn't face the cemetery germs. Hollie mumbled to herself the whole way through, as we clung tight to each other under a huge black umbrella, staring down at the chunk of engraved marble bashed into the earth:

IN MEMORY OF DANIEL ORPHEUS BAILEY
BELOVED SON OF DAVID AND BROTHER OF HOLLIE
MISSING IN BUSHLAND SURROUNDING MOUNT COOT-THA
1 JANUARY 1995
REUNITED IN DEATH WITH HIS MOTHER, LESLEY

After the service, Hollie got a bit better. At least she was talking. We both had trouble sleeping. Each night, we lay awake together, clutching each other. Hollie sobbing, me silent, numb. When I did fall asleep, I saw faces grinning from my hell-fire dreams. I was a skeleton walking through roaring flames, flesh melting off my bones, my eyes red as the devil's. I'd wake up cold-sweating into the sheets, and Hollie would hold me tight and kiss me all over until I stopped shaking.

Once my burn had healed, Randy offered me a job at his cancer-germ lab out at uni. At least when I'm working I don't think about how, if I'd told the cops about Bomber's threats, Danny mightn't be dead. Although Randy is the big cheese, he took me under his wing. He taught me how to prep petri-dishes with e.coli and how to use an electron microscope and how to record observations on the computer. It's not so bad. I get ten bucks an hour and the days go fast. I'll admit it's better than the coffee shop, although I won't be staying much longer. Of course, I missed my flight on New Year's Day but I'm still going to London. I've already booked my ticket. This time nothing's going to stop me.

It's strange being at uni again. One lunchtime, I was in the cafeteria eating lunch when Kirstie came up to me. She was in third-year law, same as I would have been if I hadn't dropped out.

'You back doing law?' she asked, inspecting her nails.

'No,' I said, my mouth full of ham sandwich.

'What then?'

'Germs.'

'Germs?'

'I'm studying germs.'

'Oh.' She smiled, real fake. 'That's nice.'

I slurped on my Coke.

'I suppose you've heard the news?' she chirped.

'What news?'

'Amber had a boy.'

'Good for her.'

'They've called him Tom. Tom Greenwood. Good strong name for a boy, don't you think?'

'Yeah,' I laughed. 'But he could still turn out faggot like his dad.'

She gave me a weird look and lowered her voice. 'I heard you'd moved in with your... friend.'

'Her brother died.'

'Yeah, but that's not the whole story, is it?' She flicked back her hair. 'Who would have thought you'd turn into ... ' She leaned in and whispered, 'a dyke,' before turning and clacking off in her kitten heels.

The weeks slip by. After the rain, the bush grows back, lusher and greener than ever. The evenings turn chilly.

Hollie and I spend the weekends re-decorating Mrs Bailey's bedroom. We paint the walls buttercup and clear away all the stuff from the night she killed herself. We hang a print of *The Lady of Shalott* on the wall and swap the satin bedspread for a big, fluffy doona, but Hollie insists on keeping the waterbed because, as she says, 'it's comfortable *and* luxurious.' The past few months, we've grown so used to living together. With Danny gone, all we have is each other, but I know it can't go on like this for ever.

I get up early and make her breakfast in bed – croissants and chocolate muffins and freshly squeezed orange juice and a pot of Russian Caravan tea.

'Rise and shine, birthday girl.' I kiss her on the lips.

She opens her eyes, sees the tray laden with goodies and smiles. As she props herself up against the pillows, my heart flares. She is so beautiful. Her face escaped the fire but her hands were badly burnt. They rest on top of the covers shiny-pink and puckered. I pull back the curtains. The sky is low and grey with fast-flitting clouds.

'Present now or later?' I say.

'Now, please,' she says.

I lean over and pull a pale-blue envelope from the top bedside drawer and gently place it into Hollie's hands. I'm dying for her to see what's inside but she takes ages to open it, her fingers stiff and clumsy. Eventually, she slips out the card – two little sepia girls on swings – and two plane tickets to London drop out. She picks them off the doona, inspects them and looks at me in amazement.

'When do we go?'

'Tomorrow.' I can't stop smiling.

'For how long?'

'As long as we want. I've got heaps of money.'

Her face drops. 'But I can't.' She hangs her head.

'Why not?'

'Danny.'

'Hollie, he's not coming back.'

She shakes her head, looks up mournfully. 'Can't we just look?'

'For God's sake, Hollie, how many times—'

'Just once more. Please.'

I sigh, heavily. It *is* her birthday. 'OK.'

I change into a tracksuit and sneakers. Hollie togs herself up in one of her mother's crêpe-de-chine cocktail dresses and heels. She pulls her hair up in an elegant French roll with wispy tendrils hanging down and wears white silk gloves to cover her hands. I spot the wicker basket at her feet and ask her what's inside.

'Oh, just some food for Danny,' she says. 'He's sure to be hungry.'

Outside, it's overcast and cold. From the top of the mountain comes a biting wind. Blustery gusts snatch leaves from the trees, flattening the spinifex. The crickets whisper, barely there, grown shy without the heat. All the way up, Hollie chats non-stop about how wonderful it'll be to see Danny again. I want to tell her how much I love her, how beautiful she looks, how much fun we are going to have overseas, but all she can think about is Danny. We reach the clearing. The wind lulls as if we have entered the eye of a storm. We turn and run, knowing the way like in a dream where you do things inexplicably, without reason. The cave appears. Hollie stops, reverent, head bowed.

'Go on,' I say, impatient to be back in the warm.

'Wait,' she says. 'Listen.' There's no sound except the wind, whooshing past our ears. I push her forward, through the young vines which are just starting to bud again, and follow her into the cool and shadowy void.

'Look,' she says as we are nearing the egg rock.

A faint, orange glow is coming from the back of the cave. I reach for her hand but she's jumped up and is rushing towards the light. 'Hollie. Wait.' But there's no reply. I step gingerly, trepidation in my heart. It can't be him. But someone, or something is there. Hollie gasps. 'Danny,' she whispers. But it's not possible. After all this time. I slip in beside her, the damp rock flush against my arm.

A man with dark skin and dark hair squats over a small fire with his back to us. He's wearing a yellow T-shirt and ragged shorts. The fire crackles and spits. The smell of burnt animal flesh fills the air. Our eyes stretch wide until they smart and throb in the fire-smoke and still I can't believe it.

Hollie speaks, 'Danny?'

He turns, slowly, as if perhaps he knew all along that we were there but was waiting for us to say something. It is not Danny. A young aboriginal man stares at us and then he speaks in his own language, which we cannot understand.

We shake our heads and he laughs and holds out his hand, but we're too stunned to take it.

'My name is Micky. Danny told me about this place. It belonged to my people.'

'But this is *our* cave—' Hollie starts, but I squeeze her hand to silence her. Micky grins and, without a trace of menace, says:

'Go, this is my place now.'

Acknowledgements

I would like to thank Richard Francis for his advice and encouragement during the early drafts of this novel. Thanks to my father for his invaluable knowledge of cricketing facts and lingo. My heartfelt thanks to Caroline Dawnay and Clara Farmer. And, my eternal gratitude to Charlie Aspinwall for his unflagging patience, faith and dedication to the cause.